HIS WILD TEMPTATION

A WILD BILLIONAIRE ROMANCE

WILD BILLIONAIRE ROMANCE
BOOK 2

C.D. GORRI

HIS WILD TEMPTATION

A Billionaire Romance Novel
Wild Billionaire Romance Book 2
By
C.D. Gorri

Copyright C.D. Gorri, NJ 2024

Before you begin sign up for my newsletter here:
SUBSCRIBE HERE

DEDICATION

For the readers willing to risk it all for one night in the Devil's arms. Don't worry. He knows how to make good girls scream.
Xoxo,
C.D. Gorri

These wild billionaire playboys are used to getting their way...

There isn't much money can't buy, especially when it comes to pleasure. But can these curvy women tame these billionaire beasts and win their love? Or will their souls be sucked into oblivion by the wanton bliss their bodies crave more and more with every surrender?

Each of our heroes wears a mask on the outside to face the world, but his disguise comes off when he runs into the one female who makes his blood run hot. Need and possessive passion abound in these books, but our heroes know only one way to control their desires.

Will they f*ck the feeling they see as weakness out of their systems, or will their needs only grow more wild with every touch, kiss, and plunge into ecstasy with the object of his affections?

Our Billionaire Heroes

Adrik Volkov
Marat Volkov
Josef Aziz
Andres Ramirez

Trigger Warnings
(I have never done one of these, so please forgive me if I muck this up.)
This series has profanity, graphic steamy scenes, voyeurism, violence, deceased parents, alcoholism (not the MCs), misogyny (not the MCs), questionable morals, manipulations, fake relationships, revenge, and romantic obsessions that may be unhealthy.

This is fictional. This is not real life.
Always take care of your mental, emotional, and physical self because you are important.

She was a temptation he couldn't afford, but letting her go was not an option.

Marat was the face of Volkov Industries. With his movie star good looks, he attracted class and money to the multi-billion dollar corporation, not to mention all the right PR. But being born with the face of an angel had its disadvantages. Expected to entertain associates, Marat's activities were anything but celestial. And yes, it was exhausting.

Sent on an errand to Sin City in the name of business, Marat needed a diversion. The curvy goddess serving drinks was exactly what this playboy billionaire craved. He was not looking for forever, but some temptations were too good to let go.

Destiny Valdez ran away to Vegas as a teen with her head full of dreams. A dozen years later, those dreams were dust. Pulling a double shift with her slimy boss giving her a hard time was not how she'd planned to spend her birthday.

But that was life.

She never expected a proposition from one of the most handsome men she'd ever seen. Daring her to take what she wanted, Marat Volkov presented the type of opportunity she only ever fantasized about. A night in his bed sounded exactly like what she needed. Waking up married? Not so much.

She thought he was playing, but keeping his curvy Dumplin' was a wild temptation he could not resist.

CHAPTER ONE
MARAT

T he breeze felt cold against the exposed skin on my arms as I stood in short sleeves, hugging Michaela to me.

My niece was warm and bundled in a pretty little frock with a thick sweater and a matching knit hat on top of her mass of chestnut colored curls, so I knew she was fine.

She pointed at the birds and spouted delightful gibberish I was all too happy to listen to. I loved my niece. That child was as close as I was ever going to get to fatherhood. Visiting my brother's house was something I made it a point to do regularly. It was like getting my own little family fix.

My brother had lucked out the day he found his Zaika, that was his pet name for my sister-in-law.

Adrik was a hard man, but Sofia fit his rough edges just fine.

He'd met her at a party and just like that, he was a goner. For a powerful billionaire used to getting his own way, Sofia was quite the challenge.

Adrik had stalked her like the wolf he was until she said yes when he proposed. It never failed to amaze me how readily she gave the wolf her heart, and now, a baby on top of that.

It was surreal in some ways. I never would have thought Adrik would find someone who not only accepted him but loved him just as obsessively as he loved her.

Sofia was truly his soulmate, and I was happy for him, for them both.

Honestly.

Of course, sometimes I felt a certain green monster sitting on my shoulder, but I did my best to ignore the miserable fucker.

I didn't want to think too much about the fact I had never been in love and likely never would be. And I sure as fuck wasn't going to voice that aloud.

How pathetic would that be? Still, I'd bet it would make headlines. Nothing set the vultures circling overhead quite like humiliation and despair.

Handsome billionaire cries himself to sleep every night in his cold, lonely, enormous bed.

Okay, I didn't cry.

But I'd been sleeping alone for months now. By choice, of course.

No, that wasn't conceit. I knew all too well if I snapped my fingers a queue would form outside my front door full of beautiful women willing to fill that empty spot.

I just wasn't interested. Nothing interested me much anymore. Life had grown stale. Or maybe just my life as a playboy. There had to be something more to it, didn't there?

"Marat?" Sofia's voice reached me.

My sister-in-law was likely looking for her daughter, but before I could answer she'd already started her next barrage of questions. The woman could yap, god love her.

"Marat? Do you have Micheala? Where are you? Oh, there you are, and I see you do have my defiant little girl in your arms outside without her shoes again," she mock-scolded before grinning and reaching for the baby.

"She's fine," I assured her.

I knew Sofia well enough to realize she wasn't

actually mad, she was simply protective. And wasn't that amazing?

Adrik and I never really had a mother. Or a father. Much less a protective one. They were both murdered by the Russian Bratva over some drug deal when I was still quite small.

My brother had taken on the burden of raising me after that. He'd used brute force, keen intelligence, and lethal cunning to get ahead in the criminal underworld. Josef had joined him soon after, and the man had been part of our fucked up little family ever since.

Adrik had always been so single-minded. But everything changed when he met Sofia.

The little Jersey girl had broken down his barriers, turning the Dark Wolf into a family man. And I got a ringside view.

It was fantastic. Also, nice to know she was as fiercely protective of their daughter as he was. I was just surprised protective parents still existed.

Either way, Sofia needn't have worried. I wouldn't have allowed my precious niece to step foot on the damp ground in only her socks.

"Hello, my sweet princess," she cooed, before turning her smiling face to me. "Thank you, Uncle Marat."

My chest tightened whenever she called me that. Sofia was the kindest person I knew, and I was grateful to have her for my niece's mother.

The terrace was still wet after the morning's rain shower, and without my arms around my niece, whom I'd been cradling, I felt the chill to my bones.

"Oh, thank you for the doll house by the way," Sofia said. "It arrived this morning. Along with the paper."

"My pleasure," I replied, before pausing.

The paper? Fuck.

Micheala just had her first birthday and though I'd already showered her with gifts at the luxurious party my brother had thrown her, this last one was a special order.

It was a replica of the house they lived in, complete with little dolls and furniture handcrafted by a master toy maker from St. Petersburg.

We shared the date, but turning one was a helluva lot more exciting than turning thirty. I kissed my niece on her soft curls before handing her over to her mother. My lips were still tingling from the pressure minutes later.

"Yes, the paper. Another headline featuring the face of Volkov Industries," she teased, and I knew she didn't mean it.

But it still struck me like a slap. The face of Volkov Industries was seen at a dinner party hosted by one of the companies I'd been looking to purchase for my new greener incentive.

I wasn't on the prowl like those damn paparazzi suggested. And the woman they'd photographed me standing beside was the wife of some young scientist. I didn't even know her name.

But the papers loved to villainize a rich Casanova, and I often made the news.

"Ooh, her cheeks are nice and warm. I thought she'd be cold," Sofia murmured, taking my mind off the headline and refocusing it on my niece.

She was too precious for words. I smiled as Sofia, good mom that she was, removed Michaela's hat and sweater now that she was indoors.

"She wanted to see outside, but I made sure she was warm enough," I explained, smiling at the picture perfect Volkov females.

How Adrik had convinced Sofia to marry him, I had no idea. But it had been a whirlwind and somewhat fantastical romance.

I couldn't believe two years had passed since then. Watching my hard, taciturn brother turn into a family man had proved interesting. I didn't think he had it in him.

Not that it was his fault. We'd simply had no examples to learn from. What I remembered of our parents was arguing and griping. I remembered being cold and hungry. I remembered being scared.

It wasn't a good childhood.

Adrik and I came from nothing. We'd literally scraped ourselves out of the gutter to get to where we were, with him doing a lot of the heavy lifting since he was ten years my senior.

After he met Sofia, and his obsession with her became apparent, change was inevitable. I stepped up, thrilled to finally be able to repay him in any way I could.

Taking a more active role in Volkov Industries proved challenging. I dove into work headfirst, eager to prove I had the aptitude for it. I hadn't been sitting on my ass, getting photographed by paparazzi, and doing nothing all this time.

I'd been learning the business, training my mind and body to keep up with my brother. Studying reports, keeping up with environmental concerns, and working on my own projects to make us more environmentally conscientious.

Finally, I was able to be of some use so Adrik could enjoy the family he fought so hard to secure.

He deserved happiness, and I would never stand in the way of that.

Besides, I loved my niece and my sister-in-law, in a strictly platonic, familial sense, of course. They were good for him. And it was my duty and my privilege to take on some of the burden of our position.

Being a Volkov was far from easy. And that wasn't me whining *poor little rich boy*. We were responsible for billions of dollars and the fates of several thousand people depended on us. Even whole governments.

Adrik always said rich men were more ruthless than mobsters and the only thing separating them were a few words on paper signed into law. He was right. I'd seen men receive honors and applause from the public who were responsible for oil spills, deforestation, pharmaceutical disaster, and the general withholding of aid and care from the public.

The world was fucked up. I couldn't solve all of its problems, but I could help my brother.

There was a time when Adrik thought I'd pursued Sofia, but I would never have crossed that line with my brother. I had to admit, it hurt that he thought I would. But I understood why.

I'd been playing the role of billionaire playboy for

so long sometimes even I believed that was all I had to offer.

After all, I was the face of Volkov Industries.

It was my toothy grin plastered on our company website. And my visage that had been splashed across the media for years.

I was the better known Volkov brother. The attention seeker. The party goer.

Sought after by women from all over the world. Some wanted to win me. Some just wanted to fuck me. Others just craved to be near me. Happy to bask in the periphery of my fame.

I'd been named the *sexiest man alive* not once, but twice.

Not a lie. Not a flex. Just fact.

My face, my name, and my net worth had been splashed across whatever magazine it was that thought putting me on the cover would sell more copies.

It did.

I paid attention to none of it. Men called me lucky. Rich men. Powerful men. They invited me to their parties, hoping I would attend, elevating their social standing with my presence.

Some even told me they wished they were me. Like being Marat Volkov was some lofty aspiration.

They wished they had this face I was born with. These features I did nothing to gain.

And I couldn't understand it. Not. For. One. Solitary. Minute.

My brother was the better man by a long shot. Adrik was brilliant. He was powerful, loyal, and ambitious. He was worthy of admiration.

Couldn't they see that?

My brother worked harder than anyone I knew. He'd battled impossible odds to bring us out of the cruel poverty we'd lived in to a level of society I could never have imagined.

Hell, sometimes I still couldn't. Back when I was a child, freezing on the streets of Moscow, food and shelter were the major concerns. But Adrik took care of it. He took care of us. Of me.

He did things that would make most people's blood curl. But now, Adrik was one of the most successful and respected men in the business world. And in the underworld, he was still one of the most feared.

A couple of years had passed since the Dark Wolf made an appearance, but no one forgot him. How could they?

The name alone represented a level of cunning, a single-minded ruthlessness that had brought governments to their knees. Adrik was the Dark Wolf, and he earned his reputation through blood, sweat, and tears—*mostly from others.*

And yet I was the one they envied.

What the fuck was wrong with people? I was nothing.

Just the fucking face of Volkov Industries. The pretty party boy. A walking billboard for the iniquitous rich we rubbed elbows with.

Fact was, I did nothing to deserve my face. My looks were not something I earned or worked for. They were just a happy accident.

A stupid fucking coincidence.

But people looked at me like I was some damn chosen one. Like I'd won the genetic lottery.

I checked my watch as Sofia kissed Micheala on the cheek a dozen more times, blowing raspberries on her baby soft skin and making her squeal with giggles. I grinned. The child was the perfect combination of her parents.

She had Sofia's softness, and Adrik's determination. Big fat curls danced around her cherubic face, but she had the Volkov eyes. Dark and intense. Micheala was going to be a heartbreaker. Hell, she was already.

Poor Adrik.

CHAPTER TWO
MARAT

Maybe envy wasn't the right emotion in this instance.

I thought of all the trouble this little one would bring my brother, and I grinned. The Dark Wolf would be completely gray before she turned three.

Not that he was the wolf with either of his girls. Those two females of his had the power to turn him into a puppy.

Would wonders never cease?

And fuck, there he was again. That goddamn green motherfucker on my shoulder.

Still, I was glad I was Michaela's uncle and not her father. I'd be terrible at parenthood. I was absolutely certain about that. But I could be a fun uncle to my niece and whatever other kids joined Adrik's brood.

I already spoiled Micheala rotten to hear Sofia tell it. My pretty little niece knew just how to capture my attention, as well as everyone else's. She was not a whiner, not a crier, but she could wrap me around her chubby little finger with barely a murmur.

Sweet little thing. Precious. Lucky, lucky Adrik to have such a beautiful family.

I would be there for her, for any of them, wherever, however, and whenever I could. I owed everything to Adrik. Protecting his family was the least I could do to repay him. And really, it was my pleasure.

But I knew nothing I did could ever be enough, and that knowledge cut me inside.

"Earth to Marat? I asked if you were staying over tonight. I could have Esmerelda freshen up your room."

"Oh, no, I'm not staying. Thanks, though."

"What's up? Seriously, you look grumpy," Sofia said, breaking my train of thought.

"Grumpy? Me? I think maybe you confused me with that growly beast you call husband."

I turned my megawatt smile on her, the one I'd

used to melt off more than one pair of panties in my lifetime, but my savvy sister-in-law was not fooled.

"Seriously, Marat. Is everything okay? Are you mad about the penthouse?"

"Why on earth would I be mad about Adrik giving me his penthouse?" I scoffed.

"I don't know," she replied.

Sofia shivered, and I moved to close the terrace doors to ward off the chilly April breeze blowing through the opening. I hated spring. It was the ugliest of all the seasons as far as I was concerned. Nothing but mud and bare branches, cold weather, and near constant rain.

Give me the greens and heat of summer or the reds and golds of fall. I even liked the stark white snow of winter. Maybe that was my Russian blood, I could not say. But springtime—*blech*.

Spring felt like a lie to me. The promise of rebirth and youth, but really, it was nothing like I wanted it to be. It was always too cold, too damp, too unwelcoming.

Harsh.

Springtime was raw. Muddy. Unfinished. Downright ugly. That was the reality of the season. But no one seemed to recognize it. It was supposed to represent youth, rebirth, but like most things, that was a mirage. Just like beauty.

Just like me.

Fuck, I was morose. I'd driven out that morning to the Long Island Sound to visit my brother and his family to cheer myself up. Also, I had to pick up some of my belongings from the mansion they now called their permanent home.

I did not mind that. Not one bit. I'd been drifting back and forth between cities, but since I was needed more at Volkov Industries these days, moving to the New York penthouse for good made sense.

I was humbled and proud that Adrik trusted me with the business, and I worked damn hard to prove myself. It was gratifying, in a way. No, we didn't need more money, but I found the advances in technology, the creativity involved in what our company did simply fascinating.

Contrary to popular belief the face of Volkov Industries was actually good for more than entertainment. I had a brain though most likely believed it lived somewhere below my buckle. But I didn't attend Princeton for nothing. And playboy or not, I was doing good work for the company and my family.

"Brother!" Adrik's bellow reached my ears a moment before Micheala let out a squeal of delight at her father's arrival. "Was traffic bad?" he asked as he nuzzled his daughter's neck.

"Same as always," I replied.

I rolled my eyes and tried not to watch as Adrik turned his head from his daughter's chubby cheek to greet his wife with a passionate kiss, as if he hadn't seen her fifteen minutes ago. I felt like a fucking voyeur whenever those two touched and it was all I could do not to grumble aloud like the fucking curmudgeon I was afraid I'd already become.

"I know you two have some business to discuss, but let's have a bite to eat before all that. I had Rosa prepare something special for you, Marat."

"Did you?" I asked, mildly curious. Like everything else, my appetite for food had dwindled lately.

"Don't act like you couldn't smell the *pelmeni* when you walked in," she said, mentioning my favorite Russian dish.

Pelmeni were meat dumplings and could be prepared steamed, pan fried, or even served in soup. Sofia was right, of course. The mouthwatering scents of onions, herbs, and spices danced in the air in of the entryway when I'd arrived a little over half an hour ago.

I winked at my sister-in-law, earning me a glare from my still overly possessive brother. Even after all this time, the man was still unhealthily obsessed with his wife. Whatever. Who was I to judge? Besides, it appeared to be working for them.

"When are you driving back to the city?" Adrik asked.

"Before rush hour was my plan," I replied, following them to the dining room.

Adrik took Micheala from his wife and strapped the baby into her highchair, quick to add some fruity puff things to her tray before she could start climbing out. She was already an expert escape artist.

"I was wondering if you wouldn't mind taking a quick trip to Vegas before you settled in the penthouse," Adrik began, and I lifted my eyes to his.

"Vegas?" I asked, my mind immediately switching from lunch to business.

"Volkov Industries is being recognized by McNeil Corp for our humanitarian efforts in providing medical supplies and food to citizens of war torn countries in Africa and the Middle East. Quite the honor, brother."

"Are we now? Interesting, those areas were where

the Dark Wolf last appeared when our mines were being threatened. Don't you think?"

"Indeed.," Adrik growled, his dark eyes flashing at me.

"Let's not discuss that at the table, boys."

"Anyway, it would be better for the company if one of the two co-chairs were there to represent us," my brother continued.

"I take it Vegas is not somewhere you'd like to bring your wife and daughter."

"Well, it's not that Adrik did not want to take us, but I am a little nervous about such a long flight with Micheala," Sofia spoke up, biting her lip.

"Of course, I will go, Sof," I said immediately, wanting to put my sister-in-law at ease. "I was just needling my brother. Force of habit."

"Good!" Adrik said, nodding his head.

Fucking Las Vegas.

Sure, it was fun ten years ago, when I was younger and carefree. But Sin City and I had parted ways, and I was no worse for wear. It wasn't my ideal, but I would go for the company, and for Adrik.

"Are they still doing an auction with the award ceremony?" I asked, mentally preparing myself.

"I believe so. Auction, dinner, gala, the whole

nine. You should bring a date otherwise Tessa McNeil might get the wrong impression," he started.

"Who's Tessa McNeil?" Sofia asked, eyes bright with curiosity.

"No one."

"His ex."

I answered at the same time as Adrik.

"Oh, I feel a story there," Sofia said right before Rosa came in with lunch.

"Rosa, darling, save me from this boring conversation," I implored the older woman who just chuckled and shushed me while she rolled a cart laden with platters of delicious smelling food onto the table.

Conversation stilted while the meal was served, and we ate in companionable silence for a few minutes. As always, time passed far too quickly when I was enjoying myself. Such a rarity these days, it was truly a pity.

"Are you sure you're okay going to Vegas?" Adrik asked and walked me to the door some minutes later.

"Yeah. It's fine."

"I could try to convince Zaika—"

"Adrik, I am fine. I've been to Vegas a million times."

"I know, but you looked sort of off before," he said, concern marring his face.

"Off? Me? I am the face of Volkov Industries. I never look off," I said, trying for humor and failing miserably.

"Marat—"

"You had them fuel up the jet, yes?"

"Yes, it is done. Marat, if you need anything—"

"Good, I'll go right to the airport. And I'll be in touch with Andres about meetings and such," I said.

"Fine. I'll have Josef meet you at the plane," Adrik huffed, clearly annoyed at me for cutting him off so many times.

"I don't need Josef—" I began.

"Nonnegotiable," he grunted, returning the favor, and not allowing me to finish my sentence. "You are not just the face of the company anymore, Marat. You are the powerful co-chair. You have gained enemies, and you would do well not to forget," he said before pulling me in for a goodbye hug.

"Fine."

I nodded, trying not to grimace as my older brother patted me on the back hard enough to jostle my whole body. The fucker.

I wished I could have done something or said something to make him relax. But I had nothing, and

I could only stand there as his heavy stare weighed down on me. He was right to be suspicious.

Lately, I'd felt off. Like something had shifted inside of me. I felt adrift most days. The realization there was nothing connecting me to the real world.

No ties. No anchors. And I was aware of my own goddamn hypocrisy. I mean, no strings was how I wanted things. It was what I demanded of my partners. The women I bedded knew the deal.

Relationships were for ordinary people, and I was not that. I never made promises or overtures. I just didn't do drama. But lately, I'd been thinking I was wrong. One night stands with nameless beauties no longer held any appeal.

Fuck.

This sucked. I needed something to steady me. But what?

"Where to, sir?" the driver asked, and I gave him the name of one of the private airports we used.

I did not need to bother to pack since an email to Andres, the administrative assistant I shared with my brother, was all I needed to ensure my hotel suite would have what I required for my trip. The only thing I had to do was get there.

Last thing I wanted was to ponder just what the fuck I was doing with my life the entire fucking trip.

I grabbed my phone and started shooting off emails. Besides, I knew what I was doing for the next few days.

I was the face of Volkov Industries and as such I'd be accepting an award in the entertainment capital of the world with millions of eyes on me. I needed to be on guard. That place was full of vipers in designer clothing. The time to indulge my sullen mood and wallow in morose fuckery was over.

It was time to roll the dice even though I knew they were loaded against me.

Las Vegas was waiting.

CHAPTER THREE
DESTINY

The day started out shitty.

I'd had a message from my brother back in Jersey and my mother's health was rapidly deteriorating. I was filled with the usual guilt and angst as I sent him my last two hundred bucks.

Money didn't make up for twelve years of absence, and I only hoped he understood how I felt. My family life had pretty much ended when I was eighteen. But that didn't mean I'd stopped caring.

Two hundred dollars didn't make up for anything, but it was all I could afford. Rent was due. My roommate skipped out. And if I didn't give in to my manager, I was likely going to get fired.

The weight of the guilt I carried was enough to

bring me to my knees. Add to it the pressure of trying to maintain my job and keep the wolves at bay, and it was a perfect recipe for disaster.

Mr. Royce's beady eyes pinned me in place, and I did my best to hide the revulsion I felt. He was a slimy creep who used his position to force women into bed.

Testing the goods.

That was what I'd heard him call it when he bragged about his *supposed conquests* to the male employees.

Not that they liked him, either. No one did. His vibe was just cringe.

Like all caps. Boldface. **CRINGE**.

What was it about guys like that who thought they needed to date tons of women to prove their manhood? And was it even a conquest if you used the threat of firing someone to make them go out with you?

It was so fucking unfair. Why did some people think this behavior was okay? But I was in no position to voice my disdain.

I just stood there, and I hated myself for it. Mr. Royce pretended to check my uniform over, but it was just an excuse to stare at my tits and ass for way longer than necessary. The uniform was a purple corset and black pants with high heels.

But yes. I was breaking the rules.

"You're wearing the wrong shoes. That's your third infraction this quarter, Destiny," he said, smacking his lips together.

I shivered at the sound, and not in a good way. Mouth noises were a serious pet peeve of mine, and somehow this man made them even when he wasn't eating. So gross.

"I'm going to have to send you home—"

"No! Mr. Royce, please. Um, my roommate skipped out on me, and the rent is due, and well, it's my birthday. I could really use the money. Please do me this favor," I whispered, hating myself for showing weakness and begging this jerk.

"Well then, if you promise to be grateful," he said, heavy emphasis on the last word. "Put on a big smile on that face, Destiny, and get your ass out there. Oh, and I expect you to kick back 20% of your tips to the house to make up for this. You can deliver them to my office after your shift, and we'll *talk*," Mr. Royce said, his gaze never rising above my tits.

I opened my mouth to say something, but what could I reply with? Shit. That was not what I meant when I asked him for a favor, but it was too late. I was going to have to run out the door at closing.

"See you later, Dollface."

Mr. Royce smacked his gums together again. I swallowed back bile. It was all I could do to stop from throwing up the two chicken tenders I'd scarfed before the start of my shift from the tray in the employee breakroom.

"Sexist pig," I muttered to myself, putting my fake smile in place as I scurried away from my asshole boss.

Mr. Royce had already reamed me out for wearing the wrong shoes tonight, but this was the first time he'd actually threatened to fire me. And docking my tips on top of the insinuation that I would give him any kind of *favor* after closing was just impalpable.

It really was a shitty day.

CHAPTER FOUR
DESTINY

Hindsight was twenty-twenty, wasn't that a saying? But it was my third night in a row on my feet and I hated the stupid high heels we were forced to wear. Besides, I was working a double.

But maybe Royce wouldn't have been such a hardass, making me work the tables in the crappy section all fucking night long if I'd worn the right shoes.

Whatever.

I'd love to see that asshole try to serve drinks in the nearly pitch black club on ice pick heels! Since he had the final say in our uniforms, I knew he was responsible for the ridiculous attire.

Sure, it was a good job. The place was always

crowded, and the clientele tipped well. But I didn't want to break a leg to make a dollar.

With everything going on in my life, I did not need the added stress of a possible work injury. So, no. There was just no way in hell I was wearing the four-inch ankle breakers Mr. Royce had made part of the official cocktail waitress uniform for the rest of my eight hour shift.

I'd been on the floor since two that afternoon and it was already midnight. Also, I wasn't lying about it being my birthday.

Swapping my shoes was a little act of rebellion. A birthday gift to myself.

It sucked, I had to work tonight. I would have much rather stayed in and read the new steamy romance novel I'd splurged on to celebrate turning thirty.

Thank fuck for eBooks and subscription services. I could never afford to keep myself in paperbacks.

But I was there instead, waiting on the rich and beautiful who came to Las Vegas by the throng to lose themselves in the neon glamor and madness of this adult playground.

Sin City. It was an apt nickname. I'd seen men and women slip on their horns and tails and do things they never would have anywhere other than in this town.

Las Vegas could get to you if you weren't careful. But I was usually careful.

I'd just served a table full of beautiful women out to celebrate their friend who was wearing a birthday sash across her hot little black dress.

There were ten of them, and I delivered their champagne with a smile. A pang of envy sliced through me, but I shoved it away. I was happy for the other birthday girl and silently wished her the best.

This was stupid. Feeling sorry for myself was a waste of time. I wasn't the only person in the world who had to work on their birthday.

Hey, at least you're not spending it alone like last year.

My inner optimist's attempt to cheer me up fell flat. No, I wasn't alone. I was busting my ass, covering twelve tables, and they were all full.

But since I was determined to be a cup half full kinda gal, I decided that was a good thing. I needed the money. Besides, I really needed to focus on a way to run out of there without Royce seeing me at the end of my shift.

"Hey birthday girl! How about a shot on me?"

Enri shouted from behind the bar, sliding a shot glass filled with pink liquid at me.

"What is it?"

"Bubble Gum Vodka! My own," he winked.

I tossed it back, even though I rarely indulged. Tonight seemed to call for an extra jolt of something, and I figured it might as well be a little liquid courage.

"Wow, Enri, this is delicious!"

And it was. My mouth was buzzing with sweet bubble gum flavor, and I grinned, thinking he should bottle the stuff.

"I know, right?" he asked, and winked.

"Yes, definitely. Hey, can I have another round for table thirty-seven, please," I called out to my absolute favorite bartender.

Enri was a character. He was originally from Indiana and his real name was Henry. But he did a mean French accent. Seriously, it was flawless.

He'd confessed one night after shift he'd increased his tips thirty-five percent over the past six months since he became *Enri* instead of plain old Henry.

Smart bastard.

The taste of bubble gum was nice in my mouth. I tapped my fingernails on the table as he got my order ready. There was a weird sort of energy in the air, but I attributed it to my nerves and all the mess going on with me. Maybe that was why I hadn't heard Royce approach.

"Move your ass, Dollface. Table forty-one has just been seated," Mr. Royce hissed.

"That's not my section."

"What was that?"

"Nothing, uh, I am going right now, sir," I mumbled, grabbing the drinks for table thirty-seven and a clean menu for my new table.

Forty-one was all the way on the other end of the second level of Lux. A VIP table, which I usually loved getting, but I was so busy already.

I grimaced. I was going to have a helluva time juggling the rest of my tables, plus this one. So much for my rebellion. Royce was always doing shit like that on purpose. Especially when he wanted to teach one of us a lesson.

He was such a total douche canoe. I'd always looked forward to the day I could give that creep a piece of my mind.

I knew I should have been grateful to have even landed that gig. But no one should have to put up with a creepy, grabby boss.

Beggars couldn't be choosers though, and in this town, I was too old to beg.

Thirty year old cocktail waitresses who were thick in the middle with fat thighs and big butts didn't typically get hired to serve the highbrow VIPs who frequented places like Lux.

A major attraction on the Las Vegas Strip, Lux Lounge was for A-listers only, which usually meant top shelf staff. It was a miracle I got the job when I applied almost a year ago.

Lucky for me, my beady-eyed cretin of a boss had taken a liking to me. He'd been trying to put the moves on me for months now, but I'd always managed to slip away no worse for wear.

His patience had worn thin, and it had always been a matter of time before things got too close for comfort. Like they had tonight.

Okay, so maybe it wasn't lucky. Like not at all.

There was always the chance he wouldn't pursue what he'd insinuated in his office. I didn't want to be one of those people who read too much into what others carelessly tossed out.

He wasn't right. And he wasn't good. But maybe he didn't mean what I thought he meant?

I was grasping at straws, and I knew it. I had plenty of practice turning down unsavory advances.

Anyone who'd worked as a waitress as long as I had could probably tell you the same thing.

There were no ands, ifs, or buts about it. I was positive Royce was going to make a pass at me after my shift, and when I refused, I was going to be fired.

Any second now.

But I wasn't done. Not yet.

Rent was due on Monday, and Cindy, my latest ex-roommate ran off with her current boyfriend, leaving me to foot the bill alone.

I needed to make some serious cash during this shift. And maybe get a line on a new job.

It seemed like I always needed more money than I was making, but I still had some pride. I wasn't desperate enough to sleep with my slimy boss to get it.

I tried to live my life by simple rules. I worked hard, didn't cheat, and I didn't steal. Honesty was important to me.

If there was one thing moving to Vegas had taught me, it was the future wasn't guaranteed. God, I'd been so young and stupid. I thought running away was the answer.

Life taught some pretty hard lessons. Losing my family after I ran away to elope with my best friend was difficult. Losing him a few days later to the disease that had stolen his childhood was even worse.

But I'd stayed in Vegas. I had no choice. I'd been estranged from my family, cut off by my parents, and I had nowhere else to go. I'd made my bed and twelve years later I was still there.

But I was more than surviving, and that had to count for something. At least I hoped it did.

Whether you were rich, poor, fat, skinny, smart, average, young, old, good, or not so good—in the end, death came for everyone.

No matter how much money or power you had, or didn't, there was no escaping that Grim mother-fucker. In the end, he was going to reap us all, so why bother?

But people were just people. Mortality was the great equalizer, and I tried to remember that as I served the hungry crowds of revelers and thrill seekers who came to Vegas searching for something they'd likely never find. It made me sad sometimes to think about it.

Everyone deserved to be happy. To feel like they belong. I knew I did. I wanted that for myself. Happiness, friends, family. I had a handful of people I was friendly with, but I found long term relationships difficult to maintain.

Everyone was always coming and going. But not me. I remained.

Stagnant.

I would never experience the carefree, lavish lifestyles the customers who frequented Lux Lounge had, and that was alright. I knew who I was, even if I didn't know where I was going.

And I was happy.

Sorta. Mostly. Ish.

So, until Mr. Royce bounced my fluffy ass out the door, I was going to do my job.

And I was going to do it in three, not four, inch heels, *fuck you very much.*

CHAPTER FIVE
DESTINY

Holy. Hell. It's the Devil himself.

I didn't subscribe to religion in the usual sense. But if there was a Devil, a fallen angel whose principal powers were to seduce, then this was him.

I didn't know his name, but I knew of this particular customer. Over the last couple of nights, he'd come to Lux with his buddy, some big as fuck bearded fellow. Each night, he chose a new table in the VIP section. He was some wealthy high rolling player, but I wasn't familiar with who.

"Welcome to L-Lux," I said, my smile faltering as I finally made my way over to table forty-one.

I just knew it was him because of his eyes. Glittering like molten chocolate, promising sin, and other carnal delights. He really was too good looking to be true.

Everyone from the busboys to the other cocktail waitresses to Enri had been chatting about this guy for the last couple of days.

The brooding playboy billionaire. Moody. Rich as Croesus. Handsome as an Angel. Tempting as Lucifer himself.

I was frozen in his onyx stare. I'd never seen such pitch black irises. And I'd been living in Vegas since I was eighteen.

I'd seen and waited on my share of famous people. Beautiful people. Powerful people. Movie stars. Heads of state. Rockstars. You name it.

But none of them held a candle to him. This man. The Devil.

He was breathtaking. Physically perfect. A face sculpted by angels. A body made for sin. Even seated, I could tell he was big and built.

He had wide shoulders and an athletic build. Chiseled features, high cheekbones and a strong jawline that gave him a sculpted look all the mewing males on social media wished they had.

He really did look like a god. That was what Enri had told me when he'd described him.

He sure filled out his midnight colored suit well enough. Like it was made for him. Of course it was.

Rich, remember?

Everyone knew the term *handsome as the Devil,* but this man, he could have invented it. It wasn't his perfectly symmetrical features. Or those gorgeous, almost black irises. Not his perfectly plump lips or heavenly body either that made him look like the closest thing to the actual Lucifer I'd ever seen.

It was the wildness behind those eyes. The complete and total lack of compassion beneath his glittering gaze. That man could eat me alive.

And that was what frightened me. Not his innate ferocity. But that I was at a point in my life where I just might let him.

Goddamn.

Those impossibly dark eyes seemed to glitter as I stood there with him staring right into my soul. I couldn't bear it for another minute. I had to look away.

Beside him was another man. Strong, silent, and not unattractive, but I could hardly see him next to *Lucifer.*

He seemed bored. Weary maybe. He had a look I recognized, and my heart squeezed for him. Like he was lonely or something.

Yeah, right, Destiny. Does he look like a guy who spends his nights alone?

I remembered myself and where I was. The heavy bass from the DJ booth blasted through the club, but I was used to that and tuned it out. The interior lighting was dark, but there was a constant glow from strategically placed bulbs and strips that made it possible to see.

I knew there was a team of professionals who were responsible for the décor. I had no idea how they did it. How they made it dark and not at the same time, but the result was pretty cool.

They changed the color palette every night, and tonight's theme made the presence of this man even more ethereal. The lights radiated cool, pale blues and whites, making the Devil look even more heavenly.

Shit. What am I doing?

I shook myself from my fanciful reverie.

Oh, right. Work. Lux. Waitressing. On thin ice with Royce.

I dragged my eyes away from the Devil incarnate and smiled at Bearded Man instead. He seemed safer somehow.

Get to work, girl, my inner voice peeped, and I blinked. Hard.

"Excuse me, sorry. Welcome to Lux, my name is Destiny, and I'll be your server tonight. What can I get for you?" I asked, making it a point to keep my eyes fixed on the bearded man.

"Vodka. Your best. One bottle. Two glasses," the stern, Bearded Man said.

"Yes, sir. Would you like any ice? Or lemon?"

He shook his head, and I nodded. I felt the Devil narrow his eyes at me, but I walked away without glancing in his direction again.

Hopefully, he wouldn't see that as a slight and give me a crappy tip. But I didn't need to worry. How many men like Lucifer over there gave two shits if his chubby waitress looked at him?

I checked on my other tables while I waited for Enri to fill the order for table forty-one, grabbing this and that and ignoring Mr. Royce's leers as I walked by.

Bottle service was a luxury seldom afforded even among the wealthy party goers of this den of sin.

I was equal parts excited by the prospect, and nervous about going back there. When you worked in hospitality, you dealt with all sorts of people, and I'd been doing this for more than a decade.

Sure, I'd seen a lot. But I had never seen anything like him.

"Destiny, you're up!" Enri called out, and I hurried back to the bar to grab the tray.

"Ouch!"

I winced as I lifted my arms, the goddamn wire from the corseted top I wore, like every other server there, had started to poke through the material earlier that afternoon.

Just my luck that it finally ripped the rest of the way and was now digging into my right boob.

"You alright?" Enri asked, concerned.

"It's fine. Stupid corset broke."

"I have a Band-Aid. Maybe you can wrap it around the wire that's poking out? But do it after you deliver that bottle and hurry, girl, Royce Rage is on his way," Enri warned, and I nodded.

"Good looking out."

I lifted the tray, ignoring the pain in my breast and pasted a smile on my face.

Who the hell still demanded their female employees wear shit like this, anyway?

Only Mr. Royce, or Royce Rage as he we called him behind his back. It was a play on *roid rage*, since his mood swings mirrored those of those who abused steroids.

All the female staff at Lux Lounge wore deep purple corsets with lace chokers that matched. The pants were moderately better. But they were super tight pants with no pockets or zippers, leaving nothing to the imagination, like at all.

And of course, on our feet were stilettos from hell. Even defying that one code with slightly lower heels, my feet were killing me.

Fuck this fucking uniform.

It was the 21st Century, but we wore purple corsets, skintight pants, and stilettos like we stepped out of some eighties time warp.

My heart started pounding as I carried the tray over to table forty-one. The two men were talking, but I saw the trio of women approaching them and hated that I'd have to interrupt in order to set their order down.

I was so not going to give any attention to the fact all three women were tall, thin, and super hot. If you Googled the exact opposite of me, those three would definitely be featured in your search results.

Thunder roared in my ears, and my stomach twisted in a knot. I had other tables to serve, and I couldn't stand behind those women forever, so I cleared my throat, murmuring an excuse me when that did not work.

"I thought that was you, Marat," one of the

blondes said, leaning over seductively. "Why didn't you come say hello?" she pouted.

"Pardon me," I whispered, trying to ignore the Devil's stare just as he ignored the woman's obvious come ons.

Interesting.

"Would you like me to pour?" I asked the Bearded Man who seemed equally uninterested in the trio of women.

"Thank you, Destiny. That would be fine," he said, and I smiled as he remembered my name.

He dipped his bearded chin, and I realized he was better looking than my first assessment. He couldn't hold a candle to the Devil over there, but who could? That man wasn't meant for this world.

He was something else. Devil. Fallen angel. Too damn beautiful to look at for very long.

Bearded Man, though, he seemed dangerous but human. He was enormous, and from my limited experience I took a wild guess that he was the muscle.

Putting on my best professional smile, I placed the glasses and the premium bottle of vodka on the table, sliding the tray to the floor as I peeled off the wrapping and pushed the crystal cork out with my thumbs.

The fallen angel must be important to have a body-guard, I mused, still not looking at him.

"Marat?" the whiny blonde continued.

"Excuse me, ladies, but I am here on business. Perhaps another time," the Devil, *er,* Marat said, dismissing the women without a passing glance.

I felt his attention on me as I poured, placing one glass in front of Bearded Man and one in front of him.

I wasn't expecting him to touch me, so when his long-fingered hand reached out to brush across my wrist, I jumped.

"Pardon me. Do I make you nervous?" he asked, a grin teasing at the corner of his ridiculously perfect mouth.

"Sorry, um, can I get you anything or do something for you, sir?" I asked, ignoring his question, and lifting the tray in front of me like a shield.

"You know, I believe you can, Destiny."

CHAPTER SIX
MARAT

It was the third night in a row we'd wound up at Lux Lounge. Fucking pretentious ass club.

But I needed a date for the stupid awards event, and I was having no luck.

Was there no one in the whole of Las Vegas even remotely interesting?

Every single simpering female who approached me gave off the same desperate vibe I'd been trying to escape.

I wanted none of them.

"The award gala is tomorrow night," Josef stated, unnecessarily explaining the itinerary to me. "You really need to settle on a date or that Tessa will eat you alive, Marat. She's a fucking snake, and she's had her eye on you too long, my friend. You know this already."

"Yeah, I know."

I got the same fucking email he did. But whatever. I'd known him forever, and he was Adrik's age.

Josef was the head of security for Volkov Industries. But he was more than that. He'd been with Adrik since his days as an international criminal, working as extra muscle. He was family. And that meant he treated me like a little brother.

It was taxing at the best of times.

"Then you know this whole thing is a fucking ploy to get the infamous Marat Volkov in her clutches again? She was the one who put Volkov Industries up for the award," he informed me.

"No, I didn't know that. It doesn't matter. Andres' efforts were good, and the company deserves the award. It's good publicity. And Tessa was last year. She knows I don't go for seconds. Everyone knows that."

"Rumor is she is looking for a husband—"

"It won't be me," I scoffed.

Funny, the idea of marriage used to scare the shit out of me. But after being around Adrik and Sofia, I realized it wasn't the institution that was so off-putting, but the idea of being tied to the wrong person.

A woman like Tessa would never suit me. I did not want a cold, empty shell of a person. I wanted someone who was real.

But in my world, I was more likely to find a fucking unicorn.

"Why not skip this?" Josef asked, interrupting my thoughts.

"The award matters to Adrik, so I will attend the gala and I will accept it. I just have to pick someone out to join me for the event," I growled, eyes prowling the establishment for someone suitable.

I was tired of this conversation. Bored with the whole fucking thing. If Volkov Industries wasn't so important to Adrik, I'd have told McNeil Corp to shove their humanitarian award up their fucking ass. I'd have been back on my jet, away from this godforsaken city.

But appearances mattered in the business world. Especially for a company whose history was as dark and shrouded in violence as ours was.

Josef understood this. It was why he was still around. His loyalty proved constant, and as such, he'd been rewarded for it with a nice chunk of our business.

A rich motherfucker in his own right, Josef did not need to work. But he loved tech as much as my brother and I, so he stayed on, heading not just physical security, but our cyber divisions as well.

"Welcome to L-Lux," she said.

Was she for real? Did sweetness like that really exist in a place like this?

I had to do a double take. Her appearance had already captivated me, but that voice of hers?

Fuck. Me.

It was husky and rich, but sweet at the same time. The dulcet tones wrapped around my chest, squeezing me until I couldn't get any air in my lungs.

It was nothing at all like the whines and pouts of insipid heiresses and cover models I usually went around with. Those were the circles I now ran in, but the sparkle had dulled.

I was tired of that lifestyle. Watching Adrik and Sofia made me want things I never had before, and looking and listening to this waitress, suddenly, I wanted them even more.

At first, it was her soft curves that called to me.

Different. Beautiful. So damn jiggly when she walked.

I wanted to bury my face in those tits. I bet they made for a soft landing. And that ass. My god. Wars had been started over less bountiful things than her perfect peach of an ass.

Then, I saw her face and confirmed, yes, she was every bit as gorgeous as I thought. But now that I'd heard her? I wanted more.

The sultry syllables she uttered floated over to me, stroking my ears like hands. I wanted her to say something else. Anything else. I just wanted her to keep talking. But she wasn't even looking at me anymore.

Look at me, Baby. Come on.

Sweet little Dumplin' was frozen in place. I made a noise, somewhere between a growl and a hum, and her gaze flashed to mine, but only for a moment.

Then her attention was back on Josef. What the fuck? I frowned. Hard.

I was annoyed. Stunned. Maybe a bit petulant. Sure, that kind of behavior was beneath me, but what could I say? Women didn't ignore me. Ever.

That wasn't conceit. It was simply a fact. But this woman was making it look easy. My sweet little temptation had no problem acting like I didn't exist.

It's a dangerous game you're playing, Baby.

I'd been called an arrogant asshole before, but for the first time I actually felt like one. This poor woman was trying to work, but I was already making plans to put every move I had on her.

Act like I don't exist? Fuck that.

I was Marat Volkov. I was accustomed to snapping my fingers and having women line up for a fraction of my attention.

This curvy little minx wasn't going to ignore me and get away with it.

I tried staring, letting her feel the weight of my stare. But she didn't acknowledge or react. I frowned. Giving someone who refused to look at you your attention was harder than it looked.

I couldn't let it go. I licked my bottom lip, a move that had made grown women moan. But she didn't notice.

Sucking in a breath, I leaned forward and tilted my head. I studied her to the point of glowering. Her gaze flitted to mine once, but she went right back to paying attention to Josef.

Couldn't give up yet. So, I just kept on staring.

It was rude. Invasive. I ran my eyes up and down her body. Stopping to pay proper homage to her big, bountiful breasts, and the delicious curve of her hip.

I made sure she felt the burn of my gaze down to her fucking marrow. I knew it was over the top.

Borderline creepy.

But I wasn't about to let her get away without feeling even a little bit of what I was going through, sitting there while she acted like I was invisible.

Me?

It was preposterous. It was intriguing. For the first time in months, something caught my attention and like a dog with a bone, I wasn't about to let it go.

"Excuse me, sorry. Um, my name is Destiny, and I'll be your server tonight. What can I get for you?" she murmured, and the effect was immediate.

My heart hammered inside my chest and my cock hardened even more. What would she sound like in bed? Would she moan and mewl or was she a screamer?

I bet I could drag sounds from her no man ever has. I want to. Goddamn, do I want to.

Thump. Thump. Thump.

CHAPTER SEVEN
MARAT

"Vodka. Your best. One bottle. Two glasses," Josef said, interrupting my X-rated train of thought.

His professional tone was the only reason I didn't do something I'd likely regret. Like slapping him upside the head for even looking at her.

Sure, I'd been trained. I knew how to fight. But I rarely engaged in physical altercations.

Why would I when I had the Dark Wolf for my brother and Josef for security?

That didn't mean I couldn't hold my own with either of them. After all, they were the ones who taught me.

"Yes, sir. Would you like any ice? Or lemon?" she asked, her sexy voice tying me up in knots.

Jesus fucking Christ.

I knew what I wanted as a belated birthday present.

This woman on her knees saying *yes, sir.* Just the thought had my cock straining against my zipper.

"No. Just the vodka," Josef said.

Destiny nodded her understanding, making her tits bounce in that goddamn corset, and Josef made a humming sound of approval.

I wanted to punch the asshole in the throat. Why the fuck was he even there?

I wasn't a child anymore, for fuck's sake. Okay, fine, I knew why Adrik insisted I had a guard with me.

Being rich and powerful drew more targets on my brother and me than being criminals ever did. Not that I was ever much of a criminal. A few times, I'd tagged along on smuggling runs and territory disputes.

Going legit was not any less volatile. Hostile takeovers, corporate espionage, and nasty business mergers were every bit as harrowing as a turf war between rival gangs. Honestly, it was a tossup which was more deadly.

But I didn't give a shit about any of that as I sat at

my VIP table at Lux Lounge, dreading the next day's events, and lusting after a curvy goddess I could not have.

I'd have given anything I had to be alone right then. Alone with her, of course.

Josef usually accompanied Adrik on trips, but since I was taking more of an active role, I supposed it made sense he was with me instead.

But that didn't mean I liked it when our sexy as fuck waitress kept her big blue eyes trained on him during both of our first interaction with her.

She intrigued me. Okay, fine. More than that.

I'd been sitting there with an uncomfortably hard dick since the second I saw her in that barely there outfit. *A corset.* Of course she had on a fucking corset.

This was Vegas, after all, and cocktail waitresses usually had some sort of getup on. The tight purple lingerie pushed her big tits up to her fucking neck, leaving her cleavage visible to everyone in the vicinity.

Fuck. The realization had me stuck between tamping down my raging desire and fighting my burning need to punch every motherfucker who could see her glorious display.

What the fuck was wrong with me? I never got possessive of women. Especially not strangers.

That was my brother's thing. Not mine. And yet, I was arguably on tenterhooks, straining to control my out of whack emotions.

She walked away, her hips twisting as she returned to the bar, and I almost fell out of my chair watching her. My cock thumped against my slacks, and I had to bite back a groan.

"Bro, you okay?" Josef asked.

I ignored the amusement in his tone. It was better for both of us. Besides, the answer was no. I was not okay.

It had been months since I shared my bed with anyone, and the truth of the matter was nothing interested me. Nothing attracted me anymore.

Well, nothing had until I walked into Lux Lounge and saw *her*.

Thump. Thump. Thump.

Goddamn. She looked positively sinful in purple satin and lace and those fucking painted on pants.

On some of the other female staff, the outfit was almost chaste. It was boring. Cliché. Uninspired.

Sure, there were plenty with silicone enhanced bosoms who filled it out. But not like her.

This woman was one hundred percent real, and

for the first time in maybe ever, I was completely captivated.

"Are you sure there is nothing wrong?" Josef asked, interrupting my staring.

"Nothing's wrong, old man. Just waiting for our drinks to arrive."

I felt excitement building in my veins as I watched our server pick up the tray with our bottle and glasses on it. I leaned forward, concerned the tray was heavy.

She was a tiny thing for all her curves, and wearing those high heels while she trounced around waiting on people couldn't have been doing her any favors.

Her hips swayed with every step, and I wanted to rip those tight pants down her thick thighs to see what she had on underneath them.

I knew it wasn't much. I could practically see her hair follicles, they were so goddamn tight.

There went my cock again. After months of nothing, this little Dumplin' was conjuring a reaction out of me even the most stunning supermodels couldn't evoke.

And believe me, they tried.

Thump. Thump. Thump.

Her skin was so pale and smooth. My mouth

watered as I watched the creamy tops of her tits jiggle with every step. I wanted to bury my face right there. To kiss those mounds. Lick them. Bite them. Push my cock between them until I came all over her. Fuck. I bit back my groan.

I want her. Jesus Christ. I fucking want her.

CHAPTER EIGHT
MARAT

Her dark curly hair was swept back from her soft face in some kind of complicated knot at her nape. She had blue eyes lined with some smoky dark shit women did to tantalize men.

I didn't know shit about makeup or fashion. Never really paid attention. The women I typically dated wore so much crap caked on their faces, the few times I'd seen them without it they were unrecognizable.

Not that I cared what a woman did to make herself feel good. *Wear makeup. Don't wear makeup.* It was none of my business what a woman did, and I wasn't so arrogant as to tell one what she could or could not do.

Then again, maybe I'd simply been uninterested in what other women wore. This woman, though, she interested me. I wouldn't mind watching her get dressed. Or undressed.

Preferably the latter.

Whatever she did to her face, the effect was stunning. But I had a feeling this woman would not look like a different person if I saw her early in the morning, her face clean of all cosmetics.

Suddenly, I wanted that. I wanted her in my bed early in the morning with nothing on. No clothes. No makeup. Nothing between us. Nothing at all.

I knew quality, and she had that. The makeup she wore was minimal. Even with the dim lights and crowd of people, I could make out her unblemished skin and glossy pink lips from across the room.

Those eyes those, they were the clincher. They fucking glowed like I imagined an angel's would, and my mouth went dry as I watched her approach.

I could almost picture them trained on me while I dove headfirst between her legs to feast on her sweet ambrosia. And it would be sweet. I just fucking knew it would.

How could it not be? She was so soft. Plump. Delicious. Tempting. *So fucking tempting.* My sexy little Dumplin' was made just to beguile and entice me.

Only me.

I wanted her. Any part of her. Every part of her. In my mouth.

Now. Right fucking now.

My line of vision was suddenly cut off, and I growled unhappily as three women, one who looked vaguely familiar, stepped in front of me. I was used to getting approached. Hell, there was a time I welcomed it. But not now.

Not when the only woman I'd wanted in too long a time was headed back my way. Only now my view of her sexy little walk was blocked by this group of skinny, uninteresting females wanting to ride my jock.

"I thought that was you, Marat," one of the three women said. "Why didn't you come say hello?"

I ignored the interruption, willing the trio of blondes to disappear. Did I know them? Possibly. But fuck if I remembered.

I knew that made me a dick. But did it, really? Whenever I bedded a woman, I made sure she knew it was casual at best.

I never pretended to be interested in anything

other than whatever we had been engaged in at the time. And I never went back for seconds.

These women should have waited for a sign, or an invitation. Neither of which they would have gotten.

Was I an asshole?

Maybe.

Fine.

Definitely.

But I sure as fuck did not call those women over to my table. They were fucking with my mood, and I wanted them gone.

"Pardon me," Dumplin' whispered.

Why was she looking down? And why was her voice so soft, so unsure? She was back to looking at Josef, and I frowned harder.

I wanted to catch her attention by any means. But she kept her gaze averted, and it was driving me mad.

"It's been awhile since you've been here," the blonde kept talking.

How fucking clearer did I have to be that I was not interested in her or anything she had to say? My face averted, I completely ignored the three women.

I brooded instead. Watching Dumplin' interact

with my bodyguard, offering him tentative glances and shy smiles.

Still acting like I was fucking invisible. My gut twisted. It left me feeling stranded, stunned even. How was I supposed to talk to her if she wouldn't even look at me?

What the fuck is up with this woman?

"Would you like me to pour?" She asked in that husky, rich voice that went straight to my balls.

My dick strained, and the blonde currently bent over in front of me eyed it like she was responsible. I restrained from telling her to fuck off.

Barely.

I kept my eyes on her, on Destiny. Cute name, but I doubted it was real. Besides, to me she was Dumplin'.

A delicious treat I wanted to devour. My wild reaction to her as she continued talking to Josef was completely unprecedented.

Fuck. I was jealous. Me.

To an outsider, my bodyguard might have looked oblivious. But because I knew the motherfucker, I could tell he was getting a kick out of her ignoring me and my reaction to her dismissal.

Simmering fury was a pretty apt description for my increasingly unbridled emotions.

Why won't she even look at me?

"Thank you, Destiny. That would be fine," the asshole said, dipping his manly bearded chin as he waited for her to pour.

Fucking dick.

He could pour his own drink. Josef had two hands. It was all I could do not to reach out and grab the fucking bottle, pluck it from the tabletop before she could, and pour his stupid vodka myself.

But I stopped myself. Forcing my brain to ask the questions I'd been avoiding. Like why I didn't want her to do it? It was her job.

Maybe it was because she was so damn petite and fragile looking. For the first time in my life, I wanted to ease someone else's burden, and that was a total fucking surprise.

More than likely, it was because I was a selfish, greedy prat who wanted her all to myself.

I made fists with my hands and watched hungrily as she moved the glasses closer to her, tucking the tray unobtrusively away as she opened the bottle.

"Marat?" the blonde whined.

Were they still there? I sighed. These women did not take hints well. It was bad enough they'd approached me without an invitation, but the fact they still stood there waiting for a crumb of atten-tion was just embarrassing. *For me and for them.*

I'd been downright ungracious, but now it was time for me to be blunt. They needed to take the fucking hint.

"Excuse me, I am having a drink with my friend here. Perhaps you'd be happier chatting with someone more attentive to your needs," I said, not giving a fuck.

I didn't acknowledge their affronted gasps. And I didn't pay attention as they walked away with promises to see me soon.

My eyes and ears were on *her* alone. My tempting little Dumplin'.

She'd just finished the second pour when I decided I couldn't wait another second. I needed to feel her.

Never one to deny myself any earthly pleasures, I reached out and touched the soft skin on her wrist with my fingers, making her jump.

"Pardon me," I murmured, encouraged by the feel of her pulse racing beneath my fingertips. "Do I make you nervous?"

"**D**o I make you nervous?"

Holy hell. What was even going on? Was the Devil touching me?

My eyes darted around nervously, waiting for Mr. Royce to come out of the woodwork to scream at me or fire me.

There was zero tolerance for fraternizing with customers, and I was pretty sure that involved touching them. Even if he was the one who reached for me.

But I couldn't move. I was frozen in place. Finally, I managed to lift my gaze to his, *and holy hotness*, the result was a flood between my legs.

His eyes glittered in the dim light like shards of

obsidian. I had to admit he was pretty damn spectacular.

Beautiful and dark. Like a fallen angel. Maybe he *was* Lucifer himself.

That he kept staring at me was incomprehensible. I had to wonder if I'd done something wrong, offended him somehow. There was no way a man who looked like that would gaze at me so intently unless I'd done something wrong.

I wanted to ask, but like I said, I was frozen in place. Caught somewhere between wanting to know if he was only touching me because I did something wrong and not wanting him to stop.

The looks he kept exchanging with his buddy were puzzling. Maybe they were a couple? Maybe this was some sort of sex thing? Like a jealousy game. Or they were looking for someone to complete their menage?

I'd never participated in an Eiffel tower, but I was not strictly against it. Of course, I wasn't about to let anyone use me as a pawn. But it was my birthday, and a little fantasizing wouldn't hurt anyone.

OMG! I can't believe I just thought that!

I squirmed, shuffling from foot to foot as inconspicuously as possible. He hadn't let me go yet, and I wasn't exactly in a rush to make him.

He was really *really* nice to look at, and I'd never been grabbed by someone with a face that could make angels weep.

Shallow much? Maybe.

But I was human, and it wasn't often a gorgeous man, gay or not, invited me to his table.

This is wrong.

"Sorry, um, can I get you anything or do something for you, sir?" I asked.

"You know, I believe you can, Destiny," he replied, gifting me with a panty-melting grin.

"Josef, take a walk, will you? I need to speak with Destiny here about something."

"Sure," Bearded Man, aka Josef, said.

"Oh, I can't—"

But he was already on his feet and guiding me into a seat. Jesus Christ, he was tall.

I had a thing for tall men. Maybe it was because I was so round. They made me feel smaller. Well, they let me pretend I was smaller.

Not that I would have to pretend with him. He was positively gigantic. Like Superman big.

I wonder if he's that big everywhere.

My eyes dropped to his lap as he squeezed in beside me and I felt my cheeks heat.

Eeek! What was wrong with me? I should have

switched tables with someone else the second I saw this devilish man sitting there.

I frowned, a certain green-eyed monster growling on my shoulder, and I shook my head. This was insane.

He was a stranger, *a customer*, and I had no reason to feel any way about him at all.

But that didn't stop my pulse from racing, or thunder from roaring in my ears. I couldn't stop my reaction to him anymore than I could stop the tide.

Besides, it was my birthday, I reminded myself again. And really, what was the harm in pretending I was there for him? Like this was a date.

How pathetic am I?

I would have groaned if I thought he wouldn't hear it. But he would have. So I didn't.

He angled his body, mostly blocking me from the crowd, and I appreciated that. The last thing I wanted was to have Royce Rage coming at me again. That jerk.

But this was a nice job, and I made more money at Lux in a night than I made in a week at my last gig. Vegas was not cheap. But neither was New Jersey.

The money I sent my brother every week helped

him pay for our mother's care. I might have been estranged from my family, but I still felt a responsibility towards the woman who birthed me.

After all, you only had one mother, right? And even if she disapproved of my running away with Timmy, she'd been good to me when I was a kid.

I didn't begrudge her a thing. Besides, it was my dad who made her cut off ties with me. He was long gone now. But I forgave him for what he did, and when I found out he'd died, I prayed that he forgave me.

All that heartache and sadness was too much to think about right then. The fact was my mother needed constant care now. The kind only assisted living could provide. And it was expensive.

So, yeah, I needed my job. I had to keep it. I could not afford to lose my head.

Even if there was something about this stranger that made my blood stir in a way I'd never felt. He was just so much.

So attractive. So masculine. So beautiful. And so sad.

Why would a man with the face and body of an angel be so somber?

Power and raw masculine energy seemed to roll

off him in waves. I had no doubt he was a man very used to getting his way.

For a moment, I wondered what that must be like. Was it as fun as it sounded?

Looking into his almost black eyes, I doubted it. There was a sadness there behind the wall he'd erected around himself like an invisible force field.

I wanted to go to him. Tears pricked my eyes, and I forced them back. I wanted to cry for him, for this beautiful man. I wanted to wrap him up in my arms and comfort him. Soothe away that haunted look. Ease his burdens and wash his troubles away.

I shook my head again. I was being foolish. Stupid. Running away with my imagination. And it was going to cost me my job.

Wake up, girl. Stop drooling over this guy and get to work.

Really, I should have asked someone to switch tables with me the second I saw him. But one look into his deep, dark eyes and I couldn't bring myself to do that.

I wasn't going anywhere. This was my table. Royce gave it to me, and I was going to ride this thing out. At worst, I'd get a lousy tip. And it wouldn't be the first time.

Yes, he looked like sin personified, but it wasn't

like I was going to rip my clothes off and ask him to take me right there. I wasn't insane.

I could handle getting drinks for a sexy man. It was what I did. I waited on people. It was my job. I was being stupid.

What could possibly happen?

CHAPTER TEN
MARAT

I licked my bottom lip, watching her throat work as she swallowed down a lungful of air.

She shivered.

Involuntarily?

Maybe. I wondered if she was cold. Unlikely since the temperature inside the club seemed to be comfortable. A relief from the sweltering heat of the Neon City.

Maybe she trembled for a different reason. Maybe she was suffering from the same primitive desire I felt burning in my veins for her.

I fucking hoped so. My pulse raced as I watched her tremble a second time. Fuck. Would she shiver like that when I undressed her? I bet I could make her legs shake.

I bet I could knock her right off her feet.

Josef said something, and reality came crashing into my fantasies. We weren't alone. If I saw her shivering, that meant others could see her too.

I wanted to cover her up. To warm her. Hide her. Make it so no one else could see any part of her.

The pulse at the base of her neck was racing. Those creamy topped tits of hers were rising and falling as her breathing increased. And my dick was harder than before.

Thump. Thump. Thump.

"Sorry, um, can I get you anything or do something for you, sir?" she asked.

I did not miss the way she placed the tray in front of her body. Like a shield. As if the small circle could somehow hide her from me.

"You know, I believe you can, Destiny," I said, grinning widely.

"Josef, take a walk, will you? I need to speak with Destiny here about something alone."

"Sure thing," Josef agreed, standing up and walking away discreetly.

"Oh, I can't do that," she argued weakly as I rose to my feet, towering over her.

With my hand on her back, I pressed her

forward, guiding her into the seat. I wanted her ass right where I'd just been sitting.

Something about having her sweet as fuck body on the same leather that I'd just warmed felt right.

She let out the cutest little squeak when I moved in beside her. Suddenly, I wondered what other noises my little Dumplin' made when she got excited. Curiosity got the better of me and I leaned closer, pressing my leg up against hers.

I turned my body blocking her from view. I coveted this creature. That was rare, almost unheard of for me.

"Look, I am not sure what this is about, and I am sorry. But I'm already on thin ice with my boss," she said, her pretty blue eyes sparkling in the dim light.

Goddamn. She was pretty. Really pretty.

I'd seen beautiful women. I'd had countless encounters with glamorous faces, perfect zero fat bodies with silicone enhancements. But I could not recall a single time that any of them made me feel this way.

There was something wholesome and entirely tangible about this woman. A quality of realness that I wanted for my own.

"This boss of yours, has he threatened or hurt you?" I asked, feeling my ire rise at the idea.

If someone browbeat or abused this precious woman, I was going to find out. And I was going to fucking gut them. It wasn't even a question.

"What? No. But he is kind of a prick, and like I said, I'm on thin ice. I need this job."

"Destiny," I started. "Is that your real name? Never mind, it's not important. What if I offered you a better job?"

"What? A job? Why do you own a hotel or a restaurant in town? Are you looking for waitresses?" she asked.

I watched her nose scrunch up adorably. She shuffled on the seat and her mouthwatering citrusy fragrance filled my senses.

I bit my bottom lip again. Fuck. This girl was so tempting. So damn sexy. I wonder if she knew it.

"No. I don't own a restaurant and I'm not looking for a waitress."

"Then what are you talking about?"

"Where are you from?" I asked, her accent seemed familiar.

"Originally, I'm from New Jersey. But I've lived here for over a decade. Why do you ask?" she canted her head curiously.

"Jersey girl, I knew it," I murmured.

Of all the luck.

"Yep. That's me. Are you from New Jersey?"

"Not exactly," I said. "But someone I care very much about is from there."

"Oh," she murmured, gaze dropping.

"Oh?"

"This person you care about, are they still around?"

"Sure. Married my brother, in fact."

"Oh my god, that's terrible. Your brother stole your girl?"

Sympathy replaced horror. Both passed over her face, and I couldn't help it, I laughed. Relief showed next, and I was ridiculously pleased at the depth of emotion I read so easily in her big blue eyes.

When was the last time I even cared to take a deeper look?

"No! Not at all," I told her truthfully. "The jersey girl I mention was always like a sister to me. Nothing romantic there."

"Oh. Oh," she said the second *oh* like she'd just discovered something or confirmed it.

I wondered what it was, but she was already saying something else, so I didn't get to ask.

"So, was there something you needed? Because I really can't take a break right now."

"I like you, Destiny. You intrigue me."

"Bullshit!"

She slapped her hand over her mouth two seconds too late to cover her snort.

She snorted. Actually snorted. How fucking cute is this girl?

I barked a laugh, my second of the night. I was just as shocked as she appeared to be. Embarrassment burned her cheeks, but I was already reaching up to pull her hand down from her mouth.

"Oh my god, that was crass. Sorry."

She winced. Her body jerked like she'd been elbowed or something, but it wasn't me. I hadn't touched her. I frowned as she grabbed at her side and looked down at her torso.

"Don't apologize. It was funny. And honest. But, uh, is something wrong?" I asked, following her gaze down her tightly wrapped body.

That fucking corset was a laced up bit of naughtiness. It made her look like a goddamn present. All hooks and ribbons, satin, lace, and peekaboo holes, revealing little swatches of pale skin.

Not to mention her glorious tits were practically spilling out of the thing. One wrong move and she'd have a wardrobe malfunction of epic proportions.

Part of me secretly wished for it. Another part of

me feared it. Because if anyone else saw her naked flesh, I wasn't sure I'd be able to control my reactions.

My emotions were rioting all over the place. I wanted to rip the fucking thing off her sexy body and discover all her secrets for myself.

But I also wanted to take off my jacket, cover her up, toss her over my shoulder, and carry her sweet ass out of there.

Both options have merit.

"No, well, yeah," she replied, biting her lower lip. "My top."

"Your top?" I repeated like a moron.

"Listen, is your, *uh, friend* giving you a hard time?" she asked, gaze darting to where Josef had been sitting.

"I mean, I'm flattered you wanted to chat, but are you just one of those bored rich guys looking for a confidant or something? Or if you need, um, *prescriptive entertainment*, Enri at the bar is better suited to help—"

"Are you asking me if I want drugs, Baby?" I asked, trying to hide my smile.

"No! I mean, no, of course not, but if there was something—"

"I need something," I agreed, my gaze still stuck on the creamy mounds of her breasts. "What's going on with your top?"

And please can I help? I wanted to add, but I didn't. I wasn't a total fucking pig.

I watched as she raised her blue eyes to mine. I didn't have a clue what was going on inside her pretty little head, but she was gazing at me intently before coming to some conclusion.

"Alright, I'll tell you because we're *friends*, and because, you know, I'm not like a prude or anything."

"Of course," I mumbled, not sure where this was going.

She nodded, then looked around, I assumed to make sure no one was watching.

"All frigging night long, the stupid under wire in this thing has been digging into my side boob, and I swear it's trying to cut me open."

She inhaled and those fucking tits jiggled, the corset pushing them so high I thought they might touch her chin. Then she exhaled roughly and winced again. Her pain made me forget my lecherous staring.

"What? Are you okay?" I asked, horrified at the thought of her being hurt, not to mention utterly baffled.

What the fuck was a side boob? Did she have more than the usual two?

I had no idea, but I was so on board with finding out.

"I just haven't had a minute to fix it. But could you do me a favor? Just sit right like that," she whispered, and I obliged, turning my body to shield her even further from unwanted eyes.

I watched, my eyes bulging out of my head as she reached into her cup and adjusted her tit.

Her whole fucking tit.

Glimpses of creamy pale skin and her dusky pink nipple filled my vision and I had to swallow down the drool that filled my mouth.

She sighed aloud, and it went straight to my cock. The sound was one of pure relief as she tucked the piece of metal back behind the fabric and rubbed the angry red spot on the side of her boob.

Side boob. Got it. Would it be wrong of me to ask if I could kiss it and make it better?

Probably.

Damn it.

Then she was back to lifting her tit and adjusting the fucking corset once more.

I went cross-eyed.

Jesus fucking Christ.

The woman was trying to kill me. She had a gorgeous body. Creamy, smooth skin, with just the right amount of jiggle. So soft and plump. Mouthwatering. Fucking perfect.

I wanted her even more.

"Dumplin', you flash those tits at me again and I'm putting my mouth on them, I don't care where we are," I growled.

"Flash my tits? Oh shit. Wait—you're not gay?" she asked, and my eyebrows went sky high.

"Gay? No, I'm not gay," I scoffed.

Admittedly, it was not the first time someone made that assumption. I knew what I looked like. Tall, built, handsome, and dressed to the nines.

But no, I wasn't gay.

"Oh my god, I just assumed that you must be gay cause you ignored the three hottest women here, and now you're talking to me. Wait. *Is* there something wrong with the service?" she asked, flitting from one subject to the next so fast it was fascinating to watch.

"Okay, first—"

"Oh, and I wasn't trying to flash you or anything! I really thought, well, never mind what I thought. I just didn't want the under wire to cut into my boob.

I am really making a mess of all this. I'm sorry. I mean that, I am really sorry," she blurted, speaking even more rapidly at the end.

Her Jersey accent was more pronounced as her stress levels maxed out. It was so fucking cute.

But I almost didn't catch all of what she said, I was so damn distracted by the heaving of her chest and her hypnotic eyes.

"Okay, first," I tried again slowly, seeing if she'd interrupt. "You don't need to apologize, Destiny. You did nothing wrong."

I placed my hand on the back of her neck, gently squeezing to reassure her. I needed her to understand I was serious.

"The service is fine, Baby," I added.

She lifted those goddamn gorgeous baby blues to mine and nodded. Then, my sweet little temptation exhaled slowly, and her body seemed to relax against mine.

"Second, just so we're clear, I'm straight. I have nothing against it. I think everyone should be free to pursue whatever makes them happy. I'm just not gay," I said, stopping again to let that settle in her pretty little head.

"Third, I'm talking to you because I want to talk

to you. And fourth—now, pay attention, Dumplin', cause it's the most important thing I'm going to say —*you* are the hottest woman here," I told her.

I punctuated the statement with an extra squeeze before releasing my grip. Call me a caveman, but I needed her to get caught up with everything I was feeling.

And I was feeling caught between actual astonishment, pure carnal hunger, and absolute delight. My little Dumplin' managed to surprise me at every turn so far, and that alone was worth the discomfort of having a hard on in tight pants.

She thought I was gay.

I shook my head. I knew what she was thinking. Why else would I chat her up? She was thicker than most of the other servers there. A little older, too. Not that she was old. She was my age.

She was probably thinking she wasn't my type. That I was running some game on her.

But she was so fucking wrong.

Truth was, I didn't even know I had a type till I saw her. Women of all sizes, shapes, and color came on to me all the time. I was a man who appreciated beauty.

I never picked, though. It was always the same everywhere I went. I'd walk in and the hottest women in the room flocked to me. But now I saw what I'd been missing.

Destiny was the sexiest woman in that place. No contest. I didn't give a fuck what society said and fuck people who thought body-shaming anyone was okay. It wasn't.

The tempting little morsel had me wanting to prove my heterosexuality right there. I wouldn't mind bending her over the table and showing her how hard she made me. How much I wanted her.

"Sorry, oh, *um*, I am *not* sorry," she said, correcting herself.

I hummed in approval. Good Girl. She remembered I said not to apologize. She was even hotter, following directions. I wondered if she would follow them in bed.

Thump. Thump. Thump.

"That's right. No apologies," I murmured.

Unable to help myself. I reached up and tucked a stray curl behind her ear, relishing the softness of her hair between my fingers.

"I just don't know what you want from me," she said.

"How about we start with conversation and go from there?"

"Um, I'm sure you're not used to being told *no*.

But like I said before, my boss is in a mood, and I need this job. I can't afford to give him another excuse to fire me."

"Why is he *in a mood*?" I asked, curious.

She exhaled and shrugged. I cup her chin between my forefinger and thumb and tipped her face back to me. Not willing to confront my need for her gaze on me at all times, I simply stared and waited.

"Tell me," I prompted.

"Well, I've been here about a year. It's a really good run for someone like me at a place like this. But Mr. Royce has been getting kind of insistent and impatient. I imagine my days are numbered."

"A girl like you?" I asked, canting my head as I waited for her to continue.

She looked embarrassed, but I wasn't going to quit until she told me. Something about her just compelled me to want to know everything I could learn.

No, this was not my normal MO. But whatever it was that was different about her, it made me want things I never had before.

"Yeah, a girl like me," she repeated, rolling her pretty blue eyes. "I don't want to shock you, but I am not the typical Vegas cocktail waitress."

"How do you mean?" I baited her.

"Oh my god, I'm short and fat, okay? And I turned thirty today, so—"

I frowned, about to scold her.

Did she just—wait? What?

"Hey, it's your birthday?"

"It is. Sorr—I mean, it's no big deal," she agreed, and blushed.

"Of course it is. I had mine a few days ago. Happy Birthday, Baby," I said, smiling widely at the pure delight that registered in her eyes.

"Thank you."

"As for that other stuff. Don't talk about yourself like that, hear me? You look exactly how a woman should look. Fuckin' perfect," I growled.

She just sat there, staring at me like she couldn't believe what I'd said. But I meant every word. She was fucking perfect, and I hated that she thought otherwise.

Sure, my past was filled with women like the ones she called hot, but I never limited myself to a certain type. I liked women of all shapes and sizes.

Contrary to her beliefs, Dumplin' was just my type. Maybe even more so because even working in Sin City, she had an air of innocence I found breathtaking.

And I was greedy for more.

CHAPTER ELEVEN
MARAT

"I wanna know more about your boss, though."

"My boss? Oh, nothing, he's pretty par for the course."

"Come again?"

"You know, he's pushy. Wants to date all the girls. Some say yes right away. Like they just wanna get it over with."

"You date him?"

"Me? No. Actually, I've been lucky. I've been here a year without being backed into a corner, but now I think he sees me as a challenge."

She made a face that said she was repulsed, and it was all I could do not to go after the motherfucker right then. She shouldn't be working in a place that made her feel unsafe. No one should have to do that.

"He's been pushy with you sexually?" I growled.

I needed to make sure I understood everything that asshole was guilty of before I went after him. He was already going to pay. That wasn't in question.

But how much he would pay? That would depend on her next words.

"Well, he's asked me out, but I'm not stupid. The girls talk. When you go out with him, he expects sex. And I am not having sex with that man."

"Damn fucking straight you're not. Hasn't anyone told the owner?"

"No way. No one wants to get a rep for being a shit stirrer in this town. You could end up black-listed and most of us are hardworking people who need these jobs," she replied, shaking her head.

"That's messed up. No one, male or female, should ever feel pressure to date or have sex with their boss, Dumplin'. That's just un-fucking-acceptable!"

"That's life. But it's not so bad, really. And I'll be fine. I didn't mean to sound like it was do or die. And I didn't mean to make you upset or angry—"

"Shit," I muttered, running my hand over my face. "Look, I have a temper, I admit it. But I'm not angry with you, Dumplin'. If someone is making you uncomfortable, though, I want you to know I'll take care of it."

"Oh no, please. You don't even know me. You don't have to do that," she said, shaking her head and trying to downplay her situation.

Most women would have tried asking me to hook them up with a different job or something at this point. They would be making promises by now, trying to gain access to people I knew, exchanging favors for favors. They'd be hustling.

But not her. She wasn't like that. Awareness crept through my veins and for the first time in a long time, I felt alive.

I interrupted her objection. There was no point in listening to her objections. This woman had me so on edge, of course I was going to do something.

"I gotta ask if it isn't about him pressuring you to date him, why do you think he wants to fire you?"

"Oh, uh, I'm wearing the wrong shoes today," she said, and shrugged.

I glanced down, checking out her tiny feet in the tall pumps. Wrong shoes?

"Their supposed to be four inches high, these are only three. Mr. Royce has a mark on the wall in his office and he checks each one of the waitresses every night to make sure we comply."

"What the fuck? Must have a foot fetish."

"Probably."

She worried her bottom lip with her teeth. I was dying to take over doing that for her, but I managed to catch myself.

"So, you're a rule breaker, I like that. But why wait to be fired? Why not leave?"

"Well, that's easy. Money," she scoffed. "I mean, the diner where I used to work never bounced back from Covid and when they closed their doors, it was hard for a while. I lucked out when my ex-roommate told me about this place. It was a long shot, but I got hired."

"That was a year ago," I said, making sure I had the timeline right.

"About that, yeah. I expected Mr. Royce to give up trying to get me to go out with him."

"And you've never?" I had to ask.

"Hell no," she said, nose wrinkled in disgust. "Even if I was tempted, which I was not the rumor is that *Royce Rage*, that's his nickname, has a teeny tiny dick."

"Royce Rage?"

"Yeah. He has mood swings," she explained, and I hated the fucker already.

"Mood swings and a small dick. That's why the steroid rumor," I said, explaining it to myself.

"Yep," she agreed.

"So, size does matter," I replied.

I had to steer the topic away from her boss before I did something dumb and acted on the ridiculous jealousy I was feeling.

"Well, if you haven't figured that out, then you can just thank god for that face of yours. I bet women cream themselves just looking at you," she replied with a candor I found both irresistible and refreshing.

"You're not wrong," I said and frowned.

I had to admit I suffered from a preconceived notion that women just enjoyed sex no matter what they got. To me it was just something that happened between mutually consenting parties.

Had I ever had someone not derive pleasure from engaging in sex with me? I didn't think so. If that did happen, would she have told me? I really could not say.

Hmm.

It bothered me that I didn't know. No, no woman

had ever complained after sex. But then again, I never asked. I never cared.

This was a bizarre conversation. Not uncomfortable. The opposite, in fact. I just never had a female speak so bluntly about sex before. Not to me.

"So, you're saying you would tell a man if you weren't satisfied?" I needed to know.

"Um, yeah," she said, accepting the glass of vodka I pushed her way.

She sipped it, made a face, and I grinned. That was probably due to the lack of lemon or ice.

"Oh wow, that is smooth, but I don't usually drink hard liquor. Anyway, lack of an O face would be pretty fucking indicative of a failure to launch, so to speak."

"Are you saying you're a demonstrative little thing, then?" I asked, and my voice dropped an octave.

"What?" she asked, her blue gaze darting to mine.

"Are you showy when you come, Dumplin'? What exactly is your O face?"

I leaned closer, one hand wrapped around her wrist, my other arm draped over the back of her chair, my fingertips brushing against her bare shoulders.

I was crowding her, but she didn't move away, so

I didn't care. I wanted to get closer. I needed to touch her.

"Wouldn't you like to know," she murmured, and I dipped my head.

"Yeah, Dumplin'. I want to know."

I was close. So close to kissing her sweet mouth I could feel her warm breath tickling my skin. Her hair smelled sweet and citrusy, like mandarins or clementines.

I couldn't get enough of it. Of her. I wanted more, and I intended to take it.

CHAPTER TWELVE
MARAT

"**W**hat the hell is going on here?!"

A stranger, who I assumed was her boss, *old Royce Rage himself,* bellowed from behind me.

I tensed.

Anger at both the interruption and his tone filling me to the point I was hissing like a steam engine.

"Listen, pal, the waitresses aren't permitted to take breaks with guests on the floor," he said, clapping a sweaty hand down on my shoulder.

This motherfucker.

"Sorry, Mr. Royce, my customer needed some, um, help, and I was just—"

Destiny tried to explain, offering a weak excuse.

"Shut it, Dollface."

That was it. I was done. He could have fucking listened. Could have been respectful. But he wasn't. And that sealed his fucking fate for him.

"Pal, I'm going to have to ask you to leave. We don't allow our staff to fraternize with customers. Beat it, you don't want me to call security. As for you, Dollface, this was your last warning. In my office, now."

Oh, this motherfucker.

I closed my eyes, allowing my fury to build.

"Buddy, I said it's time to go," he repeated.

"Mr. Royce—"

"Don't make me tell you twice, Dollface. Get your fat ass to my office!"

His sweaty fucking finger was still pointed at my Dumplin'. And that, as it turned out, was my breaking point.

The hair on the back of my neck stood on end and every protective instinct I ever had came racing to the surface. I pressed down on her hand, making sure she knew to stay right where she was before I flicked my gaze to her boss, *the manager of Lux Lounge,* or one of them.

What kind of douchebag prick would speak to a woman, any woman, that way? I was a dick, I admitted that freely. But I never abused a single woman verbally or physically. It was enough to make me hate him.

That he spoke to the woman I was interested in that way, well, that was just his bad fucking luck. I stood up slowly, turning my body to block her from his view.

I grabbed the finger he still had in the air, bent it backwards, and twisted his arm with the move. The satisfying snap of his finger dislocating reverberated through my hand, but I still wasn't appeased.

"Ow! Fucking shit man, let me go! You don't know who you're dealing with," he cried out, bending over in pain.

I snarled, pushing his useless hand out of my grip. I needed him away, far away from her. He stumbled, and I spared a glance behind me to make sure Dumplin' was okay.

Her eyes were wide, and I read the upset and panic in them. She'd mentioned needing this job and however much I wanted to fuck her, I had no business getting her fired.

Shit.

I fucked this up for her. Now, I had to make it right. Whoever the fuck this asshole was, he clearly did not know me.

That was good and bad. Good for me. Bad for him. I stood up, looking down my nose at the smaller man clad in his cheap suit.

"Who are you?" I growled.

"I'm Roger Royce, manager. Who the fuck are you?" he asked in his nasal voice, narrowing his beady eyes at me.

This asshole.

I didn't offer my name. I didn't have to because behind Roger Royce was Vince Ferragamo, the owner of Lux Lounge, and a personal friend.

"Hello, Marat. Good to see you," Vince said, and I dipped my chin in recognition.

"Vince," I returned his greeting.

"Royce, is there a problem?" Vince asked, clearly pissed at his employee. But it was still not enough to placate me.

"Uh, yeah, Mr. Ferragamo, sir. Um, I didn't know you were coming in tonight—"

"I asked you if there was a problem, Royce."

"No, sir. Yes, sir. Um, this *gentleman* was taking up one of our cocktail waitresses' time, sir, and, um, I asked him to leave?" he ended his mumbling explanation with a question.

I had to give him credit for not just breaking down and crying right there. Royce was favoring his hand, sweat beading on his forehead as he tried to meet his boss' eyes. He couldn't.

And I knew why. Vince Ferragamo had quite a reputation in Sin City. He was the co-owner of several establishments, including this one. The product of a bygone era when the mafia had their fingers in every pie in Vegas.

Ever the shrewd businessman, Vince kept his family ties. He was old school. He knew the deal. Even better, Ferragamo knew all the big players.

Which meant he knew me. He knew my brother. The face of Volkov Industries was more than just a symbol. I had money and power. And I made a terrible fucking enemy.

"You asked *Marat Volkov* to leave my club? Are you out of your damned mind?" Vince snarled, eyes blazing.

He turned to me a ready apology on his lips, which I, of course, accepted.

"Marat, please, accept my humble apologies for this fucking idiot's blundering," he began, turning his attention to where my Dumplin' was still sitting, stunned.

I liked the fact she'd moved closer to me during the slight altercation. Might have been subconscious, but I still found it endearing. Like she was looking to me for protection, and that was good.

I would protect her.

My eyes darted to Josef who'd returned when things got a little hairy. He didn't interfere, and I knew he wouldn't unless things got precarious, which I appreciated.

I was the brother of the Dark Wolf, but I was no fucking pup. Despite some unpopular opinions.

"Sweetheart, you alright over there?" Vince asked.

"Yes, sir. I'm so sorry about all the trouble."

"Don't apologize," I told her again. "This is on me Vince. You see, I have a little problem and I need her help."

"Is that so?"

"Yes. If you can see to it her schedule is cleared for the next few days, I'd appreciate it," I said rather highhandedly since she hadn't exactly said yes to the offer I had yet to make her.

Details. Unimportant details.

"Of course. Royce, clear her schedule. Then get out, you're through for the night."

"For the night?" I asked, eyebrow raised.

"Did I say that? You're through for good, Royce. Got it? Destiny, my dear, you are in excellent hands.

My man Marat here is the best," Vince assured her and winked.

I didn't like the wink, and it must have showed. Vince stepped back, hands raised placatingly as he offered to foot the bill for the vodka I didn't drink.

Unnecessary, but fuck him.

I reached for Dumplin's hand and pulled her up next to me. Not bothering to say anything else, I dragged her behind me as we left Lux Lounge.

"Wait. Hang on. I don't even know your name!" she yelled, trying unsuccessfully to slow my stride.

"I don't know your real name either," I said reasonably.

"Oh, um, it's Valdez. Destiny Valdez."

"So, that *is* your real name?" I asked, noting her slight wince.

"Sort of. I mean, I unofficially changed it. It used to be Marianna," she explained and cleared her throat.

"Marianna. Pretty name for a pretty girl," I whispered as we rode the private elevator down to street level.

She kept glancing down, and I didn't like that. I wanted her attention on me. Without thinking it through, I reached out and cupped her cheek.

Her eyes were so damn blue. So deep and bright,

they gutted me. I thought I might drown in them if I kept staring, but I couldn't look away.

The elevator doors opened, and I had no choice but to break eye contact. I turned my head, unsurprised to see Josef had already made it outside. He was waiting for us beside a large, silver SUV.

"I know you heard them, but my name is Marat Volkov." I told her belatedly.

"Merit? Like the badge?"

I grinned at her uncanny American accent as she said my name. It was better than what some others came up with. I shrugged.

"Close enough, Dumplin'."

I took the door handle away from Josef and held it open for her, placing my hand on her waist as she got inside. I didn't want him that close to her.

I was behaving like a child with a new toy he didn't want to share, but I wasn't willing to look any deeper than that.

I did not know this woman. I had no claim on her. But I wanted her.

"Do you keep calling me a dumpling?" she asked, her pretty mouth turned down as I slid in beside her.

Her lips were plump and pink, and I was dying to have them under mine.

Why wait?

I growled and pulled her close with my hand on the back of her neck.

Then I crushed my mouth to hers, tasting the wild temptation before me with reckless abandon.

"Close enough," I repeated.

CHAPTER THIRTEEN
MARAT

Now, I'd been kissing girls since I was twelve years old.

It started with a neighbor in this fucked up little building we'd lived in down in Sheepshead Bay when we first came to America. Adrik and I already knew English, among other languages.

He went to work for the New York Bratva, with Josef, and I attended school, making fast friends with the sixteen year old girl next door. Elena something. That kiss was memorable, even if her name wasn't, simply because it was my first.

I'd been sitting on the stoop after school smoking a cigarette, which I quit soon after, and giving the old man from the corner store the stink eye when Elena came home from band practice.

I was a skinny little shit. But I was already turning all the girls' heads. Elena came home, sat down next to me, and bam, pressed her cherry Chapstick wearing mouth to mine.

I was shocked. I didn't know what to do. So, I acted bored. And Elena ate it up. Like so many women had since.

Boredom was my constant companion. It was hard to feign an appetite when you had so much bounty to choose from.

But that was in the past. For the first time since I was a kid, I felt hunger. Real, honest to fuck hunger.

And it was all for her. Destiny Valdez. Curvy goddess of a cocktail waitress.

The fact her name was Destiny had me intrigued. I never thought much about mine. My future. How could I when plans were never certain?

Even making billions didn't put my little boy fears at ease. I knew what it was like to be without. To not be sure if I even had a future.

Maybe if I conquered Destiny, if I fucked this curvy little Dumplin', maybe then I'd be okay. Maybe then I'd be settled.

My dick strained, the need to fuck this woman so damn deep fueled me with desire. I needed to regain control, or I'd be coming way too fucking soon.

But that was like trying to hold on to a feather in a hurricane. Weathering the storm of my arousal for my Dumplin' was the hardest thing I'd ever done.

What was it about her that made her so damn special? It was an enigma. A puzzle. But I needed her, and I wasn't one to deny my needs.

There was no safe harbor from my feelings. No shelter from the beauty of her. I needed her. All of her.

Her plump body, her big blue eyes, her hot, sweet pussy in my hands, surrounding my cock.

Fuck. Yes.

She smelled like pure sunshine. A citrus scented goddess. She permeated my senses and took over my control.

Feeling her heat beneath my palms made me feel like a fucking conqueror. It was all so new. Just the fact I wanted to touch her more than I wanted to breathe. To cover her with my body. To worship at her altar. All of it so fucking new.

She called me a fallen angel, but she was the angel. So good. So fucking good. And I was in her thrall. A willing subject. She might not know it yet, but she was mine.

My wild temptation.

There was something about Dumplin's plump pink lips beneath mine that moved me in a way I'd never experienced.

It was like an earthquake, only it was taking place inside my body, in my brain. Like I had one of those white noise machines on full blast, and only the sounds of our breathing made it through the clamor.

I had to slow it down. It was going to fucking kill me, but unless I wanted to embarrass myself and blow my load in my pants, I had no other choice.

"Wow," she whispered, and I smiled with my eyes closed.

"Yeah. Wow. I've been dying to do that since I laid eyes on you," I confessed softly, brushing my lips against her mouth.

She tasted like pure fucking sunshine. After a lifetime of darkness, it was a welcome relief.

I cupped her cheek, gripping the back of her neck with my other hand in a totally possessive manner. I couldn't let her go, though. I wanted to own her.

Her citrus scent filled my senses, the sweetness of her lips drove me wild. If I didn't stop, I was going to take this too far in front of too many eyes.

So, I tried to calm myself. Pressing my closed lips to hers several more times in biting, plucking little kisses that left us both panting.

Thump. Thump. Thump.

"Um, where are we going?"

"You're coming with me."

"Okay. I mean, oh my god. I can't believe I'm doing this."

"Doing what?"

"I shouldn't even get in a car with you. You're a stranger—"

"Don't say that, Dumplin'. You feel this too, I know you do," I whispered.

"I don't even know if I'm fired, and I don't have my purse—"

"You're not fired," I said, even though she wouldn't be going back there to work.

No fucking way.

"Here you are, Miss Valdez. I collected your personal items from your locker," Josef said, leaning past me to hand her a purse I assumed was hers.

"Oh, thanks," she whispered.

She took the purse and the small backpack Josef held out and I noticed her wince with the movement. That fucking corset. I was going to burn that thing the second I got it off her.

If she let me take it off her. Goddamn. I really hope she lets me.

I'd never doubted my ability to get a woman in bed. It never mattered to me before. The women I slept with were fillers.

If one refused, there was always another waiting behind her. A never ending queue of nameless, faceless bodies to pass the time. But none of them mattered.

Until now.

She mattered. And that made all the difference. I'd never wanted anyone like I wanted Destiny Valdez.

"Step on it," I growled.

Suddenly, I was pissed. Angry that she'd reduced me to this. To wondering if I was good enough. But that wasn't going to stop me from trying.

I kept her hand in mine, my eyes on the window for the duration of the drive. Familiar with the area, my driver had us there in minutes.

Depending on my mood, I sometimes used back entryways. Lately, I preferred less noise when I traveled, and I was glad Josef had instructed the man to deliver us to the back entrance of the hotel.

"Come," I ordered.

Tugging on her hand, I made it so she had no choice but to slide across the seat and exit from the same door as me.

It was an overbearing move, but I never said I wasn't a prick. I needed to figure out what this was between us, and I needed time to do that.

"Marat, I think maybe you have the wrong idea about me," she started as we stepped into the elevator.

"Take the next one," I told Josef.

I sucked in a great gulping breath, closing my eyes as I tasted her citrusy sweetness on my tongue. I needed control or this would be over before it started.

"Now, what was that?" I asked, turning towards her once I was steady again.

I spoke too soon. Even in the stark light of the elevator, she was stunning. Just looking at her had my pulse racing, dick throbbing, and my mouth watering.

I was right about the makeup. Hers wasn't caked on or overdone. She looked positively delicious. Her rounded face was prettier than I'd thought.

Her skin looked so soft. My fingers itched to touch it.

"I said, I think maybe you have the wrong impression. I don't do this sort of thing. I don't go back to hotel rooms with strange men."

"Glad to hear it," I said. "But I'm not a strange man. And I know you want to come with me. I can feel it."

It was all bravado. I had no idea if she felt the same wild temptation to be with me that I felt for her, but I hoped. I really fucking hoped.

"Well, I mean, that may be, but I shouldn't—"

"Haven't you ever done something just for yourself?" I asked, stepping closer to her just as the doors slid open to reveal the exclusive penthouse I'd rented.

Destiny stepped backwards. She kept on retreating until her back met the wall. I watched her throat work, swallowing down her nervousness.

"Haven't you ever taken what you wanted with no questions asked?"

"No, not me. I always ask questions. It's probably why I'm alone. I just can't help it, Marat. I don't live in your world," she said, lifting her hands as if to stop me.

Instead, I crushed them to my chest as I pressed my body into hers, moaning at the way her softness welcomed me.

Goddamn, she was so sexy. So real. My heart squeezed inside my chest, and I gazed at her with covetous eyes, drinking in every inch I could see. It wasn't enough. I needed more.

"Maybe that's why I'm so attracted to you, Dumplin'."

"Before we do this, tell me more about what you told my boss."

"Your boss?" I asked, annoyed she'd brought up that asshole.

"Not Royce, I mean Mr. Ferragamo. You said you needed me for a few days," she said.

I struggled for a minute to get my brain to work. It was a little difficult since at the time, all my blood resided below my belt.

Destiny was biting her lower lip, her small hands clinging to my waist, and fuck, she felt good.

Thump. Thump. Thump.

The temptation to press my hips against her, forcing my cock into contact with her soft stomach was too much to resist. So, I didn't even try.

I groaned at the sensations, noting with pleasure the way her blue eyes glazed over with lust. She squeezed my sides, rubbing herself on my body.

I was so turned on, I almost forgot what we were talking about.

"Oh, uh, I need a date tomorrow night. Award dinner. And maybe a few more things like that after," I groaned.

"But you can have anyone—"

"I want you. Only you."

"I see. Do you do this a lot?"

"Never," I said, and it was the truth.

"What do I have to do? Like sign an NDA or something?"

She gasped as I ran my hands up and down her sides, needing to feel her sweet softness.

"What? We'll talk about it later. Now, I just need one thing."

"Okay. Good. I think I need it too," she moaned, lifting her pretty face to mine.

"Kiss me, Dumplin'. Now," I commanded, loving the way she lifted her face and met my lips.

Desire pumped through my veins, and I growled as I swept my tongue inside her mouth. She tasted so fucking good.

"Yes, Marat, yes."

"Yes?"

"Yeah, yes."

"To what?"

"To all of it. To right now. To going with you tomorrow. To the NDA. I mean, it is my birthday, and since I didn't get anything else this year, maybe you're right. Maybe it's time I got something for myself," she whispered as I dropped my lips to her throat.

Victory rang through me like a fucking bell, and I wanted to toss my head back and crow my victory out loud.

"Good," I growled, wanting to roar in victory. "I'll be your present."

"You think you can give me what I need?" she asked coyly, and I growled, nipping her earlobe between my teeth.

"I know it. I can give you what you need, Dumplin'. I got exactly what you crave," I said, and I believed it.

I'd never been shy. I never skulked or hid in the shadows. Sure, my world was dark, but I was too fucking pretty to remain unknown, and I knew it. Adrik reminded me of it all the time.

It was why I was the face of the company, and he was the wolf. But I was more than my face, and for the first time in my life I wanted to prove it to someone.

"Marat," she moaned as I marched her backwards, down the hall, towards the king-sized bed.

She whimpered and moaned, tugging on my tie,

helping me remove my jacket. I undid the fastenings on her corset, groaning as her glorious tits tumbled free. She had a body made for sin. A body that begged to be worshipped. And it was mine.

But it's not permanent, my inner nagging voice shouted in my head. That might be true. But it didn't have to be.

I could keep her. Make her mine for good.

I was rich, handsome, and I would be good to her. Better than her shitty boss and her ex-roommate who ran out on this month's rent. I could be to her what Sofia was to my brother. Then I'd never have to come to one of these fucking things alone again.

I wouldn't have to fend off unwanted advances from desperate women, bored debutantes, and unhappy housewives. With Dumplin' on my arm, I could be happy.

Sure, I didn't know much about her, but I already had Josef working on a background check. Besides, I trusted my gut and my gut told me she was honest. That kind of thing was a rarity in my world.

Honest, sexy as fuck, smelling like clementines and sunshine, tasting like heaven. Yes, I wanted to keep her. An idea formed fast in my mind as I felt her up against the wall, swallowing down her throaty sighs and needy whimpers.

I could make her want this. Make her want me. Get her addicted to my cock. To the idea of being mine.

This could work.

CHAPTER FOURTEEN
DESTINY

Things like this did not happen to me. I mean, did they happen to anyone? Thoughts like that plagued me the entire ride to his hotel.

I mean, did big, sexy, rich men—*he didn't have to tell me he was rich, the suit, car, bodyguard, and penthouse kind of gave it away*—who looked like gods often swoop chubby little waitresses off their feet, kiss them senseless, and carry them back to their lair to have their wicked way with them?

Snort. Okay, so I'm a dork, but whatever.

Besides, I wasn't wrong. I was pretty sure stuff like that was reserved for romance novels only. It certainly never happened to me.

I was a simple person. Not in the sense that I was

dumb. Far from it. Degrees didn't equal brains, but I was proud I'd earned a BA in English Literature from an online university.

I worked hard and was currently enrolled in three graduate classes, all virtual. They were the only kind I could take with my work schedule. But I'd been a bookworm since forever.

Reading was always my go to back when I was a kid. Hell, I used to devour the written word faster than my fat tabby cat Horace ate his Tender Vittles.

Books were my escape. They were my special hiding place from a reality that was far too often cold and callous. I read everything from poetry to novels to plays, and more.

When I was younger, I dreamed of being on the stage and I used to practice reading aloud. My family was working class. We never had money for recreational activities or fancy lessons like the kind some of my schoolmates took.

Reading helped pass the time. My best friend Timmy and I poured through old copies of the Hardy Boys and Nancy Drew books his grandmother had given him. After that, I used to act out scenes from plays I loved. God, it seemed like forever ago, but Timmy and I used to read together all the time.

Running away to Sin City had seemed like the answer for a couple of kids from New Jersey whose parents stifled their hopes and aspirations. The only place we could think of that would give us some freedom to make our own choices.

Years had passed since then, and everything was different now. But I never went back. I didn't know how to.

In the twelve years since I'd moved to Vegas, I'd stopped dreaming. My silly childish fantasies were nothing but dust and memories. Reality was so much worse. The world I'd imagined full of pretty words and colors was a cruel, dark place more often than not. And I'd learned some pretty hard lessons.

Not a day went by that I didn't stop and say a prayer for sweet Timmy. Leukemia had ended his life far too soon. It was unfair. It fucking sucked.

But it taught me something. Ever since then, I tried to live my life without regret. I never wanted to waste a single minute or opportunity. I worked damn hard to be happy and to keep my outlook on life bright.

It wasn't easy living in a place that offered so much temptation. But I was honest and diligent, and I tried not to grasp for more than what I needed or deserved.

I didn't know if Marat fell into the latter category, but I damn well needed him to quench the desire raging inside me. The lust he'd spiked with his fallen angel looks and possessive display back at Lux.

I never had a man stand up for me like that. Seeing him grapple with Royce and hearing his crisp, explicit instructions to Mr. Ferragamo—*a man I knew was connected*—without worry or care, did something to me inside.

Marat made me feel special, important. He made me feel like someone worthy of his attention. And I wanted it. His eyes, his hands, his lips, his focus. I wanted it all.

Yeah, I was being dumb. I mean, he probably slept with a different woman every night, but knowing that didn't stop me from wanting to be next.

Maybe I was pathetic. Needy. Desperate. Or some combination of all three.

It made no difference. Opportunity had knocked, and I was answering.

I might have been completely out of my depth. I mean, I knew I was.

Hell, I wasn't even in the same category as Marat. But I was the one he brought to his penthouse suite. And the feeling that gave me was pure elation.

He could have had anyone at Lux tonight. And there were plenty of beauties. All lithe and lean and decked out like goddesses.

But he chose me. *Me.*

I couldn't help the thrill of excitement his touch gave me. Chills raced up my spine, and my blood heated just being near him.

How long had it been since I had an orgasm? It must have been months.

Sure, I had a drawer full of toys, but up until a few hours ago I'd lived with a roommate, and I never felt comfortable doing *that* when she was home.

I couldn't remember the last time I had an orgasm with a man. But the second Marat touched me, it was like lightning bolted straight through my body, right to my clit.

I was seconds from spontaneously combusting. And that never happened.

His body was so hot, so hard. And I didn't just mean the enormous bat in his pants. My hands roamed over the expensive material of his suit, searching, seeking, needing to feel him, and goddamn, he was fine.

"Um, I think I should probably warn you I am

not really good at this," I confessed, my head fuzzy with lust.

"Not good at what?" he asked, his attention on my body.

"At this. At sex."

"What do you mean?" he asked, stopping his sensual assault on my overwhelmed system.

He looked mildly amused, and I wasn't sure if I wanted to kick him or myself for interrupting.

"It's just if I don't come, I don't want you to be upset," I told him.

"You think I can't make you come? Did you just say that?" he asked, eyebrows raised.

"Look, I'm not insulting you, and the fault is probably mine, but I just have a difficult time and I wanted you to know it's my problem not yours," I tried to explain.

His eyes glittered at me, and I could literally see the moment he decided to act.

"Dumplin', I'm going to make you come so hard you don't remember your name," he growled and flexed his hips, pressing his thick dick against my soft belly.

The resulting flood in my panties made me want to bet on him.

"Just hold on, Baby. I got you," he growled, licking his way from my cleavage to my mouth.

"Oh god, you smell good," I moaned, my face buried in his neck.

His scent was divine. Spicy and exotic. Like the man, but more. Like he was caught somewhere between heaven and hell. Angel and devil.

He was so beautiful, and when he moaned, it was like a heavenly host.

Marat licked and sucked on the sensitive skin below my ear.

"You smell good too, Dumplin'. So fucking good. I can't get enough of you," he moaned against my neck and the sound went right to my core.

Maybe he really would succeed at getting me off. Miracles happened, or so they said. And it was my birthday.

The man made me shiver with just kisses and some petting, I could not imagine what he would do once he got me naked. He was good at this.

Too good.

And really, it should have made me self-conscious, but it didn't.

I felt desired. Coveted. And as crazy as it sounded, I loved it. I wanted him to cherish me. To make me feel good the way his eyes promised he could.

I read romance novels, not Forbes. So no, I had no idea what he did or how he made his money. He was rich, obviously.

I didn't recognize his name, but he was someone if Mr. Ferragamo was bowing down to him. That old mobster didn't cater to anyone.

The one thing I did not want was to think about the total playboy Marat Volkov was. A man didn't walk around with that face and body without having a flock of females at his disposal.

I could never belong to a man like that. But for one night, I could pretend. I could take the pleasure he offered and give to him in return. I knew he wanted me.

Why? I had no idea, but there was no denying he was as into this as I was.

By some minor miracle, I'd claimed Marat's attention, and I was so down with reaping the bene-fits of his sensual assault. It had been way too long since I felt so good.

Truthfully, I never felt such a pull towards someone.

I wasn't joking earlier when we'd discussed sex and how I'd candidly told him that I was all for letting my few and far between partners know when I wasn't satisfied.

I was starting to think part of the problem was the lack of attraction. I mean, I'd never wanted anyone the way I wanted him.

My entire body was pulsating with my need for him. I was actually close to coming, and we were still dressed.

I couldn't believe I talked to him about sex and my O face. But with any luck, Marat was going to get up close and personal with my favorite elusive expression. Hopefully, more than once.

Please let it happen. And because I was a greedy bitch I added, *and let it be multiple times.*

I sent that last bit out into the universe, desperate to reach the ears of any waiting deities in the area.

Hopefully, they'd answer my prayers.

CHAPTER FIFTEEN
DESTINY

Marat's room was in one of the ritziest hotels on the Strip. I'd been in the lobby before, but never in a room, and sure as fuck, I'd never been in the penthouse.

But I couldn't divert any attention to my surroundings. He claimed all of it. The elevator ride was a blur. And as for the décor of the penthouse suite? I had no fucking idea.

I was a fan of beautiful things. I liked art and nature. Even the neon signs and the riotous, sometimes gaudy, interior design of hotels, bars, clubs, and restaurants in Vegas were pretty.

But if someone asked me right then what color the walls were or what flooring was beneath my feet, I would have had no fucking clue.

I could have been anywhere standing on anything and it wouldn't have made a dent through the fog of passion shrouding my brain.

All I saw, heard, and felt was him. Marat Volkov was everywhere. He was everything. For someone who'd been alone most of her adult life, I hadn't even put up a fight.

This big, sexy man had walked into my life, and I literally and willingly handed him the reins. At that point, all I could do was hope to god he knew how to drive this thing.

"Goddamn. You taste so good. Why do you taste so fucking good?" he growled against my soft flesh.

My body tingled with desire. It was like someone had flipped a switch and I was buzzing with electricity, vibrating with need. I didn't know what was crazier, that I wanted him so much, or that he seemed to want me with equal fervor.

I'd never felt sexier or more desirable in my life. I knew very well what I looked like, what I offered. I was plump, short, and not exactly a spring chicken. I had cellulite and stretch marks, my belly was soft, and my thighs were jiggly.

Sure, my face was pretty enough. But I wasn't in his league. And no, I didn't have a poor body image. I'd learned early to love myself because it was unlikely anyone else was going to if I didn't. But I wasn't delusional.

Marat was a vision of physical perfection, and I was short, chubby, and at best, cute. I was half a second away from panicking. That nasty bitch doubt threatened to creep in, making me second guess myself.

But it was like Marat sensed my growing hesitance. He grabbed onto me, pulling me flush against him, making sure I felt the hard evidence of his heightened arousal.

Chubby or not, he liked what he saw. I could feel it in the way his cock pulsed against me. He growled, the sound deep and sexy. Then he moved faster than I could track.

We moved from the elevator to the hall to the master bedroom on the other end of the suite. His hands were everywhere, cupping my tits, squeezing my ass, and gripping my pussy over my pants.

"Let's get this fucking thing off," he said, and popped the hooks of the corset, allowing my tits to spill free.

"Goddamn. Fuck."

His forehead pressed against mine as he cupped my breasts, feeling their weight. My nipples were so hard, I whimpered when he lowered his head, closing his mouth around one and sucking it into his hot mouth.

"Marat," I moaned, arching my back.

While he lavished attention on my breasts, his hands were busy. I heard clothing tear and felt him tugging the fabric away from my overheated body. But I was too absorbed by what he was doing to worry about how I looked.

Marat had me stripped down and sprawled before him on top of black satin sheets like some sort of pagan offering in no time at all.

It was fitting, really. From the moment I first saw him, Marat looked like the Devil to me. Perfectly chiseled, sculpted features highlighted by the soft glow of the wall sconces. His obsidian gaze pinned me, and I gasped at how beautiful he really was.

He undressed quickly, and I was completely taken aback by the raw power in his body. The man could have been carved from marble. A living, breathing monument to what a man should be.

He was bulkier than I'd thought. Muscles roped around his long frame. And even more shocking was the enormous tattoo that traveled from his left ankle up his entire side.

The thick tribal pattern called to something primal in me and when he twisted his hips to drop his clothes on the floor, I saw a wolf inked across his ribs. The beast's hackles were up, the entire tattoo done in black, except for the eyes. Those were red.

The Devil is a wolf.

Need pooled between my legs. My pussy was practically waving a flag and begging him to fill me already.

I'd been teasing him earlier that night when I'd said women probably creamed themselves by just looking at him. But staring up at him from my position on my back I realized that was a very possible likelihood.

How amazing and awful that must be.

The thought pained me, and I reached up, tracing his face from eyebrow to jaw with just my fingertips. I moved up higher, combing them through his thick, glossy hair, then cradling his cheeks as he leaned down.

His breath hitched in his throat, and I was moved by the sudden evidence of his humanity.

He wasn't some cold ethereal being. He was a man. And I wanted to gift him with some of what he'd given me.

It was dumb. I wasn't some sex kitten. I was literally no good at this. The few times I'd indulged it was embarrassing, quick, and unfulfilling.

But I wanted to show him how good he made me feel and offer him some of the same.

I pulled him down for a kiss, and miracle of miracles, he allowed it.

But only for a moment. His tongue snaked out, licking into my mouth before he groaned and broke the kiss. Marat moved down my body.

His lips burned with intensity, leaving evidence of his claim in hot, wet trails over my body. His tongue lashed across my skin, awakening a fiery desire I'd never known.

He made me shiver and moan, unable to comprehend the sensations rolling through me.

"Marat," I moaned his name.

It must have been a good thing, cause he moaned too. He tasted like sin and desire, dark, exotic, forbidden, and I wanted him so damn much.

His fingers were demanding then, and he pushed my legs open, revealing my soaked sex to his obsidian stare.

"Fuck, you're so goddamn wet. Fucking soaked," he groaned, his fingers spearing between my legs.

I yelped a surprised sound at his invasion. His fingers delved deeper, curling inside my sheath, and my pussy rippled around his thick digits.

"S'going to be tight, but you can take me. You're

going to let me have you, aren't you, Dumplin'?" he growled the question, stilling his hand.

His fingers slowly retreated until just the tips remained inside. He pressed his lips against mine, kissing me sweetly.

A deep, guttural sound spilled from his lips. Like it was killing him to go slow. Then he licked along the seam of my lips, begging entry.

He was right. I was going to let him in. I was going to give him everything.

"Give it to me. Let me in, Destiny," he growled, calling me by name.

I opened my lips, and he hummed in approval. The sound so deep in his throat, it sent shivers reverberating from his chest to mine. Fire spiked through my veins.

All at once, Marat pushed his fingers all the way inside my channel and thrusted his tongue into my willing mouth. I grasped his shoulders, needing something to anchor me.

Without him to hold on to, I might have combusted in an explosion made of sheer desire. I'd never been so completely turned on, and it scared the hell out of me. But I was so fucking glad I said yes to him.

I knew better than to trust a stranger, but the

truth was, he didn't feel like one. There was something so sad and beautiful about the dark-eyed man. The way he looked at me, the way he made me feel seen, was extraordinary. And having him touch me? Well, that was just a bonus.

I knew I shouldn't acknowledge the connection I felt to him. It was stupid. I was kidding myself. Setting myself up for heartbreak.

But I'd only just found the courage to take something for myself, and I wanted to enjoy it.

No, I wasn't sure what would happen when I woke up tomorrow, but I was in it for now.

"Going to fill this wet pussy, Baby. Going to make us both feel good. You ready?" he asked.

"Yes. God, yes, I'm ready."

"Not God. Marat. Call me Marat when I'm about to fuck you."

His huskily whispered command sent pleasure spiking through my veins. His hands were everywhere. But his attention was all on me.

He made me feel special, cherished, and even if it was a lie, I wanted to believe it. What was the harm in that? It felt so good to be touched. To pretend he cared.

I gasped, rolling my hips as he brushed his thumb

across my needy clit. I was on the precipice of pure pleasure. I just had to let go and it could be mine.

I only had to trust him. I could do that. I would do that. For the promise his eyes were giving me right then, I damn well could be brave and give in to the desire we were both feeling.

Just for a little while.

"Marat, please," I moaned, and the sound of something tearing filled the air.

He moved back, and I watched as he rolled a condom onto his long, thick cock. Holy. Fuck. He was big. Like *was he even going to fit* big, and I had never had that.

"You can take me. My sweet Dumplin', you were made for this right here," he growled, reading my reticence more accurately than anyone ever could.

I nodded, meeting his heated gaze, since he seemed to be waiting for confirmation. I could take him. I was made for him. He said so.

"Please, Marat, I need you now," I begged.

I had no idea what was going on inside his head. My body was so much softer than his, flushed all over, and swollen with need. But I refused to think badly about myself.

After all, he'd pursued me. The lust in his eyes as

he watched me bounce and jiggle said he liked what he saw, bolstering my confidence.

I wasn't that kid with a fragile ego who'd run away from home all those years ago and fled to Sin City. I was an adult. Had been for a while now. So what if one night stands weren't my norm?

Did that mean I couldn't indulge this one time? I was old enough to embrace the fact I was an independent woman, and I had needs. Needs that had gone unmet for too long.

But Marat could meet them. He'd said so. And I believed him. I trusted him to make me feel good. The promise of it shone there in his impossibly dark eyes. Besides, it was my birthday. I hadn't even had cake.

But this. What he was offering to give me? This I could have. This I could take.

Yes. I would like one orgasm for my birthday, please. Maybe two.

"With me. Stay here with me, Dumplin'," he growled, eyes flashing black lightning before he slammed his lips against mine.

The man had the Devil's talented tongue, for sure. I could hardly keep track of my own thoughts. Marat's obsidian stare bore into me as he notched his blunted head at my entrance. Then he pushed, and all logical thought left my brain.

A long, slow groan accompanied the action, but I was uncertain whether it was his or mine or a combination of us both. He was so fucking big. So thick. So hard.

And it was all for me. *For me.* I couldn't contain my response. I raked my nails down his muscled back whimpering as he practically split me in half with his fat cock. Dear god, he was hung.

"Good girl. You're such a good girl, taking me so fucking good," he grunted, pulling back, then slamming all the way inside till his hips were flush with mine.

The delicious burning sensation ebbed and flowed, drowning me until all I could see, hear, breathe, and feel was him. Marat surrounded me. He encompassed me.

"Goddamn, you feel so good. Like coming home. Let me in, Baby. That's it. Take it. Take me," he grunted, rutting inside me like a madman.

The ferocity of his movements shook the bed, or maybe that was an earthquake. I wrapped my legs around him, unable to do anything but hold on and take everything he gave me.

I was noisy. I knew I was, and the sounds I made

reverberated inside the decadent bedroom. Eyes open, I saw the mirrored ceiling and the black, gold, and red design. It was rich and glamourous, but we could have been in a shed for all I cared.

He outshone everything.

Hugging me tight to him, I could feel Marat move, like he was trying to touch every inch of me. He ground his pelvis against mine, rubbing my clit just hard enough to send me catapulting off that preface I'd been teetering on since he shoved that big dick of his inside me.

And. It. Was. Spectacular.

"Fuck, your pussy is squeezing me so tight, You're going to suck the cum right from my balls," he groaned, his movements growing jerky.

With a strained growl, Marat reared back onto his knees, spreading my thighs further apart. He looked feral then, beast-like.

His sharp cheekbones were more pronounced as he gritted his teeth, and those black eyes zeroed in on me. I felt that stare down to my toes, but I couldn't look away.

Then, he started to move. His thrusts deeper than before, and my mouth gaped open.

Holy. Shit.

Grabbing both my hands in his, he slammed

them over my head. His knees were wide, forcing my legs to open even more.

Marat pressed down, crushing me with his weight, slamming his thick dick home again and again. He pistoned his hips, faster, harder, and goddamn, I was coming again, and so hard, I almost blacked out.

But I forced my eyes open, not wanting to miss the look on his face as he exploded inside me. And it was worth it. So fucking worth it.

I might have made the right assessment the first time I'd gazed upon Marat Volkov. The man was the Devil.

And I'd just been fucked stupid.

CHAPTER SIXTEEN
MARAT

"My attorney already drew up the papers. I just need you to print them and bring them to me."

"Are you serious, Marat? Does Adrik know?" Joseph's voice sounded even more gruff than usual.

"Yes, I am serious, and this is one matter that does not concern my brother."

I clicked end call, grabbed two bottles of water from the fully stocked refrigerator, and walked back to the bedroom where I'd left my sweet Dumplin' after fucking her until she passed out.

Once hadn't been enough. After the very first time I felt her sweet pussy pulse around my cock, I knew I needed more. One time. That was all it took, and now I was addicted.

All I could see was her. All I wanted was more of her. More of her perfect body. More of her sexy sighs. And more of her O faces.

Those were mine. The mere idea of her leaving my hotel room and gifting that sight to any other man sent me into a murderous rage.

Yeah, I was being crazy. But that was a side of myself I'd come to terms with long ago.

My Dumplin' was a vision of pure carnal sin when she was engrossed in passion. Her plump lips parted, those stunning blue eyes glowing brightly, and her creamy skin all hot and flushed.

I fucking loved the way that dusky rose color spread across her cheeks, down to her big, glorious tits.

Each time I'd brought her to orgasm, I watched a myriad of expressions cross her face and that stroked something primal inside me. Something dark and possessive.

Her O face was mine.

I'd earned it. I wanted to keep earning it. And I felt a homicidal fury at the idea another man might ever see it.

I wasn't about to let that happen. Not now that I'd had her. She was mine.

My Destiny.

My sweet Dumplin'.

And I had no plans to let her go.

I paused in the doorway just taking her in. I wished I could tell you I stood there grinning like a rooster in his henhouse, but I was too dumfounded to do that.

Destiny's dark hair spilled over the side of the bed, her nudity partially hidden by the sheet carelessly covering her. The temperature was moderate, so I knew she wasn't cold.

I pressed a hand over my heart. I didn't know her well enough for what I was about to propose. Not really. Hell. Not at all.

But we got along so far. She was gorgeous and sweet and kind. Plus, we set fires between the sheets, which was more than most people had.

Goddamn beauty. So sweet and giving. When had anyone ever wanted to give to me? It was always about what they could get. What I could give them.

But not with her. The way she reached for me. Clinging to me. Gave me her mouth. Offered me comfort. Oh, I'd felt it when she traced my face and combed her soft fingers through my hair.

Dumplin' was everything I never knew I needed. She was unique in my world, and I was suddenly obsessed with the need to keep her. To cage her in and throw away the key.

But how?

I supposed keeping it simple was best. I wanted her. And I always got what I wanted. I moved away from the doorframe, feeling like a creeper just staring at her.

I placed the water bottles down on the end table. But before I could touch her again, the sound of the elevator pinging alerted me to Josef's arrival.

I cast one more look at her sleeping form, then I went to meet him, to retrieve the papers I'd asked for and to ask him and the bodyguard he'd brought with him to witness what I was about to do.

It was fucked up. A sick shortcut to getting what I wanted. But something inside me demanded that I claim the woman sleeping in my bed as soon as possible. It was an urgency I'd never experienced.

I needed to make her mine before something took her from me. To bond her to me in as many ways as possible.

I wasn't used to being so fucking emotional, but this woman left me unhinged. She'd opened up something inside of me, and now she was the only thing who could fill it.

But I wasn't going to look too closely at that.

"Is that everything?" I asked.

"Yes. But Marat, don't you think maybe you should run this past Adrik?"

"No. This is not my brother's concern. Just stand by the door and make sure you and your man avert your fucking eyes or I'll take them. And make sure he shuts the fuck up," I said.

I was talking like a jealous fool, but I couldn't help it. I did my research. In order for the marriage to be legal, a ceremony had to be conducted in front of witnesses. But these particular witnesses knew better than to cross me.

My brother was the one with the better known reputation, but I was no fucking slouch. I was Volkov. The wolf was in my blood.

I was every bit as predatory and ruthless as Adrik, I just never had a reason to show my hand. But Josef knew. He could see the wolf in my eyes. He nodded once in recognition.

"He'll do as he's told. Just take a moment to consider the danger here. You do not know this woman, Marat. What if she has skeletons in her closet? I mean, marriage? This is a fucking mistake."

"I didn't ask you for your opinion, Josef," I growled, then relented, knowing he was just showing concern. "I know enough. I've never wanted to keep anyone before. But I want to keep her. And I will."

"She's not a pet. She's a person," he said, but I was past listening to reason.

"You ready?"

"Fuck. Yeah. Let's fucking do this."

I turned my back, leaving Josef and the body-guard to follow. I did not repeat my instructions, trusting them to do as I said.

Josef was more than just an employee, and I knew he meant well. But he knew me. He would only go so far with his objections.

There was no reasoning with a Volkov once his mind was made up. And mine was. Definitively so.

"Dumplin'," I whispered, sliding into the bed beside her warm, soft body.

I roused the object of my desire. The woman I was about to trick into marrying me, loving the feel of my immediate response to her nearness.

How fucking long had it been since I'd experienced a reaction like that? Too fucking long. My cock was straining beneath my boxers, and precum was already leaking from the slit.

Life had grown stale. I'd become bored with the state of things. Nothing roused my appetite. Not till

I saw her walking towards me in that fucking corset and those painted on pants.

Goddamn. She was fine as fuck. And the way she made me feel? I was already addicted to it. I needed this woman, and I was smart enough to recognize that.

"Mmm? I'm sleeping," she mumbled adorably.

She'd already warned me last night she slept like the dead, but I was still surprised by how many times I had to shake her to get her to even this mild state of awareness.

Fucking adorable.

"Want some water, Baby?" I asked, holding the bottle to her lips and brushing her hair back.

"Mm, thanks," she murmured, barely opening her sleepy blue eyes, smiling up at me.

That act alone was enough to make my heart hammer in my chest. When had anyone ever offered their smiles so freely to me?

Invitations to fuck?

Sure.

But smiling at me just because? Simply for the sake of expressing joy?

Never.

I tilted the bottle again, and she pressed her mouth to it, accepting the drink.

I was surprised by how much I liked the act of providing for her. It was strange, but I'd never taken care of anyone. Never wanted to. Till now.

"I need you to sign this, Dumplin'," I instructed, handing her a pen.

"What is it? An NDA?" she asked, and my eyebrows flew up.

That was as good an excuse as any. I should've thanked her for supplying it, but I wasn't a total moron. I didn't want her to be suspicious before we were finished.

"Sorta," I said, pushing the pen into her hand.

"I won't tell anyone anything about you. Marat," she said, mumbling a little.

"I know."

She wouldn't. She wasn't like that.

I tilted my head, signaling to Josef. This was the part that had to be said before it was official. I'd had him take an online class, making him ordained.

"Hmm?" she mumbled when I shook her again. "What's that sound?"

"Nothing, Baby," I growled, sliding my hands down her soft body, over her belly, down to the curls covering her sweet cunt.

She moaned, arching into my touch, and I loved it.

"Marat," she whimpered my name. Ducking. Whimpered. And my cock thumped in response.

"So fucking wet for me already."

"Mmm, please."

"What is it? What do you need? Do you need my fingers inside your tight little cunt?" I asked, whispering my words so only she could hear,

"You want me to bury them deep? To make you come?" I asked, nuzzling her neck, and running my hands over her soft, warm skin.

"I do, Marat. Please, I do," she murmured, and my fingers slid between her thick, parted thighs.

"I do, too, Dumplin'. I do," I growled, loud enough for my witnesses to hear.

I blocked the view from the door with my body, making sure to keep what I was doing from the men watching us to make sure we said our *I dos*.

After the *ceremony* was finished, nice and legal, I raised my free hand, dismissing them, catching Destiny's next moan with my mouth.

Victory rolled through me like a freight train, and I wanted to tilt my head back and roar it to the world.

This woman was my wife now. My sexy as fuck wife. She was delicious. And all it took was a few whispered words to make her mine.

I pulled my waistband down and freed my dick, sliding back to line myself up. Lifting her leg higher, I notched myself at her entrance. On a groan, I slid into her from behind, rocking my hips as her wet sheath constricted around my cock.

Fuck, she felt so good. She was so wet. So hot for me.

Destiny keened. Her small hands reaching back to scratch against my hips as I fucked her in long, hard thrusts.

"That's it. Take it, Baby. You take it so fucking good," I growled, my lips by her ear as I started to pound into her.

I had one goal right then. My entire being was focused on one thing and one thing only.

Making my wife come.

I pushed my hand between her writhing body and the mattress, coating my fingers with her slick and rubbing her bundle of nerves.

Three swipes were all it took for her sweet pussy to contract, and I followed, emptying my balls into the woman I'd just made my wife without her knowledge.

Til death do us part, Dumplin'.

CHAPTER SEVENTEEN
DESTINY

Waking up to find the exquisite suite empty was not nearly as bad as looking at myself the next morning. I squeaked at the hot mess I saw reflected in the ceiling to floor mirror while I peed.

Did Marat wake me up in the middle of the night to sign something?

I had a blurry memory—*or was it a dream*—of him teasing me with deliciously naughty words after shoving a pen in my hand and telling me to write my name on a piece of paper?

After that, he fucked me so good, I came until I passed out. But that part was not a dream. The ache between my legs was proof enough.

Ugh. My reflection stared back at me, and I was a

total mess. My hair was sticking up on one side and flattened on the other. The eye makeup I wore to work was smeared down my face.

I supposed after countless rounds of sweaty, coma-inducing sex, looking like a drugged out raccoon the morning after was a fair price to pay.

There was nothing to be done for it except a hot shower, which I was definitely going to take. I spied a fluffy white robe hanging on the back of the door and grinned.

Surely, Marat wouldn't mind if I got cleaned up before making myself scarce. He'd said something about a gala, but I doubted he meant it. Besides, I had to go see if I still had a job.

I cringed at the idea of having to put my work clothes back on. But whatever. It wasn't like I had a choice.

Finding a new toothbrush in a package, I opened it and used some peppermint toothpaste to clean my teeth. A complimentary mouthwash sat on the vanity, and I used that next.

After that, I pulled back the glass door to the enormous shower. Playing with the knobs for a few minutes, I finally figured it out and had all six heads pouring luxuriously hot water from different directions to the middle of the stall. Then I stepped under the spray and sighed.

I used muscles I'd ignored for way too long last night, and the water did a fantastic job of massaging my sore spots. Maybe Marat really was a fallen angel with all the mystical powers of one.

No one had ever made me feel like he did. It was stupid of me to feel attached to the man.

Last night couldn't have meant much to him. He was like the walking, talking definition of a rich playboy. And I was just a fluffy waitress.

Yeah, he definitely didn't mean the invite. I'll just shower, dress, and leave.

Refusing to let uncertainty taint the memory of last night, I concentrated on getting clean. Morning afters didn't have to be awkward. I was an adult. We had sex.

A lot of it. But no biggie.

The soap lining the shelf inside the shower stall was decidedly masculine, some upscale brand I'd seen in magazines. Next to it were bergamot and lavender scented bottles of shampoo, conditioner, and body wash supplied by the hotel.

I used all of it. I knew it was silly, but I could not resist the temptation of smelling like Marat when I left his penthouse suite. So, yeah, I used everything I could find.

Sure, I mean, I showered to get clean. Washing off sleep and everything else that clung to my skin from the night before was just necessary. But I didn't want to lose him just yet. Keeping his scent on my skin seemed like a good way to delay the unexpected pang of impending loss I was experiencing.

Using one of the thick towels to pat myself dry, I took the small bottle of lotion from the vanity and rubbed it on my skin. It felt really good, and it was unscented, which was a bonus. It didn't take away from the scent of Marat's soap.

When I was finished, I wrapped my hair in a towel and shrugged on the thick robe. I never had the time or the money to pamper myself with expensive toiletries, and it was an experience.

Money couldn't buy happiness, but it could buy a lot of cool shit. Like a night in a really nice fucking suite.

I frowned, thinking of the sad, empty look I'd caught in Marat's impossibly dark eyes last night. I wondered if all the money in the world was worth feeling that way.

I did not know him well enough to make assumptions, but that didn't stop me. Marat was so damn handsome. But I imagined it wasn't the gift everyone assumed.

I never really understood the meaning of the word charisma, but thinking of Marat as I combed my hair, the word just popped inside my head. And it fit.

He had charisma in spades. That special something that made everyone want to be near him, to touch him, to take from him. Protective feelings I never knew I possessed rose inside me.

No wonder he looked so bored and aloof when I'd first laid eyes on him at Lux. He must have gotten used to keeping himself detached just to stave off disappointment.

For some reason, that made me terribly sad. It made me want to hug him tightly and tell him everything was okay.

As if someone like me could somehow offer someone like him comfort or solace.

Fuck.

I was so dumb. What could I possibly give him he couldn't get from someone else?

Besides, I was clearly just a once off in his book. Marat hadn't even bothered to stick around to say goodbye.

I sighed and shook my head, wondering if the

hotel left any complimentary deodorant. I found his and used it.

Las Vegas was in the middle of a fucking desert. Even though I was leaving the hotel to go home, I was not about to attempt it without the stuff.

I shook the towel around my head, used his comb once more, then opened the bedroom door, ready to put my clothes on and get back to my life.

I had no idea there was a surprise waiting for me on the other side.

CHAPTER EIGHTEEN
MARAT

I slipped out of bed a couple of hours ago, leaving Destiny asleep while I used the private gym on the penthouse floor.

After my workout, I showered in one of the other bathrooms and donned a pair of joggers before meeting the hotel concierge with double my standing breakfast order. He'd also brought a selection of clothes, shoes, and other items I ordered from the hotel shops for Destiny.

My wife.

The word filled me with inimitable pride. I rubbed the hollow spot over my heart, wondering at the surge of emotion I was feeling. It had been a very long time since that particular organ got any sort of exercise.

What is the woman doing to me?

I had no idea, but I liked it. I wanted more of it. More of the new, different, real things I was feeling.

"Good morning, sir." The concierge interrupted my train of thought, and I frowned at him.

"Is everything good, sir?"

"Yes, but I don't want anyone coming inside the suite without me present. Is that understood?"

"Yes, sir. Apologies. I thought you meant the bedroom was off limits."

"I meant everywhere," I growled.

There was no way in hell I was letting anyone inside the suite with my Dumplin' still asleep and vulnerable. Especially not while I was otherwise occupied.

I already took a risk using the gym, but I had no choice. I woke up still amped and ready. But she was exhausted, and she needed to sleep. Especially for what waited for her today.

The workout helped get rid of some of my energy, but I was still fired up. Just thinking of Destiny lying in bed, her soft, sweet body all relaxed and warm from sleep had my cock thumping inside my boxers.

And here I thought I wouldn't go at her like a rutting beast today.

Yeah. Right. I had hoped she'd remain in bed while I was gone. Truthfully, I didn't know what I would have done if she'd tried to leave.

That wasn't exactly true. I know what I would have done. I'd have stopped her. And if by some miracle she got away, I would have tracked her sweet ass down.

Not that she could get far. Unless she wanted to go naked.

I'd already gotten rid of that pitiful excuse for a uniform. It made me angry just thinking about her wearing that fucking corset with the under wire digging into her soft flesh.

Ferragamo was a fucking pig for making his servers dress that way. I'd already set the ball in motion to buy out the club and set up new management. He wouldn't know it was me. Not yet anyway. But it was the least I could fucking do.

But back to my unwitting wife. Unless she didn't mind being butt ass naked, my sweet Dumplin' stayed right where she was. Where she belonged. In my bed.

The thought of her trying to leave me filled me with a myriad of emotions from anger to hurt and I was not ready to delve into that fucking mess. I frowned and hurried my pace.

Luckily for both of us, since I had no idea exactly how unhinged I was regarding this woman, the sounds of her in the shower told me she was still in the suite.

Thank fuck.

"Will you be needing anything else, Mr. Volkov?"

The concierge—*Bradley, according to his nametag*—offered me a slight bow.

"No. Did you get everything I asked for?"

"Yes, sir. Would you like me to arrange the articles in the closet?"

The closet was in the bedroom. *That was a hard fucking no, Bradley.* Of course, I did not want the greasy fucker in there.

"No," I growled, taking the shopping bags from him myself. "I'll do it. Leave. Now."

The asshole was probably looking to get a name to sell to some tabloid. It wasn't the first time the face of Volkov Industries had company in Vegas.

But every fucking time I did, the vultures circled, looking for carrion to feed their frenzied hunger for gossip. Fucking paparazzi.

"Yes, sir," the man said, taking way too long to walk his skinny ass to the elevator.

I waited for Bradley to leave, sending a fast text to Josef to check the man out. I trusted in the hotel to do background checks on employees, but I had a different standard.

The fact my brother and I owned a significant percentage of the place meant the general manager would do what he was told, but I would not have Bradley fired until I ran my own check.

I did not like fucking with people's lives unless necessary. But if it was necessary, if Bradley was trying to sell information about me to the press, then I'd rip his life apart with my bare fucking hands.

I walked to the bedroom, placing the shopping bags on the chaise lounge that sat against the wall when you entered. I sat at the foot of the bed and waited. It didn't take her long. Just a few minutes. But when she opened the door, all the air left my lungs.

Goddamn, she was so fucking pretty.

Standing there with her dark, damp hair around her shoulders, all wrapped up in a soft robe without a single drop of makeup—I'd never seen a more beautiful woman.

She was stunning. And she was mine.

"Good morning, Wife."

Her smile faltered. She almost tripped walking across the carpeted floor towards me and I frowned, reaching out to steady her with sure hands.

"First Dumplin' now Wife. You got a thing for nicknames or something?" she remarked, looking at me like I was nuts.

"Not a nickname. You signed the marriage license last night, Josef and Stan, one of my guards, heard you say I do. We can write vows to each other later, but that would be just for us," I said and shrugged, wondering for a moment what vows she would write for me.

"Wait what?" she asked, her voice going high at the end.

"You're my wife. We're married. Congratulations."

"Be serious."

"I am serious," I said, watching her closely to gauge her reaction.

Confusion. Disbelief. Shock.

But somewhere in there I saw something else. Somewhere in there I saw pleasure. And it was enough to give me hope.

"Okay, I need you to slow down. Take a breath. Now, what are you saying?" she asked.

"Would you like a diamond or some other kind of stone for your wedding band? I was thinking sapphires to match your pretty eyes, Dumplin'."

I ignored her sputtering. Her gasp of outrage.

The way she tried to shy from my touch. If she wasn't careful, she was going to hurt my feelings.

"Marat, we can't be married. That-that's crazy."

"It's not crazy. It's fact," I said, handing her a copy of the marriage license, which I'd already had sent to the proper authorities.

"You. Are. My. Wife. Marianna Destiny Valdez now Volkov."

I let that settle before I continued, watching her shocked face for any sign she might pass out or throw something at me.

I'd been hoping for a different reaction, but stunned silence was fine for now. She'd have plenty of time to make it up to me later.

"I had the concierge deliver some clothes from the boutique downstairs. I hope you don't mind, I selected them for you," I explained.

I did not tell her how I'd obsessed over the color and texture of each object. How I'd envisioned her in blue silk dresses with nothing but sheer panties beneath.

Thump.

I cleared my throat.

"Anyway, it will hold you over until we have time to do some real shopping. Oh, and your license and passport with your new last name are being printed now. They will arrive before we go back to New York."

"New York?"

"Yes, it's where we live."

"No, I live in Vegas."

"You lived in Vegas. Past tense, Dumplin'. You'll get dressed, then we'll discuss terms."

"Terms?" She raised her eyebrows, shock widening her blue orbs until they practically drowned out the rest of her face.

Goddamn.

She was so pretty. Like a Disney princess when she looked like that.

Well, a Disney princess with a pinup model body and fuck me mouth. I opened one of the bags, grabbing the first aid ointment I'd ordered.

"Come here."

It was an order, not a request, and I was pleased when she shuffled forward. I unscrewed the top of the tube, focusing on the task at hand and not on the fact I'd just forced this woman into marriage.

"Open your robe, Dumplin'."

Heat flared in her gaze. She tried to hide it, but it was too late. I saw, and I was not unaffected.

Thump. Thump.

I bit back my groan as she obeyed my order,

untying the knot at her waist. I wanted nothing more than to fulfill the need I saw sizzling in her sky blue eyes.

But we had things to talk about. So, I resigned myself to being content with just that one thing. I squeezed a drop of antibacterial ointment onto my fingertip and ran my gaze over her delicious body.

Her skin was pink and warm, flushed from the shower. She was beautiful. Breathtaking. So goddamn tempting.

"Come here, Dumplin'. That's it. Poor, Baby," I murmured, my voice sounding like I swallowed a mouthful of gravel.

I lifted her plump breast, revealing the angry red mark caused by the under wire from her corset last night. I frowned. The bruise was already there, but I suddenly wished I'd burned the fucking thing that caused it.

I did not want to hurt her, but I had no choice but to run my fingertip over her marred skin. Destiny gasped.

Her eyes were huge in her face as she watched me tend to her. It was a level of intimacy I'd never known. It made me feel useful, needed.

That was heady. That was new.

I'd been wanted. Desired. Craved by many. But

needed? That was something out of my realm of experience.

She needed me to take care of her. This was a woman I'd known for less than a day, but I'd spent the better part of last night going through her purse. Unlocking her phone. Hunting for any bit of information I could find.

Sure, it might be unsavory. But I really had no choice. I was keeping her. And I needed to know everything I could.

Lines had been crossed, but it was too late now. This was unfamiliar territory for me, and it made me so damn excited. I stroked her skin, loving how she submitted to me, allowing me to tend to her.

My cock was so damn hard, but I wasn't going to fuck her again. Not yet.

"Better?" I whispered.

My careful ministrations took a turn as I ran my fingers down her sides, to her hips, pulling her closer to me. She was so soft. So different from the women I usually took to bed.

They were all hard lines and angles. But my Dumplin'? She was all rounded curves and sweet temptations.

My mouth watered for her.

"Yes. It's better," she whispered.

"Good. I have breakfast if you're hungry."

"Just coffee for me in the morning," she replied.

"Cream?"

"Yes, please."

"I'll bring it to you. Now get dressed," I repeated, allowing myself one plucking kiss on her lips before putting her gently away from me.

CHAPTER NINETEEN
DESTINY

The man was insane. Not just insanely gorgeous, but actually, irrevocably insane. Married? We were married. I was married. To him. Marat Volkov. A quick internet search after he left the bedroom allowing me some space told me exactly who my new husband was.

Younger brother of business tycoon Adrik Volkov. Co-owner of Volkov Industries. Billionaire. Bachelor. Playboy. Heartbreaker.

How the hell did I end up married to this man?

I couldn't even comprehend what was going on. Oh, he'd explained and showed me the marriage license. Apparently, the NDA I thought I was signing was really a marriage certificate.

When he'd been teasing my slick pussy with his

fingers, asking me if I wanted him to fuck me, I'd answered with an *I do*.

Of fucking course I did. Who the fuck wouldn't?

But while that was happening his buddies, Josef and some other dude, were in the doorway, facing away from us, of course, but still witnessing our nuptials.

Gulp.

Marat explained it after he brought me some coffee with the perfect amount of cream. I never had a man make me a cup of coffee and deliver it. And definitely never one who was as handsome and dark-eyed as Lucifer himself.

I was struck dumb by the picture he made. I mean, I must have been, because while he explained what happened, I didn't offer one single protest.

Not even the part where he glossed over the naughty things he'd done and asked of me while I was half asleep. I'd been caught between dream and fantasy, unsure if his hands touching me, his seducing me with his body and words were even real.

But they were. Marat had been touching me. He had, in fact, been whispering deliciously decadent things in my ear, asking questions that required just the right answer.

He also happened to be marrying me at the same time. Without my knowledge.

Can you say red fucking flag?

When he'd asked if I wanted to be his, I'd replied with *I do.*

I just didn't know I was saying I do *I do.*

My heart hammered inside my chest as I processed everything he said.

"So, the witnesses?"

"There were witnesses present. Josef, and another bodyguard," he told me.

"If they were there, did they see me like that? With you, um, touching me?"

Humiliation at the idea of someone other than him seeing me in the throes of passion threatened to fill me, but Marat took my face in his hands, making sure I was looking right at him before he answered.

"No. Never. No one sees you but me."

It shouldn't have turned me on. But it did.

There was something about his possessive turn of phrase that made my legs shake and my pussy ache to be filled.

Oh my god, I'm married!

It was surreal. Fantasy. I mean, the sex we'd shared was good, there was no doubt about it. But was it good enough to make him lose his mind?

I exhaled slowly, looking back at the door he'd just walked through, my body aching with unfulfilled need. I pressed my fingertips to my lips, remembering the soft, tender touches he gave me while applying a first-aid ointment to my breast.

Fuck. Me.

There was nothing else on the planet Marat could have done that would have affected me as deeply as that tiny act of caring. It completely wrecked me.

My heart was beating like a runaway train. When was the last time someone took care of me? I couldn't even remember. And I knew it was no big deal in the greater scheme of things. But it was to me.

I bit my lip and turned to look at the ridiculous number of bags in the chaise. I didn't know how he did it, but he'd managed to get everything from lingerie to shoes and all in the right size.

I grinned at the silky blue dress with the crossover neckline and flared skirt. The material felt heavenly against my fingers. Deciding on that one was easy. I found a bra and panty set that wouldn't show beneath it and began to dress. Sliding my feet into a pair of moderately high, strappy heels, I grinned at my reflection.

I hadn't bothered drying my hair, so a loose French braid was the best I could manage. He'd even ordered a beautiful assortment of makeup in several shades.

The quality was exquisite, and I tried not to think of the expense as I dusted my face lightly with powder adding mascara, some highlighter, a touch of bronzer, and a smear of lip gloss.

The sound of Marat clearing his throat caught my attention, and I turned to him, caught unawares in his predatory gaze. He was wearing a linen jacket over a dark shirt and slacks.

He looked fresh, debonair. The man was sex on legs. His powerful body moved effortlessly with all the grace of a big cat. Lithe, sensual, like a tiger. He seemed to exude sex appeal, and he was so goddamn handsome.

Okay, I shouldn't have put my panties on just yet.

"You look stunning."

"I do? Um, thank you," I said. "I can pay you back—" I started to talk but didn't bother finishing my sentence.

The cold, hard truth was I couldn't pay him back. There was simply no way I could afford it. And I wasn't a liar.

"Money is not an issue," he said, dismissing me.

"I wish that was true for me, Marat. And I know I can't afford any of this, but I have some money in my savings account," I replied.

"It *is* true for you. You're my wife."

The way he kept saying that I wondered if it was for my benefit or if he needed the reminder.

"Money is no issue for either of us," he continued before I could lose myself in thought.

"Marat," I whispered, shaking my head.

I wasn't materialistic, never having the funds to indulge, but I liked nice things. I admired beauty and quality. But it was the *how,* not the *what* that was important to me.

How you treated someone. How you showed you cared. Not what you were wearing. Or what you could get next.

"I don't want you offering me any of yours again, okay?" he continued. "Now, I've already had some funds transferred to your checking account, and credit cards have been ordered. But they will take a few days to arrive. If there is anything you need while we are here, just ask me or have it charged to the room. The hotel manager knows who you are," he said.

"Marat, this is crazy."

He hummed but said nothing. His dark gaze

roamed over me, and I stood up straighter, taking pride in the way he couldn't seem to take his eyes off me.

I had to admit, the clothes felt nice. If they looked half as good as they felt, I was doing alright. At least I would not embarrass myself standing next to him.

"Come. We have an appointment at the jeweler's."

I started shaking my head, but he'd already moved, taking my hand before I could do more than squeak. Marat led the way to the elevator, and all I could do was follow.

"Oh, here," he said, grabbing something off the table and handing it to me.

I stared at the beautiful bag, mouth gaping. I couldn't be sure, but it looked like a Birkin. The shiny blue leather felt like butter beneath my fingertips and I almost moaned.

A moderate estimate for the cost of that bag was more than I made in a year. The fact he gifted it to me without so much as batting an eyelash rendered me speechless.

But there was more to it than just the bag. Looking inside, I saw he'd replaced my cheap wallet with a matching one. My phone had also been upgraded to a newer model, all my contacts transferred. And there was a key to the hotel suite in there as well.

"You went through my things?"

He nodded.

"W-when?"

"When you were asleep."

"Marat—"

"We'll talk, Dumplin'. I promise. But outside our room, there are too many ears listening. So let's not saying anything we don't want splashed across the news and social media, alright?"

"Alright," I whispered, brows furrowed.

There was a lot to unpack with all this. The invasion of my privacy was a minor thing in retrospect.

Marat's heavy-handedness was perhaps the most shocking. Picking me up for the night was one thing, but tricking me into marriage? Why? Why would someone like him want someone like me?

I didn't know if I was emotionally equipped to handle looking too closely at that. Maybe he was just a bored billionaire, and this was some way to blow off steam?

I shouldn't let him use me.

I knew that already. But he made me feel so good, it was hard to remember why I should argue or fight against this. Against him.

No regrets, remember?

That voice from my past spoke inside my head and I closed my eyes, feeling Marat's hand squeeze mine as we rode the elevator down. The last sixteen hours had been a roller coaster ride, and for all intents and purposes I was still on it.

I was still strapped into my seat with no other recourse than to simply hold on to the bar for all I was worth and enjoy the ride.

Maybe I'd let go when we got to the big dip.

Maybe I'd throw my hands up in the air, and scream as I fell.

Maybe.

Just maybe.

CHAPTER TWENTY
DESTINY

"This ring is ridiculous," I said, staring at the enormous blue sapphire on my left hand.

"I thought you liked it?" Marat asked, brows furrowed as he leaned over the table to take my hand.

"I did. I do like it," I assured him.

The princess cut cornflower sapphire in its platinum setting was huge. Just over four carats and surrounded by diamonds on either side. Marat picked it out, and afterwards, he told me it was because it reminded him of my eyes.

Tremble. The man makes me tremble.

"Blue suits you," he repeated, looking from my hand to my dress, then back at me.

"Hmm, lucky it fits," I replied.

"Not luck. Destiny. Just like your name. Just like finding you was my destiny."

I felt my face flame and bit my lower lip. We'd skated over the whole part where I changed my name to Destiny during our conversations the night before. But I hadn't told him all of it. Not yet.

We were sitting at one of the discreet booths reserved for VIPs in one of the hotel's premier restaurants. I hadn't paid much attention when Marat led me inside, dazzled as I was to simply be with him.

Imagine me having the attention of a man who was tempting as the Devil himself, only better looking and infinitely more seductive. It was like being on one of those shows where they pluck ordinary people and drop them into extraordinary circumstances.

After spending an hour in the jewelry story, he'd insisted on another stop at a boutique for an evening gown. I was stunned speechless by the first price tag I saw, and noticing, Marat made sure to keep me from seeing the rest.

I'd almost forgotten about the award ceremony, which was apparently why he was in Vegas. I supposed I should be grateful to whoever was giving his company the award.

In reality, I was nervous as fuck. But—*and this was the really bizarre part*—I trusted him. He was a stranger. Out of my league in every way. But I trusted him to take care of me, and he did.

Something about the cool, calm manner in which he operated put me at ease. He didn't bark commands, he simply told the people working at whatever restaurant or shop we entered what he wanted, and they fell over themselves trying to get it for him.

Men and women alike. It didn't matter. When Marat spoke, everyone listened. It was like they couldn't help themselves. He held the masses in his thrall, and I wondered if I wasn't just another mindless minion.

I hoped not. I mean, I really hoped I meant something else to him. And I wasn't just another willing subject.

Marat lived in a completely different world than most people. I still didn't know why he chose me to go back to his room last night. And I sure as fuck did not know why he'd gone through all the trouble of tricking me into this marriage thing.

Maybe it was time I asked.

"Here you are," our server interrupted the second I went to open my mouth, appearing out of nowhere with beautifully plated dishes.

Aside from the glitz and glamour of Vegas, the one thing I loved about this place was the food. It was just out of this world good. And there was so much of it.

"Hungry?" Marat asked, a grin tilting the corner of his lips.

"Yes, actually," I said, not shying away from it.

I was a woman with a healthy appetite and whether or not I was married now, that was one thing that would never change. I liked food. Obviously.

"Good," he said, and I looked up at the heat I'd picked up in his tone.

I dropped my gaze, taking in the several small plates the server brought. I recognized some dishes.

Scallops. Foie gras. Tuna tartare. Burrata. Golden beets drizzled with a wine reduction. A charcuterie board.

My mouth watered. I hesitated though, uncertain what to choose and not wanting to make an ass of myself.

I didn't have to worry. The feel of Marat's leg beside mine as he squeezed in beside me settled over me like a security blanket.

His chest rumbled, and I closed my eyes, loving the animalistic sounds he made. He lifted his fork, using it to cut into one of the dishes before us, then presented it to my lips.

"Try this," he murmured, his voice like rough silk against my ears.

It was like sensory overload. His chiseled good looks were even more devastating up close to the point I had to close my eyes to stop myself from dissolving into a puddle of hormones at his feet.

Then there was the way his chest vibrated with his words. The sound of that growly rumble. The purely masculine scent of his soap flowed through the air, and I breathed him in wholeheartedly.

The sound of his suit brushing against my clothes as he pushed in closer had me clenching my thighs tight together beneath the table. Marat pressed the steel pronged fork against my lip, and I opened, using my tongue to slide the morsel free.

It was the sexiest thing I'd ever experienced to date. Being fed by this man who looked like a fallen angel and fucked like the Devil himself.

I didn't know what I was eating. The flavors of each bite he fed me burst inside my mouth. And it was good. All of it was good.

Bite by bite. Plate by plate. Marat fed me. Each

action was a sensual form of foreplay I'd never engaged in. By the time we were done, I was panting.

"Are you finished?" he asked me, and I nodded, incapable of speech.

I felt hot and swollen. Needy. Desperate. We needed to talk, but it could wait. I wanted him too much for words.

"Let's go."

CHAPTER TWENTY-ONE
MARAT

oly. Fuck.

Who knew feeding someone could be so fucking sexy? Every moan was just another log tossed on the fire. Every hum stoked the flame of my already wild desire for the sexy little minx I had the foresight to bind to me through lawfully wedded marriage.

Eyes locked on my wife's sexy as fuck body draped in silk, I had to adjust my dick just so I could stand. That steady thumping that started the minute I first saw her was harder now, the tempo faster.

Thump. Thump. Thump.

My pulse raced wildly as I looked my fill, leaning close so I could breathe her in. She still smelled like my soap, and that was probably because the stuff I ordered for her hadn't arrived until after she'd showered.

But that was more than okay.

I liked her smelling like me. Liked the way my spice mixed with her natural citrusy scent.

Dumplin' was a feast for my senses.

And I meant *mine*.

I practically snarled at every man who had the audacity to check her out as she walked beside me. They were only human, and she was a fucking knockout, so I understood. But that didn't mean I liked it.

Jealousy was another new emotion for me. I held her left hand with my right one, flashing that little ring on her finger whenever someone stared too hard.

Fuck.

Maybe she needed a bigger one? Maybe she needed a fucking sign. A t-shirt. Or a tattoo. Something that declared her as taken. By me.

I was suddenly possessed by the need to ensure everyone knew. The whole goddamn world.

Was it too late to take out an ad? Maybe I could call our publicist.

We barely made it into the private elevator before I had her pinned against the wall inside. My aching cock felt so damn good against her soft belly.

"Jesus. Fuck. Open up for me, Dumplin', I need your fucking mouth," I growled, crashing into her with none of the finesse I was known for.

I'd been called suave, smooth as silk, and seduction itself. But with her, I was a rutting animal. A mindless beast acting on feeling alone.

"Are you wet for me, Baby?" I growled, crashing my mouth to hers as I hoisted her off the floor.

Her ready submission had my dick thumping double time and I couldn't wait to be buried inside her again. I loved having her in my arms. The weight of her felt different. It was real, heavy, anchoring me to the present.

Perfect. So fucking perfect.

"Y-yes. My panties are soaked. I feel it dripping down my thighs," she whispered her response, and it drove me wild.

I groaned, forcing her mouth open wider with one hand on her chin. She was so fucking sweet. So good. So ready.

I thrust my tongue inside, tracing her teeth and her tongue, leaving no inch of her untouched. I wanted to ravage every inch of her. To plunder her secrets. Conquer her for my own.

I'd never felt anything like this before. And I didn't know why, but I was used to getting what I wanted. So, I didn't question it. I just took.

Thunder roared in my ears, and I was deaf, dumb, and blind to everything but this over-whelming passion I felt for her. I couldn't fucking wait to be inside my sweet Dumplin'.

The elevator doors opened, and I carried her to the table, dropping her on it as I tore at her clothes.

"The dress," she protested weakly.

"I'll buy you another one," I growled, yanking her skirt up.

The sound of fabric tearing met my ears with primordial satisfaction as I revealed her thick, pale thighs.

This might be my new thing. Ripping clothes off my sexy wife.

Hell, I'd buy her a closetful just so I could rip them off her. See the excitement burning in her blue eyes as I showed my hand, letting her see how much I wanted her.

I wanted to bury my face between her legs. Lick her until she came, screaming my name.

But that could wait till later. Right then, I needed inside her hot pussy.

I was fucking desperate to feel her hot, wet cunt tight around my cock. Fuck. She was damn good. I needed her. Desperately. I needed to feel her walls squeezing the cum right out of my aching balls.

Thump. Thump. Thump.

My clothes were next. Well, my pants, anyway. I dragged the zipper down, pushing the material along with my boxers until my cock sprang free.

I'd wait till round two to take off my fucking jacket.

"Fuuucckkk," I groaned, sinking into her slippery sex without pause.

"Goddamn!" Destiny gasped.

"Fuck, you feel good. Need it. Need more. Wanna feel you come on my bare cock, Baby," I growled.

"Oh god," she moaned, gripping my hips with her fingers.

"Not god. You say my name when I fuck you."

"Marat. Marat," she moaned like a good little wife, repeating my name in her husky voice.

It was like music to my ears.

It was a novelty for sure, fucking someone without a condom. There were just too many damn variables, but I knew I was clean. I had regular checkups.

Besides, I never did that. I always practiced safe sex. It was a huge deal for me. I didn't want children born out of wedlock, and I definitely didn't want a disease.

But the background check I ran on Destiny overnight told me all I needed to know. Josef had even hacked into her health records.

I knew she'd had her last checkup just this month, right before her birthday. Her lab results were good. I knew she was on birth control. And after a deep dive into her social media I knew that her last relationship was half a year ago. The stupid bastard had skipped town, lucky for him. But I still asked Josef to track him down and make sure he stayed in whatever hole he'd crawled into.

Did I always run background checks on women I fucked? No.

But Destiny was not some woman. She was my wife. I needed to know everything about her.

Yes, it was another invasion of her privacy. Another thing for me to explain later. Much later.

Lucky for now, she was just as far gone as I was. Lost to the pleasure building between us like an inferno.

"That's it, Baby. Come for me. Let me feel your sweet cunt flutter around my dick," I grunted, bottoming out as she came apart at my command.

"Marat," she keened, and I moaned at the sensation of her cunt fluttering around my length.

"Good Wife."

CHAPTER TWENTY-TWO
DESTINY

"I guess we should start getting ready," Marat said after returning to the bedroom with my newly arrived gown in hand.

The concierge had buzzed the room to alert us the gown was ready, after a few modifications I needed to accommodate my shortness. Apparently, it was Marat's decision, not mine. So, I didn't bother pointing out that he was being a touch overbearing.

It was all too new for me to tease him just yet. Even though I wanted to. But I did not know my husband well enough, so I just waited for him to retrieve the gown.

I watched him walk back into the bedroom clad only in his black silk boxers. It struck me again how beautiful he was. I mean, I never thought I would call a man that, but he was so much more than handsome.

I was leaning against the padded headboard in the luxurious king-sized bed. The sheets were rumpled, pillows scattered on the floor in disarray. But I felt sated, good even. We'd moved to the bed after our table sexcapades, and I fell asleep with Marat's arms around me.

It was insane how easily I slept with him. And I meant slept, not fucking. I mean, anyone could see why dropping my panties wouldn't be a chore for a man like Marat, but I never rested so easily beside another human being before in my life.

"What's going on?" he asked, taking in my stiff posture.

"We need to talk."

I was nervous and fidgeting. This man had tricked me into marriage. But I wanted him. Things happened for a reason, right? I picked my name for a reason.

I believed in fate. I believed in destiny. Maybe this big, sexy man was mine. We were already hitched, so what was wrong with trying?

I really wanted to try.

"About?"

"Well, if you're serious and we're really going to do this, we need ground rules."

I bit my lip, waiting for him to reply. Marat didn't disappoint, he cocked his head and nodded.

"This? As in our marriage?"

"Of course, this, as in our marriage," I replied, rolling my eyes.

"I already told you, Dumplin', I'm very serious. You're mine. We're married now, and I have every intention of us remaining that way."

"I understand you feel like that now, Marat. But Vegas is hardly the place to make such a commitment," I argued.

"Are you serious? It is precisely the right place. Millions of people come here for that very reason, Baby."

"Yeah, but not like this. I mean, you hardly know me. And you tricked me into marrying you," I stated, laying it all out.

I watched as he hung my gown in the closet. His long fingers traced the plastic garment bag as he turned, coming back to the bed to sit across from me.

"Maybe. But you can't tell me you're really angry about that, can you?"

Smug bastard was right. I wasn't angry. But I was worried.

"Okay look, I'm willing to concede circumstances were a bit unorthodox."

"That's big of you," I teased.

"And I think I see what you mean," he continued, ignoring me except to pinch me on my thigh to which I squeaked. "So, what are your ground rules?"

His mien was different. Like the defenses on his invisible shield had shifted somehow. This was a Marat I hadn't glimpsed yet.

The beautiful billionaire playboy was now the shrewd businessman. He looked powerful. A little scary, truth be told.

I took a moment to simply drink him in. He was a mystery. This man was my husband, but I didn't know him at all.

"What is it, Dumplin'?" he asked, reading me so well.

"I was just thinking, I imagine a lot of people take you for granted. They don't bother to look beneath your shiny exterior to the intelligent and ruthless man you really are, do they?"

"You're astute," he remarked.

"I pay attention."

"Ground rules, Dumplin'. What are they?"

"Yeah. Ground rules," I repeated, licking my lips.

"Alright, I'm ready. You go first."

"Fine, rule number one, I think it is important we are always honest with each other," I said.

"I am honest—"

"No, I mean, we tell each other everything. This is new. We don't know each other. So, if I snore and it bugs you. Or you leave the toothpaste uncapped, and it bugs me, we tell each other, then we work on it. Deal?"

"I like your soft snores," he said with a grin.

"I do not snore!"

I pretended to be outraged, but his rich laughter surprised me into shutting my trap. My stomach tensed. My heart stopped.

Holy. Crap.

He was even more gorgeous when he laughed. How was that even possible?

"I promise, Dumplin' only honesty between you and me. What else?"

"I went first. It's your turn," I said,

"Okay. Rule number two, no cheating. Ever."

"Cheating?"

"Yeah, no other women or men, or both, or either," he growled.

"That's easy for me. Will it be easy for you?" I asked, letting some of my self-doubt creep in.

"There is no one else," he said, and my heart stuttered in my chest.

"Alright, well, when I said we needed honesty, I meant it. So ground rule three is no half-assing this."

"Half-assing it?"

He smirked. His gorgeous lips tipped up, making him look even more like the Devil than usual. Sexy, dangerous man.

"Yeah, no half-assing. No half-truths or lies by omission. So, you know, when you get your mind back and you want out of this marriage, just say so. Don't leave me to figure it out."

"I won't want out, Dumplin'," he said, and my heart thudded inside my chest.

"Also," I continued. "If you're going to call me pet names cause I'm chubby, be prepared for me to retaliate with some names of my own. You with all your fallen angel beauty, I'm going to call you Lucifer."

I meant it to be funny, but Marat's face dropped into a glare, and before I knew it, he was pushing me back onto the bed, his hard body pinning me down.

"First, you think I'm beautiful?"

"Oh my god, you know you are, Marat."

"Fine, we'll get to that later. More importantly, there's been a serious miscommunication, Wife. Allow me to explain," he growled, and I moaned at the hardness I felt growing between my thighs.

He'd just made me come twice. I couldn't possibly be needy for him again, could I?

Fuck, yes, I could.

I moaned, flexing my hips, trying to bring him closer.

"Fuck. Pay attention and stop squirming."

"I can't help it. I'm so wet," I murmured, unashamed of the state Marat had driven me to.

"Goddamn. Such a dirty little wife," he groaned, pressing his hips hard against mine.

I whimpered, and his eyes rolled back in pleasure. I never had that kind of no holds barred instant attraction with anyone else.

It was like the second we touched, our simmering passions were reignited to towering fucking infernos.

Hot. So hot.

"I said knock it off," he growled, and nipped my neck with his teeth before raising his head and freezing me with his obsidian stare.

"Now, what did you say about my, what was it,

my *pet name* for you? That I said it cause you're chubby?"

"Yeah," I nodded, a little more than flustered. "I mean calling me Dumplin' is like you're calling me fat, isn't it? Like that movie?"

"I have no idea what movie you are talking about. Or why you think Dumplin' means fat."

"Because they are fat," I said, embarrassed and exasperated.

His body was still pressed against mine. But without him moving, it was like torture, making me crazy. I wanted him to kiss me. To touch me. I was desperate for something, anything, other than this conversation.

It was humiliating talking about that with him. But I was the one who started it, and I supposed having Marat's gorgeous self, half naked and teasing, was my punishment.

"Yes, definitely a miscommunication," he growled. "I call you Dumplin' because *you* are fucking delicious. Like a dumpling. And they aren't *fat*. They are the best fucking food."

"What?"

"Dumplings are my favorite. They come in all flavors. Sweet and savory. They're soft," he said, kissing my cheek. "Juicy," he continued, kissing my neck. "And fucking addictive," Marat growled, licking a trail down to my cleavage.

"Oh god," I moaned, closing my eyes.

I was so turned on. Whether from his words, his lips, his body, or all the above. My body was stoked, and I needed him so damn bad.

"That's why I call you Dumplin'. You. Are. All. Those. Things. For. Me."

"You're addicted to me?" I gasped.

"Ever since I had my first taste, Dumplin'. Addicted and always wanting more."

His voice was so rough, so deep, I didn't know if it was from rage or desire or some potent combination of both. My clit twitched, and I ached, needing him so badly.

"Oh." My reply was so fucking soft, I barely heard it above the sound of my heavy breathing.

"Yeah. Oh," he grunted.

"Marat," I begged, pleading for something I didn't even understand.

"Now, I want you to take that sheet off, Baby. Spread those soft, thick legs wide. That's it, hold yourself open for me," he growled, kneeling between my legs, his dark eyes on my pink pussy that I'd just bared for him.

"I'm fucking starving and it's time for my dinner."

I hated this. I hated pompous galas of any kind. Awards dinners filled with dishonorable dick-heads pretending to be better than they were, patting themselves on the back for accomplishments not of their own making.

It was ludicrous. It was grotesque. But it was business.

Sometimes I wondered if we had remained on the path Adrik first took, pursuing criminal endeavors instead of legitimate ones, if things would have been any different. Really, the more I became involved with the company, the more I saw how difficult Adrik's struggle to keep us legit really was.

The line between the business world and the

underworld was truly fine. So damn thin it was impossible to see in certain places.

Volkov Industries had several divisions. I was currently working on a plan to decrease our carbon footprint overseas, to make our mines green, safer for the environment and for our employees. It was a huge undertaking, but one Adrik approved of.

I'd already discussed the possibility of moving Andres from assistant to manager on my green team. That was the nickname I chose for the group I'd handpicked for this project.

Spending the last few days in Vegas had put a hold on things, and I was eager to return to work.

"Marat, old boy, how are you?" some stuffy, white-haired businessman I'd forgotten the name of stopped on his way to the restroom and I merely nodded, uninterested in conversation.

I pulled on my collar, stopping myself when I realized what I was doing. The tux I wore was custom tailored and fit me like a glove. It wasn't uncomfortable in the least, but I was on edge.

I waited outside the main ballroom for Destiny to rejoin me after she'd excused herself to the ladies' room. Not wanting her to be uncomfortable, I escorted her.

This whole event was alien for someone with her

lifestyle, and I was not judging or bragging. Before she was my wife, she was a waitress. That was simply a fact.

Although, when I thought about it, our worlds were probably not that different. She worked in Sin City, and this town was full of morally compromised people.

The type of people who attended events like this were often the worst of the elite, congratulating themselves for whatever fake fucking accomplishments some publicist or other set up for them. I didn't want anyone of those fucks looking at her. Not without me there to provide a buffer.

At least I knew Volkov Industries had done the things we'd been given a humanitarian award for at this thing. After the ceremony, I'd handed the small statue off to Josef, who in turn gave it to one of his men.

My speech was hardly memorable. All I could see was Destiny's big blue eyes following me, and for once in my life, I wanted to make someone proud. I mean, yeah, I shared in the successes of the company I co-owned and chaired with my brother.

But these were Andres', our assistant's incentives, and accomplishments. Another reason I was behind his latest raise. I'd gone through accepting the award mechanically. All the while, I played back in my head the rest of the ground rules my wife had surprised me with.

"I want you to promise to meet me in the middle, Marat."

"What do you mean?"

"No half-assing this marriage. You did this. I should be mad. I should demand you get it annulled, but I'm not that smart, I guess."

She'd been joking. But it still made me mad.

"You're smart. Don't say that about yourself. And I told you, I am not half-assing anything. I want this."

"Fine, if I'm not dumb, then I must be crazy. Cause I want to stay married too. But it's going to be a group effort. I won't be bought, so no more outrageous presents."

"What are you talking about? You needed a ring."

"And you're not wearing one, I noticed."

"You're going to make me work for this aren't you?"

I had to admit I'd been pleasantly surprised to hear her say she wanted me to wear a ring. It was a symbol of ownership I'd never given anyone over me. And like everything else about my Dumplin' it was tempting.

"You're damn straight I am. I know what I'm worth."

And because I did too, I made her come again, that time on my dick. She was so fucking sweet, I could not get enough of her. It was a new level of obsession for me. I had never felt that. Not for anyone.

I wanted to stay alone with her locked in our penthouse suite away from everyone else. But that fucking award was why I was there in the first place. I had no choice but to show up and accept the thing.

I thought about the way she mentioned a ring and looked at my bare hand. She was right. I needed a ring on my finger.

Maybe we could go right now? The jeweler would open for me.

We'd been at the gala long enough. But what was Destiny doing in the ladies' room? How long did women take to pee, anyway?

Patience was not one of my virtues. While I pondered the timeless question of what females did in restrooms that took so long, someone tapped me on the shoulder.

I spun around, frowning at the grinning face of Tessa McNeil. The thin, blonde socialite was a few inches shorter than me and way too close for comfort.

"Marat, there you are," she purred, placing one hand on my chest over the jacket of my tuxedo.

I stepped back, causing her hand to fall. The

confidant smile that had been on her face a second ago faltered, and something caught her attention. I turned my head, my eyesight landing on Destiny as she approached slowly.

I was unsure what to expect. A scene? Would she freak out because another woman's hands were on me? I didn't like the idea of causing her discomfort or hurt in any way.

Without too much thought, I reached for my wife. I needed to touch her. So, I pulled Destiny to my side, and wrapped my arm around her waist, securing her to me before she had the chance to react.

For some reason, with her in my arms, I felt grounded and present. I didn't want to be there, in that room, at that gala, or even in Vegas. I didn't want to make small talk with Tessa.

I just wanted her.

My wife. My sweet temptation. My Dumplin'.

"Marat, who is this? A friend of yours?" Tessa asked, and her voice held an edge I did not like.

"Hello there. Sorry for this one. We're technically honeymooning. I'm Destiny," my wife answered for me, pressing against my side, and extending a hand to Tessa.

"Tessa McNeil. I'm sorry, did you say honeymooning?" she asked, mouth gaping and closing like a fish out of water.

"That's right," I said, speaking up. "Destiny is my wife."

I watched Tessa absorb that fact, the woman seemed shocked. But honestly, I could not care less.

Volkov Industries might have catapulted my brother and me into superstar status, but I did not like those people. No more than Adrik ever had.

"Are you ready to go?" I asked her, taking in the midnight blue evening gown she wore.

"Is it over?"

"Mm," I hummed a noncommittal reply.

She said something else, but I didn't hear her. My attention was elsewhere. It was on the pounding of my heart. The roaring in my ears. How could she talk when I felt like the entire world was shifting just from looking at her?

Fuck.

She was a vision. All in blue, like an angel. Blue matched her eyes. It contrasted the warmth of her skin but complimented her dark hair and the purity of her smile.

The color was a common theme in the clothes I'd chosen for her. She brought me calm and tranquility.

Like a piece of heaven. I dressed her in blue for that reason.

The gown alone might have been considered plain, but not with her curves filling it out. Destiny looked delicious.

The deep V showed off her ample cleavage, and the long slit up the side revealed flashes of creamy white skin when she walked.

Her hair was styled in long, dark ringlets that hung past her shoulder, and all night I pictured wrapping it around my fist as I shoved my cock past her plump, pink lips.

I'd married a gorgeous woman. Just looking at her turned my cock to steel. My breath caught in my lungs and pleasure surged inside me as she turned her wide smile towards me.

I wondered if it was possible to come without ever being touched.

Her beauty went so much deeper than her pretty skin. Every second I passed in her company, every drop of information I learned about her left me craving more.

"Are you ready to leave?" I repeated, needing to get her out of there.

"Sure. If you want to go, I'm ready."

"Yes. I want to go."

Destiny didn't ask questions or pout and beg me to introduce her to movie stars, or musicians, or any of the other rich men there.

We'd been assigned to a table with more than one headliner, but she'd kept her eyes in her head. Even better than that, she'd kept them on me.

I'd never wanted someone as wholly, as completely, as I wanted her. And I wanted her now. I wanted her out of there. I wanted her home. With me.

"Come on."

Impatience spurred me on. I needed to get her alone. Thoughts of my wife consumed me. I wanted to punch every single person at that gala for looking at her with even the mildest curiosity or interest.

She wasn't for them. She was for me. Mine.

My. Wife.

CHAPTER TWENTY-FOUR
DESTINY

"When you asked if I was ready to leave, I thought you meant the party, Marat," I said, hardly believing I was sitting aboard a private jet, flying to the east coast for the first time in twelve years.

"Oh," he murmured. "I told you we'd live in New York."

"Yeah, but I didn't expect to leave so fast," I replied.

It was really fast. Like category five hurricane wind fast.

In less than forty-eight hours, Marat Volkov had completely turned my life upside down.

Enri had called me crazy when I told him what was happening. How my one night stand with the

Devil turned into me waking up married and moving across the country. But at least my favorite bartender wished me luck.

Other than him, there was no one else to call. I had no close friends in town. My ex-roommate had already left.

Marat took care of my landlord and hired someone to box up the items I wanted to keep. I packed a small suitcase of my clothes, toiletries, and cheap jewelry I'd collected. But there was nothing really keeping me in Vegas.

No roots. No ties.

The thought should have been depressing. But I was still vibrating from the last time Marat had fucked me stupid, so I made an executive decision to just hold on and enjoy the rollercoaster ride that my life had suddenly become.

"You're okay, right?"

Silly man. Asking if it was okay that he tossed me into the literal lap of luxury. Like I was complaining.

"Yes. I'm okay. I guess I'm nervous about meeting your brother and his family."

"Don't be nervous. They're going to love you," he said, going back to his laptop.

Apparently, maintaining the Volkov brothers' billionaire status meant Marat actually worked. A lot. I napped for a little while on the plane. But now I was awake, and my thoughts were heavy.

They're going to love you.

His words repeated in my brain and my chest grew tight. It was the first time he'd said the *l* word and the sound of it left me craving more.

I knew better than that. We weren't a love match. We were just an intense physical attraction. I looked at him as he worked, traced his features with hungry eyes, as I realized I was in big trouble.

"Why did you marry me?" I blurted.

Marat's gaze flashed to mine, but I could read nothing in the dark depths of his irises. He blinked twice, his unfairly long eyelashes brushing against his cheekbones.

"Because I wanted to," he said, as if that summed up everything.

"Yes, but what if you fall in love with someone someday," I said, trying not to choke on the words.

Marat blinked again, and all the hopes and dreams I hadn't even realized I'd been building froze in place.

Seconds ticked by like hours as I waited for him to respond.

"You have nothing to worry about, Dumplin'. I've never been in love, and I don't expect I ever will be."

He turned his black gaze to the screen of his laptop, efficiently dismissing me. I'd asked him earlier what he was doing, and he'd said something about mines and the environmental impact of certain techniques.

He mentioned eastern Europe and Asia. But I admit, I was too enamored by the fact he was even talking to me about his work to pay attention to the details.

I'd done my own Google search on Volkov Industries, and I knew enough that most of their business was in mining rare earth minerals, whatever the fuck that meant.

I sat there stunned for a whole minute before excusing myself to the restroom. It was a very good thing my husband was so intent on his work.

That way, I knew he never saw the first tear drop roll down my cheek. I could keep some of my pride intact.

It was cold comfort, but it was something.

Inside the tiny stall, I sobbed in silence, fixing my face as best I could after I'd calmed down a bit.

What the hell had I gotten myself into?

The Devil tricked me into marriage, that was what. And instead of fighting him, I just went with it.

I was even dumber than I thought.

After everything I'd been through in my life, I still thought fairytales were possible. But this wasn't a storybook. There would be no happy ever after ending for me.

Stupid, Destiny. How can you still be so damn naïve?

Marat would never love me. That was the cold, hard truth. I'd married a man with the perfect exterior, but it was just a shell. Inside he was a black void. Incapable of feeling.

I sucked in a sharp breath. I knew going in he didn't love me, but somehow hearing it out loud made it so much worse.

But what did I expect?

This was a man who barely had to crook a finger for a line of willing women to form. All of them desperate to be at his beck and call.

I should have been flattered.

I mean, out of so many possibles, he'd picked me. Only, I wasn't flattered. I was rattled. I was confused.

What kind of woman allowed a man to simply take her from the place she'd called home for the last dozen years, completely uprooting her life, and all on a whim?

Me. I was that kind of woman, apparently.

Sometime during the last forty eight hours—*had*

it really only been two days—I'd begun imagining myself a heroine in my very own romance novel.

I'd been wasting time on pipe dreams and fantasies, pretending this whirlwind romance was real. Two days was not enough time to fall in love with someone.

That would be ridiculous.

Don't do it, Destiny. It will be the end of you.

My inner voice was always full of good advice. Usually, it was too late. I didn't love him. Not yet.

But I was starting to.

And when Marat walked away—*and he would, I knew he would, it was just inevitable*—it was going to crush whatever parts of my soul I'd managed to salvage over the years.

It was going to hurt like a sonovabitch.

I closed my eyes and sat on the closed toilet seat. I took a deep, cleansing breath. And another.

I was still in the restroom when my phone buzzed, alerting me to a text. It was from my brother, and I frowned.

Shit. I guess I did have someone else to tell about my move. I read through his text and sighed. He needed money.

Of course he did.

That wasn't kind of me. He was providing for our

mother, the woman who'd pushed me out of her life years ago, but I was the one who told him I'd help.

I'd just sent him two hundred dollars a couple of days ago. At the time, it was all I had. But circumstances had changed.

I wouldn't touch the money Marat had put into my account. My new husband apparently did whatever he wanted, and he'd transferred the ridiculous sum without even asking me.

Even if we stayed married, I wouldn't take his money. I never wanted him to question why I was with him. I would not admit I loved him. Not even to myself.

But I did care. I cared a great deal.

I was a hopeless romantic. And I wanted to embrace this rollercoaster ride and shout my impending fall to the world. But now that I knew he didn't believe in love, I had to keep that piece of me buried.

I sent my brother a reply. I told him I was on a plane and would be able to see him in person soon. Just the thought had my stomach twisting in knots.

I hadn't seen my brother, or any member of my family, in twelve years. Maybe it was time. To see him and my mother.

Biting my lip, I started making plans in my head.

I would need a job once we got settled. Then I could figure out a way to help with my mother's care more regularly.

I opened the door to the bathroom and finished sending the text. So engrossed in what was doing, I almost walked right into Josef.

"Oh! Sorry, I didn't see you."

I blinked up at him. Like Marat, he was tall and imposing. His bearded face seemed to always be frowning. But unlike Marat, he didn't offer me any hint of kindness.

"You were looking at your phone. Talking to someone?"

"What? Oh, yeah. These things are dangerous," I replied, smiling tightly as I scooted past him.

It was funny to think I'd first thought Josef was the safer one between him and Marat. But right then, the look in his cold eyes was enough to chill me to the bone.

I returned to my seat beside Marat, complying when he reminded me about my seatbelt. Then I leaned back and closed my eyes. We had a few hours left, and I could use a nap. Clutching my hands together, I listened to the sounds of Marat's fingers clicking away at his laptop.

After a few minutes, I drifted off into a restless

slumber as an uneasy feeling settled in my soul. A loveless marriage was not what I'd envisioned when the beautiful billionaire tricked me into marrying him. It wasn't what I wanted, but I didn't see how I had any choice.

I should have paid more attention when we made those ground rules. I should have thought about my feelings. But it seemed too soon to bring up love, and it was too late to make amendments now.

Hope fluttered inside my chest like a dove with a broken wing. I wondered how long we could continue together. How long could I stay with someone who I now knew would never love me?

"We're landing. Put your seat up, Dumplin'," his whispered words penetrated my slumber, and I woke with a start.

Sadness filled me as I opened my eyes and watched Marat's perfect profile as he put away his laptop. He was colder now somehow. Distant.

I put my chair upright and made sure my seatbelt was buckled. Going through the motions of landing like my heart was not breaking inside my chest. I'd been such a fool. Tears tracked down my cheeks as the plane touched down.

Where was my inner optimist now?

Josef and his team exited the plane first, leaving me and Destiny to follow. She'd been fiddling with her wallet, reorganizing the new ID that came rapidly after I'd pulled some strings in Las Vegas.

I noticed her ring glittering in the light and felt the emptiness on my left hand even more keenly. We never stopped at the jeweler's in the hotel. But I made a mental note to call someone to meet me at the office the following day.

"Don't be nervous," I told her, but she just looked at me like I was an idiot.

Of course, she was nervous. She bit her lower lip, and that was when I realized I was nervous, too.

"It's just my brother and his wife," I said out loud,

as if that would make it better.

Josef had tattled like the big fucking baby he was and now Adrik was demanding I bring my bride to his house for an early dinner. The plane ride was smooth, but traveling was never really easy for anyone.

Still, I didn't dare tell Adrik no. He could be a ripe bastard when he wanted to be, and I was not inviting that kind of attitude from him. I took Destiny's hand, pulling her along with me. Touching her made me feel better.

"Do you live near your brother?" she asked, and I ignored the choked cough coming from the front seat of the SUV.

Fucking Josef. Always the clown.

"No. We live in Manhattan. Adrik and Sofia live on the Long Island Sound. But it's closer to the airfield than our penthouse, so we'll stop there for an early meal, make introductions, then I'll show you your new home. Okay?"

I was trying to be gentle, but I sounded like a damn general even to my ears. Destiny nodded her understanding, turning her head to look out the window. Something was wrong. I didn't know what, and it worried me.

My gaze roamed over the silk blouse she wore,

and I groaned. The flimsy material did nothing to hide her delicious curves from my eyes, which meant others could see her pebbled nipples as well in the cold interior of the vehicle.

"Did you bring your sweater?" I asked, suddenly mad as fuck.

"What? Oh, yeah," she murmured, and looked down at the space between us.

"Put it on."

"What?"

I looked at her breasts pointedly, and she followed my stare, her cheeks turning bright red when she saw what I had already noticed. I watched her throat work as she swallowed, and I couldn't understand her expression.

It was tense. Stressed out.

Is she mad at me?

"Dumplin'? Dumplin', look at me," I said, my voice low. "I love looking at your body, but Adrik's home is heavily guarded. If one of his men looks at you, I won't be able to control my reaction. I'll have to hit him. And if I hit him. I won't stop. Do you understand?"

"No," she replied. "But I'll wear the sweater for you, Marat. You just had to ask me."

I nodded, lifting her hand to my lips. I kissed her

soft skin, reveling in her citrus scent. The soft cashmere sweater was navy blue, and it complimented the patterned dress she wore.

Spring in New York was way cooler than Las Vegas, but my Dumplin' was born a Jersey girl. She knew all about East Coast weather. The pale periwinkle blouse she wore tucked into a pair of navy blue cropped pants that matched her sweater was pretty and perfect for the weather.

Her dark curls were piled on her head and secured with a hair clip. She looked fresh and innocent and I wanted so badly to take it down, run my fingers through it. I wanted to mark her so everyone knew who she belonged to. The sparkling ring on her finger wasn't enough.

"Is this your brother's house? Wow, it's beautiful," Destiny said.

I couldn't believe we'd arrived already, but I guess time flew when you were busy obsessing. I heaved a sigh and she tensed.

"You alright?"

"Oh, yeah," she started, but my frown seemed to stop her. "Honesty, ground rule one. Okay, you sighed, and I thought maybe you were regretting this whole thing. Bringing me to meet your family is probably not a good idea yet, Marat," she explained.

"It's a great idea. And I am not regretting a thing, are you?" I asked, not sure if I wanted to know.

The entire plane ride, I'd buried myself in work, refusing to give my riotous nerves even a fraction of attention. Adrik could be a real prick when he wanted to be, but this one area of my life was off limits. He wasn't getting a say in who I married.

Adrik had his bride. He'd hunted Sofia with all the precision of his wolf alter ego. But me? I wasn't a wolf. I was not my brother. And I knew that.

It was true, I did not know a lot about my wife. But Destiny and I made a promise to be honest, and I knew if I asked, she would tell me anything I wanted to know.

The thing was, if I did that. If I pushed this thing from almost purely physical to emotional, everything would change. And I did not know if I could handle that.

Am I being a coward? Maybe.

But for now I was fine letting sleeping dogs lie. I had my Dumplin' in my bed, by my side. She settled something inside of me. Filled a void I'd lived with for so long, I had no idea it was there until suddenly it wasn't.

That was enough for now. It had to be.

"Marat, welcome home!" a loud voice boomed from the top of the opulent staircase.

I clutched Marat's hand and felt his responding squeeze all the way to my toes as we walked up the stairs towards a man who could only be his brother. Marat released me to embrace him, and I stood to the side and waited.

"Hello, you must be Destiny," the man said, his voice revealing a trace of an accent I'd never picked up from his brother.

"It's a pleasure to meet you, Adrik," I said, wondering if I should offer my hand, but settling on not when he made no move to touch me.

"Come. Zaika moya is beside herself to meet you,

but little Micheala needed changing," he explained and turned, leading the way inside.

"How was the trip, brother?"

"Good. Josef has the award. He'll bring it to the office tomorrow."

"Where is Josef?" I asked, wondering where the bearded man had disappeared to.

"He's checking in with the security team, but he will join us to eat," Adrik explained.

The sounds of a baby fussing and a woman cooing reached my ears as we walked into an enormous living room. It was done in shades of black and silver.

Expensive furniture was expertly placed to maximize the space. But what shocked me was the sheer amount of baby toys and books mixed in with all the lavish belongings.

I would have expected nothing short of military order judging from the enormous, intimidating man that was Adrik Volkov. But this space seemed lived in. It looked loved. And my smile was real as I took it all in.

"There she is," Marat said, walking away from me towards a beautiful woman dressed in a silver patterned jumpsuit, holding a perfectly angelic baby in her arms.

The baby squealed, jumping from the woman's arms to Marat's. He lifted her high in the air, speaking another language that sounded suspiciously like Italian, and I almost tripped. I'd never heard him speak anything other than English.

Was it getting hotter in there?

"Hi, I'm Sofia," the woman said, as Adrik moved next to her and wrapped an arm around her back.

"Nice to meet you. I'm Destiny," I said.

I was smiling so hard with nerves my cheeks hurt. Taking pity on me, Sofia offered me a glass of white wine, which I accepted. I was trying not to react to the spectacle of Marat holding and charming his formerly fussy niece so effortlessly.

"Well, Destiny, my brother has told me nothing about you," Adrik began.

"Adrik, she's not interviewing for a job," Sofia scolded gently.

"I know this. And please, you must forgive me, but I have questions," Adrik said, but I had a feeling he was not really asking for my forgiveness.

"Of course you do," I replied easily.

"Is dinner ready?" Marat interrupted, walking back over to us.

He met his brother's somewhat hostile gaze and handed Sofia the charming baby. Then he took my hand in his, lifting it to his lips, and I felt his claim settle my nerves.

"Yes, of course," Adrik said, staring at the place where our hands were joined.

Dinner was easier than the tension I'd felt before. I sat between Marat and Sofia. Adrik was the more reserved of everyone, with Josef following closely. But he was gentle with his wife, and I appreciated that they had a true love match.

"So, what was it like living in Las Vegas?" Sofia asked as we were served delicious platters of rare roast beef, sauteed broccolini, and mashed potatoes.

"Oh, busy, noisy, expensive," I blurted, then laughed. "Sorry, I'm not sure what you want to know."

"No, I'm sorry. You see, I'm a writer and my mind is forever working on the next story. I was thinking of setting my next book there," she said, and I smiled.

"Oh my god, that is awesome! Are you published? What's your pen name? I devour books. Seriously, I read all the time."

"Me too," she whispered conspiratorially. "I am self-published. I write under the pseudonym Z. Wolff."

"Shut up! I just finished your *Billionaires Over Broadway* series!"

"You did not!"

"I did," I squealed.

We chatted about books and the publishing world while we ate, and the men discussed business. Time flew by and I felt completely at ease because of Sofia. Adrik excused himself to take a call, and Sofia left to put the baby down for her nap.

Josef remained, but his attention was on his coffee. When my gaze darted back to Marat, I found him watching me curiously.

"What is it?"

"I didn't know you liked to read. I didn't see any books at your apartment," he said, frowning.

We'd stopped at my place before heading to his private jet. Marat had some people meet us there, and we went over instructions on what they were to pack and ship to New York for me. He was right. I did not have any paperbacks.

"Oh, I read on my phone. Or using an eReader. I mean I love all books, but print copies are expensive. Not to mention they take up space, which, as you saw, I didn't really have."

"I see," he murmured.

We left soon after, and the ride to the penthouse

took over an hour with all the traffic. I sucked in a huge breath when the elevator doors opened, revealing the space. I'd expected it to reflect his wealth, and it did.

It had that sparse but opulent vibe. The butter soft couches were black, the floors were polished to shine, and the art on the walls was authentic. But it was the floor to ceiling windows that really got me.

"You can see everything from here," I whispered reverently, and walked across the room to look down at the city below.

"Yes," Marat agreed, startling me with his nearness.

"Do you want to rest? Take a bath?" he asked, head canted as he watched me.

We were alone in the penthouse, and night was falling on the city beneath us. No, I was not tired, and I did not feel particularly dirty. There was only one thing I wanted. One thing that would soothe the unease I'd been feeling all day.

"No."

"What do you want?"

His voice was deeper just then, and it stroked against my skin like hands. I faced him, the window at my back, and shrugged out of the sweater he'd asked me to wear when we were in the car.

Next, I kicked off my sandals and unbuttoned my pants. Marat hummed. The growly sound sending spikes of desire soaring through me.

I was never a stripper. Didn't have the body or the gumption to perform as those women did. And I'd never undressed with a man watching me so intently.

But he'd asked me what I wanted, and what I wanted was this. To be the object of my beautiful husband's attention. To bring him peace and contentment. To erase that sad, weary look I sometimes saw behind his obsidian eyes.

I wanted his eyes on *me* tonight. I wanted this right here. His awareness. His unwavering focus, following my every move as I revealed myself to him, one article of clothing at a time.

Sex wouldn't solve the turmoil I'd felt earlier on the plane ride. It was rash and stupid. The act of a desperate woman, some would say. But sex was also a form of communication. It was a means to deliver comfort.

For him and me both. I wasn't sure who needed it more. But after his revelation about love on the plane ride, I thought maybe I was in first place in that particular race.

My body ached, and my soul cried out for a connection.

Okay, fine, I could admit it. I needed my husband. Desperately.

"Fuck."

I dropped the last piece of clothing, shaking my hair loose from the clip holding my curls in place.

"Look at you, Dumplin', so fucking hot," he hummed the last word, raking me from head to toe with his gaze.

"You teased me all day with that body of yours in that thin fucking shirt. Then we get home, and you strip for me. Sexy little thing, showing me what you want," Marat growled.

His words made me squirm. Each syllable he uttered had the same effect as hands on my skin. My nipples pebbled. My breathing came in short, trembling bursts. Like panting and gasping but all mixed together. The butterflies in my stomach were beating their wings to the symphonic strings playing in my head.

Still fully dressed, to my completely bare, Marat never looked more like the original fallen angel, Lucifer, himself than he did right then, with all of Manhattan laid out below him and me on my knees.

His black on black suit was immaculate despite

all the traveling we did that day. He could have just walked off a photoshoot. He was so fucking hot.

"You want me, Baby?"

"Yes. I want you," I confessed, not bothering to deny it.

"On your knees," he commanded.

I dropped down, panting with desire. Marat unzipped his fly, not even bothering with the buckle. He reached inside, took out his hard cock, already leaking precum.

I moaned, leaning forward. Mouth wide, I sucked his tip inside and swiped my tongue over his slit. The salty, sweet taste of him had my pussy clenching on air, needing to be filled.

But not yet.

I wasn't done sucking my husband's cock. The small taste I'd had wasn't enough. I needed more. I needed it all.

"You going to swallow me down, Dumplin'? Show me what you got, baby."

Marat pulled on my hair. I lifted my head, nodding as I opened wide. Then he grunted, shoving his hips forward and pushing his thick dick all the way in.

Tears burned my eyes, and my gag reflex activated. He was so big. So thick. But I wasn't giving up. He made to move his hips away. But I grabbed his hand, holding it onto the back of my head. I covered Marat's hand with mine, adding pressure as his palm cupped me. I pressed down more firmly, making him hold me in place.

"Goddamn. You want me to fuck your throat? Is that what you want, Dumplin'? Want to swallow my cum?" He was panting by then.

I couldn't nod, but I kept that hand over his, squeezing to let him know *yes*, that was what I wanted. My other hand stayed on his hip to steady myself. Moisture pooled between my legs, the wetness dripping down my thighs as I bobbed my head up and down, taking him deeper with every pass.

"Fuck. So good. So fucking good," He grunted, his hand holding tight to my head.

Never in my life had I felt anything close to what I felt at that moment. Who knew giving head could be so damn hot? But seeing him like that, my fallen angel at my mercy, made me feel powerful.

It made me feel prideful. His mouth was open, and his eyes glittered as he watched me suck his dick. It was the sexiest feeling in the world. I felt slick arousal pool between my legs, and I moaned around his cock.

"Oh, fuck, Dumplin'. Mm. Moan again. That's it. Good girl. I'm going to come now, Baby. You ready?" he asked, his words so low I could hardly make them out.

I'd never been into the idea of swallowing, but I needed to. With Marat, I needed every drop of his cum down my throat.

"Fuccckkk, Dumplin'. Fuck!" Marat shouted, and I moaned as I swallowed him down.

Eyes wide, I looked up, his cock still pulsing in my mouth as he clenched his teeth and hissed, his orgasm still going, filling me with his essence. He was so goddamn beautiful.

Moaning one last time he dropped his head forward, eyes still closed as his breathing slowed. My heart squeezed and pride filled me, knowing I was the one who offered him this, who brought him relief and peace.

I wasn't supposed to feel like that. I shouldn't feel like that. Not about him.

I knew if I grew more attached to him, I was going to suffer. But it was like trying to stop a roller coaster in the middle of the ride. There was no way. Simply nothing I could do about it.

Might as well go down smiling.

CHAPTER TWENTY-SEVEN
MARAT

The first few days back in New York, things were good. Every day I woke up with Destiny naked and warm, curled up beside me, my arms wrapped around her sweet body.

I never did that. I never stayed the whole night with a woman, and I certainly never stayed more than that.

But even though there were other rooms in the penthouse, I couldn't bear the thought of leaving her side after sex. And that we had every night as well. More than once.

My mind raced with memories of what we'd done that morning, and I couldn't breathe for the tightness I felt tied around my chest. Like a fucking vise.

"What are you smiling at, Wife?"

"Just admiring my gorgeous husband. You look like a dark prince in the moonlight," she whispered to me in our bed, her blue eyes sparkling.

Fuck. She was pretty. But her words bothered me.

"This isn't a fairytale, Wife. I'm no prince. I'm not going to give you poetry or flowers."

"No? What are you going to give me?" she asked, so fucking trusting.

But I wasn't trustworthy. I was the Devil. the sound of her voice hitching at the end as she swallowed her nerves was like a balm to my soul. But I didn't want to believe it. I didn't want to trust it.

"Marat," she moaned my name, looking at me with such affection.

I did not deserve that. How could she give it to me so freely? How did she do all the things she did?

My wife was a mystery to me. I thought if I fucked her every night, this feeling I had inside to consume her would go away.

But it wasn't gratified. The more I had of her, the more I wanted. I'd been rough with her. Taking her hard and fast with no preparation at all. I'd been inconsiderate. Even rude.

The way I rutted into her sweet fucking body I was little better than an animal. Spurred on by hunger. Insatiable. Starving for her.

I fucked Destiny with a ferocity I didn't know I had in me. I worked for it with her. Needing her pleasure as much as I needed my own.

I lashed at her cunt with my tongue first. Then my cock. Filling her with my cum until we both passed out. But it still wasn't enough.

How did she do it? How did she fuck like that but still look so damn innocent?

Her face. Her hair. Her pretty smile.

She haunted my every moment, waking and not. She made me hunger. She made me crave.

I wanted to devour her. I was a fucking glutton for my wife.

But that morning I'd been out of control.

"Give you? I'm not going to give you anything," I said, answering her question.

"W-what do you mean?"

"Exactly what I said. You get nothing. It's my turn. And I'm going to take from you."

I told her when her eyes widened at my thinly veiled threat.

"I'm going to take everything you have. Your kiss, your touch, your sighs, your pleasure. They're mine. Tell me."

"They're y-yours, Marat. Only yours."

"That's right. I'm going to stuff you with my cock and take everything you have. I'm going to fuck your tight little hole until you give me everything."

I grunted my demand before impaling her on my dick. My wife who told me she wasn't good at sex the first time we fucked was coming before my second thrust.

It should have made me proud that I was the only man who brought her to such heights. And it did.

But it also made me fucking furious. I wanted to know who her past lovers were. Who'd touched her body? Who'd left her unfulfilled? I wanted to exterminate them. I wanted to kill them with my bare hands for daring to touch what was mine. And for touching her and failing her so spectacularly.

It was madness. I knew that. And yet, I couldn't stop my feelings.

"I know you said this isn't a fairytale, but that was a pretty great ending," Destiny sighed after we both finished panting.

"That's where you're wrong, Baby. That wasn't an ending. It was the beginning. Now turn around and get

up on all fours. That's it. Show me that tight little asshole."

Fuck. She was such a good girl. Such a filthy little girl, doing what I told her.

God, the way she tasted. Like pure fucking heaven.

Like mine.

Thinking about the way she keened when I lashed my tongue between her round globes had my cock thumping inside my pants. Of course, she'd never done that before.

Ass play was new for her, and I wanted to beat my chest like a fucking barbarian that I was the first. I couldn't wait to fuck her there, but we had time.

I needed to prepare her for it. And I needed it to be me who initiated her.

Filled with thoughts of my wife filling my head, I went into the office to find my latest project in shambles. I needed to refocus my attentions on my greener initiative and not my wife's tempting little asshole.

After that encounter, things had cooled dramatically. It was my fault. I'd put up a wall.

Days blurred. Every morning, I woke up early, went to work, tried to ignore the fact my wife had started to smile less with every passing day.

Destiny was one of those naturally happy people. I'd seen it shining in her beautiful blue eyes the first time I looked into them. She had a brightness about her.

Like she was always looking for the light no matter how dark it was.

The evidence of her unhappiness weighed heavily on my conscience. We said we would be honest with one another. But to have honesty you needed communication. And I'd been nothing but cold and distant since we'd landed.

Another week passed, and we'd been isolated in our own little bubble. I thought it might be okay then. That maybe she'd let my bad behavior go. And for the most part, she did.

Destiny did not complain or nag at me. She didn't push me away when I reached out for her in the dark. When we were together like that, she was all I could see. Her throaty moans were like music to my ears and the way her body always welcomed mine was unparalleled.

But in the light of day, I became someone else. I was all business. And I was cold. I went to work at Volkov Towers every day. Putting in fourteen to sixteen hours. Coming home well after she'd gone to bed.

I was a coward. Doing anything I could to not have to talk to my wife.

Fuck. I was so fucking guarded. I hated myself for it. But I couldn't deal with the possibility of her asking me for something I couldn't give her. Or worse, for her wanting out of our marriage.

I couldn't do that. No way. She was mine. And to remind her of that, every night I came home and fucked her. Sometimes we had dinner together, other times we barely said a word.

I couldn't keep my hands off her. And by some miracle, by some goddamn fucking miracle I didn't want to look too closely at, Destiny had yet to tell me no. She welcomed me with open arms, just as hungry for my touch as I was for hers.

Hell, I didn't even know what I would do if she said I couldn't have her. I wouldn't play fair. That was the only certainty. Need buzzed in my veins like a swarm of bees, and I'd yet to get my fill.

Would it stop? Would I wake up one day cured of my desire?

Truth was, I had no fucking clue. She was the only woman who ever made me feel that way. I didn't even try to fight it. Denying my desires was not something I'd ever done.

But the world had gone dark for a while. It was

tasteless, colorless, and then suddenly, she was there. Like my own personal sun bringing warmth and soft light to my otherwise cold and listless existence.

Fuck. I needed to do better. I had to make an effort with her. Talk to her. Take her out. Show her how good things could be between us. I had to do something, or I was going to fuck this up. And I couldn't have that.

I was addicted to her. She was mine. My sweet Dumplin'. And I had no intention of letting her go.

"What are you doing here? It's Saturday," Josef said, eyebrows raised as I walked down the hall to my office.

"You're here. Adrik is here. Why shouldn't I be?"

"Because it's fucking Saturday. Who the hell are you?"

"Fuck off, Josef."

"No, seriously—" he started, but Adrik opened his door at the same time.

"Marat? What are you doing here? It's Saturday?" my older brother asked, truly puzzled.

"Oh my fuck," I growled, raising my hands and slapping them down on my sides. "What the fuck is the big deal? You are both here! Andres is probably here, too. Why shouldn't I be here?"

"Uh, maybe because you never gave a fuck about business before?" Adrik said.

"Maybe he is having problems with that hot new wife. Problems at home, Marat? Your wife disappearing on you already?" Josef taunted.

Red crept into my vision. They could talk all they wanted about me, but no one was allowed to talk about my wife. I growled, lunging for him.

"Don't fucking talk about her," I growled, as we exchanged punches.

He was stronger, I would give him that. But I was faster. And when a heavier opponent threw his weight into a punch, it was simply a matter of turning at the last minute to maximize his wasted effort. Add to that my own right hook, and Josef went down.

"ENOUGH!" Adrik roared.

He pushed his way between us, shoving Josef in one direction and me in the other. The anger rolling off him was enough to silence us both, and we stopped going for each other's throats.

"Fuck you, you little prick," Josef said, spitting blood into his handkerchief.

"You're the one who taught me that move," I grunted, wiping my new split lip with the back of my hand.

"Enough from both of you. My office. Now," Adrik commanded in clipped phrases.

"Sit," he said, and Josef took the chair on the left, leaving me the other.

"Adrik, it's nothing you wouldn't do if someone said something about Sofia," I began, not wanting to get into this.

"My Zaika is not the issue. Besides, my relationship is not the same. I love my wife," he said, eyes narrowed, and I felt those words like a punch to my gut.

I knew he loved his wife. Everyone fucking knew it. What did that have to do with me? My brother had everything he ever wanted, and he worked hard for it. I would never begrudge him his happiness.

"I am not you, Adrik. But my marriage is not up for debate. And I won't listen to a bad word about her. Destiny is my wife. She will be treated with respect," I said, brooking no argument.

"Not up for debate?" Josef spat. "Do you know where your wife goes every day? When you're working, does she tell you where she goes?"

"What the fuck are you talking about?"

"Marat, I asked Josef for a copy of the background check you ran on your wife. Then I asked him to put her under surveillance."

"What?"

"You are my brother. I will do anything to protect you. Even from yourself," he said, handing me a manilla envelope.

My heart thudded painfully inside my chest as I opened the thing. I did not want to look inside, but I was powerless to do otherwise. I dumped the contents onto my lap, pawing through them.

Photos of Destiny on a bus to New Jersey. Copies of public transportation schedules. Screenshots of text messages from someone named Bear.

Last was a copy of an old marriage license.

What. The. Fuck?

Anger dotted my vision with red. Jealousy making it impossible to breathe. She was married before. From the date, it looked like she was just eighteen when she'd married someone else. Someone named Timothy Gallo.

A fucking dead man.

More photos of her in some greasy diner, sitting across from a stranger who looked her age. Copies of a couple of checks from her account made out to cash. The amounts were small, but I could not explain them.

"Did you have any idea about this?" Adrik asked.

Fury and pain like I'd never felt filled me as I looked

through the evidence of my wife's secret life. Failure and me, we were old friends, but I'd believed Destiny when she said we would have honesty between us.

I'd been a fool. A stupid, gullible fool. She was just like all the rest.

Manipulator. User. Liar.

I felt Adrik's pity, and it was the last straw. I wasn't the Dark Wolf. I was not cunning. And I clearly didn't have a fucking clue about my own wife. But fuck him for making me feel like less. And damn her for playing me like that for all to see.

With a fury I'd never felt before roiling through me, I turned to Josef.

"Where is she now?"

He looks at me, then Adrik, then back at me. Taking his cell phone out of his pocket, Josef huffed a breath and sent a text. Seconds later, he received one back.

"I have an address. The car is waiting."

"Do you want me to come with you?" Adrik asked.

"No. Josef will come with me."

I left my brother's office with long, angry strides. Who was the man she was meeting? This Bear? What was my little wife up to?

It was not lost on me that whatever Destiny was doing, she didn't have to try hard to hide. I never asked her a single question about herself.

Ever since I brought her here, moved her into my penthouse, I'd put up a wall between us. The only time I took it down was to fuck her. But the second emotions threatened to spill over, I brought it right back up.

I did not want to feel that way about anyone.

I'd wanted her from the second I saw her. Who wouldn't? She was beautiful. A wild temptation. Out of the ordinary. Making me lose control. I could understand now how my brother had become so unhinged over a woman.

But I was not like him. Love was not something I believed in. Hell, I didn't think I was even capable of it.

Obsession, well, that was something else. Something understandable. But I'd never been moved to such a state before.

You could imagine my surprise that a curvy little cocktail waitress brought that out in me. I was possessed by the desire to make Destiny mine. To get her in my bed. Keep her there. Force her to wear my ring. Take my name. And I'd done all that.

I couldn't just allow her to take root inside my soul.

And now that I knew she'd lied, I was grateful for having the foresight to shield myself. She'd called me beautiful once. Told me I looked like a fallen angel with my dark eyes and perfect features. She'd said I looked like the Devil.

Well, Wife, you're about to find out how like Lucifer I can be.

The Four Star Diner hadn't changed in twelve years. It still smelled of stale oil and greasy burners and floor cleaner. I shook my head and watched the rain as it fell outside.

Spring was so damn wet on the East Coast. How had I forgotten? But the desert did that to you. Made you forget.

Sitting in a booth, I tapped my nails on the chipped tabletop while I waited for Bear. His name was Orson, but we'd always called him Bear. Ever since he was a kid.

My memories of him were a little mixed. He was older. He had his own life and drama when I was a child going through mine. But he was trying to be a good brother, and I needed family, so I was trying, too.

Things with Marat had started out promising. I thought the craziness of our marriage might actually work out.

But my husband had been steadily pushing me away since the first day we moved into his penthouse. I probably needed to do or say something, but I was terrified of him asking me to leave.

See, I'd done something really stupid. I caught feelings for the Devil, and I was going to burn because of them. But Marat wasn't why I was sitting in that old ass diner.

Bear was just getting off his shift, and we had a meeting. Sometimes he got out late, so I ordered my coffee already and waited.

I was so proud of my brother. He'd worked hard to stay out of trouble after a brief fuck up when he was a teen. He'd served eighteen months for car theft, but after that, he went back to school and got his diploma. Now, he was gainfully employed and doing well.

"Hey, little sis. Good to see you," he said, shaking off his jacket and dropping it on the hook outside the booth.

"Hey Bear," I said and stood up, accepting his hug.

"I can't get over it. I mean every time I look at you. You look just like Mom," he said.

"Yeah? I don't see it. Speaking of Mom, I want to see her, Bear," I told him, tears making my voice thick.

"Yeah, yeah, no, we can do that."

He dropped his motor oil stained hat on the booth where he sat and heaved a sigh. He always liked cars. That was probably why he stole one. But I thought it was cool my older brother worked on them now.

I frowned, thinking about my own dismal job experiences. I needed to do something with my time. I did not want to waitress, but I couldn't just sit around the penthouse and wait for my husband to come home.

Considering how late he'd been doing that just lately, it seemed like a bad idea. If it wasn't for the fact, he still seemed interested in sex with me, I'd think he was already drawing up divorce papers.

The whole thing made me furious. It wasn't like I'd trapped him or tricked him into marriage.

Dammit. Why did I have to like him?

I lived for those rare, unguarded moments where

he let me in and showed me something real. It was quite a shock to discover the Devil had interests other than temptation.

Marat liked movies. He was completely obsessed with John Hughes films, and wouldn't you know it? They were my favorite. What was better than watching an awkward Molly Ringwald fall for the wrong guy?

Sigh.

"So, what's going on with you?" Bear asked, and it was just the distraction I needed.

"Nothing. I'm good. What happened with Mom's tests?"

"It's not good. I tried, but the doc says Mom is in the late stages of dementia. I can't take care of her cause I work so many hours. She has to stay in a care home permanently," he choked on the words.

I reached across the table and clasped his hand. This was so hard. Bear's tears matched my own. We sat there, trying to comfort one another for a few minutes before we discussed long-term care plans for our mother.

"I appreciate it, Sis."

"She's my mom, too," I whispered, even though we both knew that wasn't entirely true.

Mom and Dad had both shoved me out of their

lives because of one desperate decision I'd made before I even got my license. But that was the past. I'd learned to live with it. Besides, I needed to worry about my future.

I noticed movement at the front of the diner and turned to see what the fuss was all about. My mouth dropped open. Bear was saying something, but I didn't hear him at first.

"Destiny? What's the matter? Who is that?" he asked as the last person in the world I expected to see at that moment came striding right toward us.

"I'm her husband. Who the fuck are you?" Marat asked, but his eyes were on me.

Josef filled the space next to him. Disdain made Marat's angelic features that much harder to look at as he glowered at me. His anger was positively palpable.

"I'm Bear," my brother said, narrowing eyes as blue as mine at my husband.

"Like the animal?" Marat asked.

"No, like the teddy bear he wouldn't go anywhere without when he was a kid," I answered, not liking his tone at all.

I stood, toe to toe with my angry husband and gestured to Bear who was looking at us both like we'd lost our minds.

He wasn't wrong.

Josef was the only one not betraying any emotion, but I was pissed at him, too.

I knew all about the background check, and the gross invasion to my privacy when Marat had ordered him, most likely, to change my name and pay off my landlord.

Everything had moved so quickly, I never questioned it or even allowed myself a minute to think how freaked out I should have been.

Ever since we got on that goddamn plane, the whirlwind romance I'd been building up in my head had burst into flames. For weeks, I'd waited for Marat to turn back into the man who'd relentlessly pursued me. The one who wanted me and made me feel special.

But that man was gone. My husband was as much a stranger to me now as he was the first time I saw him in Lux.

Stupid, stupid girl.

"Marat, this is Orson, or, as we've always called him, Bear. He's my big brother."

Silence stretched for a few long minutes, and I had the pleasure of seeing Marat's anger dissolve into embarrassment.

Served him right, the know it all jerk.

My husband nudged me back into my seat, sliding into the booth beside me. he should have looked ridiculous in his ten thousand dollar suit. But he moved with the same self-assured elegance as always.

Bastard.

Josef just grunted and sat next to Bear. And my poor confused brother just looked between the three of us like he was waiting for a punchline.

"So, you're married? To him? How long?" Bear asked.

"Yes, she is married to me. Three weeks now," Marat answered for me. "Forgive me, I did not recognize you from your nickname."

"I see. Uh, so, sis, how do you like married life?"

"It's been interesting," I muttered because really what could I say?

I couldn't tell my brother I had no idea what married life was like because all my husband did was work, come home, have sex, sleep, rinse and repeat.

It wasn't a bad life. But it wasn't what I'd thought it would be. Suddenly, I felt dirty. Used. And so fucking stupid.

Anger and humiliation filled me as Josef and Marat made small talk with my brother. I hummed a response when the topic of my mother came up, and it was revealed why I'd been visiting with my brother in the first place.

"Come, let me arrange for a car to take you home," Josef said to Bear after a while.

He dropped a couple of hundred dollar bills on the table and Bear shook his head like the man was nuts. He wasn't wrong.

We hadn't ordered anything but coffee. But we had taken up time and space and that was worth somethin, I supposed.

Our unlikely foursome walked outside together. I hugged Bear goodbye and told him I'd see him soon to which my husband growled.

Whatever.

"It was good seeing you. Make sure you call me if you need anything," he said, kissing my cheek before he got in the car Josef ordered for him.

"Dumplin'," Marat said, but I was too rattled to talk just yet.

I shook my head and got in the waiting SUV without waiting for him. My old blue jeans looked ratty inside the expensive vehicle, and I frowned. I wore my old clothes when I took the bus to see Bear.

It just didn't feel right to be dressed in designer clothes when I walked to the Port Authority station a few streets away from Marat's penthouse. The bus to Jersey took an hour each way, more or less, depending on traffic.

"Destiny, we need to talk."

"Talk? Is that what you want to do? Why don't you just ask Josef? He knows everything."

"Mrs. Volkov, your security is important, I will not say sorry for doing my job, but I will for insulting you or insinuating you were doing something wrong. Please accept my apologies," he said, surprising me with his bluntness.

"Dumplin', why didn't you just tell me what was going on?" Marat asked, and he sounded confused, not angry.

Oh, he'd been angry when he walked into the diner. When he thought I was cheating on him or paying my dealer. Or whatever the hell he imagined a woman did when she met a man outside of her home.

This bitch.

I wanted to scream. My feelings were so fucking hurt, but I was the only one to blame.

"We have ground rules, remember?" he said, and fuck him for being right. "Talk to me, Dumplin'."

"This is all my fault," I whispered, closing my eyes.

"Please don't cry," he whispered, cupping my

cheeks with his hands, and tugging my face towards his lips. "Don't cry, I can't fucking bear it. Shhh."

He kissed my cheeks, my mouth, my chin. He nuzzled my face with his, kissing away my tears as I cried in his arms.

I was so tired. And lonely. I was really lonely. Seeing my brother and not having anyone to talk to about it brought all those old feelings back.

Years of hurt and disappointment, loneliness, and despair. That wound I'd thought time had healed was still raw beneath the scar.

Seeing Marat and Bear in the same place just brought everything to a head. I'd been running from my life for too long.

Marat was my husband. He'd wanted this marriage, even though he hadn't been acting like it lately. But he made those ground rules with me, and we both agreed honesty was the most important one.

He said he wouldn't want out. He knew about my past, or whatever it was Josef had dug up on me, and he was there, asking me to explain. It was time I fessed up. Time for me to evaluate this marriage, our lives, my husband's resolve, and maybe mine, too.

It was time I told Marat about my first husband.

By the time we returned home, it was dark outside.

I held Dumplin' in my arms as she cried for the better part of the drive. She'd exhausted herself, nodding out sometime in the last fifteen minutes.

Whatever stress she'd been dealing with, the pain of her turbulent past she'd been carrying alone, it must have been tremendous.

She didn't wake up when Josef parked in the lot beneath our building. She didn't stir at all. Not even when I picked her up in my arms, princess-style, and carried her out of the vehicle.

I entered the elevator with my wife's warm weight and felt grounded in a way I never had. She belonged with me. Whatever was going on, we would figure it out.

Selfishness was part of my nature and shitty husband or not, I couldn't give her up. I wouldn't.

The elevator jerked to a stop, and her eyes opened abruptly. Destiny jerked awake. She whimpered and pushed against my chest. But I squeezed her, keeping her in place.

"Put me down. I'm too heavy," she said, her voice scratchy from all her crying.

"Hush. You're fucking perfect. And I got you," I replied.

I didn't want to put her down. Didn't think I could if I tried. Not just yet.

Something about her tears, the way she'd sobbed her heartbreak all over me, made me want to hold on to her. I wanted to help ease her burden. To carry some of the weight and lift the pressure off her.

Goddamn, this woman with her big blue eyes and her even bigger heart was doing things to me. She was changing how I felt about a lot of things, and that was unexpected.

Another surprise that came with marrying a stranger. Whether or not it was a good surprise was still up in the air.

I carried her to the couch, not trusting myself to leave her be if I took her to the bedroom.

My cock was half hard already, and I knew that made me a sick fuck. But I would never not want her, and that was something I just needed to accept.

"Want a drink?"

"Yes, please," she whispered.

"Soda? Vodka? Water?"

"Got any wine?"

"Yeah. Red or white?"

"Um, red, with a splash of lime soda if you have it," she said.

I nodded and went to fetch her drink, pouring myself a vodka. I went back, handing her the glass I filled halfway for her, and taking the seat beside her.

"Will you tell me now?"

She nodded, taking a long sip before placing her glass on the table.

"I was four when Timmy and his family moved in next door," she started. "He was my age, but I was bigger than him. He was so thin and pale, weak most of the time. He was diagnosed with acute myeloid Leukemia when he turned seven, and it was a long fight from there to remission. I stuck with him through it all. I read to him. Collected his schoolwork. Brought him get well cards from our classmates."

My heart squeezed inside my chest.

Fuck. What the fuck?

Of course, my sweet Dumplin' made friends with the sick boy next door.

She's a fucking angel.

My wife had a heart so fucking big she could hold the whole damn world inside it. She wasn't finished with her story, and I didn't want her to stop, so I listened.

I. Me. Marat Volkov.

For the first time in my life, I shut the fuck up, I bit my tongue, and I listened to someone else's story. But it was more than that.

I not only listened, I was riveted. I was hungry for her words. Greedy for every detail she could remember. I paid close attention to the nuances of her voice as she spoke. The feel of her in my arms as she sobbed and spilled her soul to me.

And I absorbed it all. I took it in. Every so often, I squeezed her reassuringly. I kissed her head. I hummed my understanding. Cradling her face, rubbing the nape of her neck, I needed her to feel me. I had to make sure she knew I was there for this. For her.

Always. I'm keeping her. I'm not letting her go.

"We lived in an apartment building that had two apartments on each floor. So, our bedrooms were next to each other, sharing a wall. Bear helped us drill a hole through the wall so we could run a string, and he made us one of those tin can phones so we could chat, and I could read to him at bedtime."

I watched her face, tracked her expressions. God, when she remembered something happy her eyes fucking glowed. And when the sadness came, they welled with tears. And I sat there, taking it all in, greedy for every nuance, every facet of my wife.

"When he was sixteen, he fought with his parents to allow him to attend school and he got better. Timmy did really well for a little while. We went to prom," she said and smiled, big, fat tears running down her face. "He wore a ruffled shirt just to make me laugh. But soon after that, he got sick again."

"I'm so sorry, Baby."

And I was. So fucking sorry. I couldn't even imagine.

"I know. He was so good. And he didn't have a chance, Marat. He was running out of time, and he knew it. Timmy wanted to get married. We were best friends, shared everything, and he wanted to marry me. To do something he'd always dreamed of," she said and sniffed.

I let her have her moment. Pushing down the jealousy that stirred in the periphery of my soul. She didn't need the weight of my idiotic emotions right then, so I remained quiet. A shoulder for her to lean on. An ear to listen to her story.

It was a heady thing being needed, and when I thought about it, I realized I maybe liked it. Okay, fine. I really liked it. Being needed. Being useful. Not just being a face to look at or a body to fuck.

Dumplin' needed me for more than that, and I fucking needed her to.

But it wasn't my time to talk, so I just let my feelings simmer as I tried to be there for her.

"His parents were dead set against it. My parents, too. They refused to allow it. But we both turned eighteen that year, and we'd just graduated. I had some money saved, presents from family. So, we ran away."

"You ran away?" I asked, thinking how fucking hard that must have been.

"We took our savings, combined them, and got on a plane to Las Vegas. We found a cheap motel, put our bags away, and got married that afternoon in a little chapel. That's when I started going by the name

Destiny. Timmy said it suited me. He told me I was destined for great things," she whispered.

I closed my eyes, processing and absorbing what she'd just said. I hated that another man had given her the name she went by. But I understood. Or I tried to.

I didn't know Timmy. But he was right about one thing. My Dumplin' was destined for great things.

She was going to have a wonderful life. And I was going to provide it.

"And your parents?" I asked.

"It took them a little while to find us. Just a couple of days. I was a stupid kid, I used my bank card to pay for a motel room."

"You weren't stupid, Dumplin'," I said, and she petted my chest, comforting me.

This woman is too good. My Wife. My sweet temptation.

Destiny was baring her soul. She was sharing every raw detail of her heartbreaking tale, and she was trying to make me feel better.

The shit she'd gone through when she was just a teenager. I couldn't understand.

Where was her brother? He was six years older than her. Plenty old to protect her, stand between her and four angry adults. Why didn't he do something?

Adrik would have. He would have done that and more, just like I would do for him. But I didn't ask her.

She needed to get this out, and I needed to listen. It was the least I could do after tricking her into marriage and moving her back across the country. For the first time, guilt hit me over what I did, and it hit me hard.

Fuck. She's too good for me. She deserved better. I have to make this right.

"When our parents landed in Vegas, it was a bad day for Timmy. I was working at a shitty little truck stop when he started throwing up. He'd been alright the first few days," she said, her voice scratchy.

My heart broke for her. I just could not fucking imagine. He was her best friend. Her first love.

I had to force myself to look at it like the observer I was, and not someone involved with one of the major players in her story.

Her story. A tragic childhood romance.

The organ inside my chest pumped slowly. I never thought much about my heart, but I felt it contracting and releasing as I held my wife. I felt her pain through every fucking beat.

It should have been sweet and innocent, but it was tainted with sickness and death, hurt and abandonment.

My poor Baby. Sweet Dumplin'.

She had such a beautiful heart. I couldn't even understand that kind of selflessness. She'd abandoned everything she knew, gave up her home and family to try to give her friend something he wanted.

The fact my wife had been married before was like a nail through my chest, but I forced myself to understand it from her point of view. First, she didn't know me back then. Second, she married a dying boy, granting him his last wish, and breaking her whole life apart in the process.

She's too good for me. I don't deserve her. But I'm keeping her. I. Am. Keeping. Her.

"Timmy had a lot of energy on the plane ride to Vegas," she said, interrupting my spiraling thoughts. "Someone staying in a neighboring room at the motel called an ambulance after they heard him getting sick. He was rushed to the hospital and there, they called his parents. They arrived later that night with papers to transfer him back to the East Coast."

"They moved him?" I asked, confused why anyone would think that was a good idea.

"The doctors argued to keep him there. I argued.

My parents came. Our marriage license wasn't official yet, so the police said I couldn't decide for him legally yet. I was young and stupid and scared, so I let them have their way. I just wanted what was best for him."

She took a deep breath, and I squeezed her tighter.

"I just wanted him to be happy. He'd asked me to marry him when he was sixteen, and he thought he was going to be better. He thought he had time. When they told him he was terminal, he begged me to elope. He said it was one thing he wanted before he died. To be married to me."

"I can understand that," I whispered so low I didn't think she heard me.

"My father and mother came to Vegas. They were so mad. My Dad called me a whore. He told me he and my mom would never speak to me again because of what I did. He was so ashamed of me."

"Fuck. You know that's not true, right?"

"I couldn't believe they just thought we wanted to run away to have sex. I tried to explain. Timmy was my best friend. I loved him. He loved me. I just wanted to give him the thing he wanted. To experience what our future could have been like for a little while, you know? To say he was my husband, and I was his w-wife," her voice cracked with the last word.

She cried in earnest then, and I held her tighter.

"While my father was yelling and distracting me, Timmy's parents were busy packing him up and taking him away. I didn't know. I didn't realize until they'd already gone. My father told me it was what I deserved. He said I was too young and stupid to understand being a wife. He said I would learn how hard life was without them. Said I'd made my own bed."

"Fuck. Shit. I'm so sorry," I repeated impotently.

Rage boiled inside me. No longer simmering on the edge of my awareness. I wished her father was still alive so I could track him down and shout at him. I wanted to tell him he was wrong for what he'd said.

What kind of father pushed his own daughter out of his life? What kind of mother allowed it?

They should have been there for her. Should have lifted her up, praised her for what she did for that poor dying kid.

But he was long gone, and her mother was sick. It was a moot point, I supposed, but that didn't make it any easier to swallow.

I wondered when her father died. How many

years had he let pass without talking to her? Checking on her?

I made a mental note to find out. She'd obviously forgiven her parents, and that was her choice, but I knew she hadn't been back to visit. Not in the twelve years she'd lived in Sin City.

I knew she still spoke to her brother, and she'd been sending him money for her mother's care. But when did that start?

The idea of my sweet Dumplin' waiting tables and dealing with her asshole ex-boss had me seeing red again. She'd worked so fucking hard.

Did her family know the shit she'd been through on her own? Did they care?

At least I could make sure she never had to do that again. I felt proud that I could ease at least part of her burden. Make her life easier. Better.

I can make her happy if I try. I know I can.

"Timmy died the day after they landed in New Jersey," she whispered.

Her voice was hoarse by then. Her tears were running like a faucet, staining my shirt, breaking my fucking heart.

"I never got to say goodbye. It was years before my parents reached out to me again. My father was sick, but I was still so mad. I wasn't there when he died, either. My mother told Bear she would never forgive me. She said I did it. I killed my father by breaking his heart. But I, I didn't mean to. I was so hurt. I didn't understand how cruel and fragile life could be," she sobbed.

I couldn't take it anymore. This fucking woman. She'd been through so much.

She carried all this guilt on her own for so long, and there I was putting more stress and blame on her, none of which she deserved. I pulled her to me, lifting her until I had both arms wrapped around her, crushing her to my chest.

"Shhh. Please, Baby, don't cry anymore. I'm so sorry you went through all that alone. My sweet Dumplin'. My brave girl," I told her, kissing her hair, her cheeks, everywhere I could reach.

We sat like that for a few more minutes, wrapped around each other, me rocking her back and forth while she cried.

"You already know this, but Mom has dementia. I've been sending Bear whatever money I had extra to help pay for her care, but the doctors say she needs to be in assisted living. He found a place, and that's why I've been meeting with him this week, to talk about her diagnosis and discuss her care," she explained, and I felt like an even bigger piece of shit.

"I know Josef had me tailed, so he probably knows I've been giving Bear money for Mom. But I need you to know you and me, we were never about money."

"What? Dumplin', I never thought you wanted my money," I said, needing her to know.

"The money I gave Bear was what I had in my account. It was the rent money. But y-you canceled my lease, and I never got to pay it. Then you transferred all that money to me," she said, shaking her head against my chest.

"That was for you to do with what you wanted. Baby, that was a gift."

"I never asked for it. And I didn't touch it. The money you put in my account was too much, Marat. I don't want it. I don't want you or your family to think I stayed married to you for that. Please, just take it back—"

"Shhhh. Shhh," I whispered, holding her tighter, and closing my eyes when I felt her small hands clutching my sides. "Don't you think I know that? You're so good, Dumplin'. So fucking good. Your heart is pure gold. Shhh. It's okay. I got you."

That money was hers. She could do whatever she wanted with it. It meant nothing to me. I gave it to her just so she would have a cushion until her credit cards arrived.

But fucking appearances made it look like she was maybe taking advantage of me. Like she was capable.

Destiny was the most honest person I knew. Even when she withheld information from me, it was my fault. I was the one building walls, keeping distant. I was the one who'd tricked her into being my wife.

Like the spoiled fucking child I was, I saw her, wanted her, and took her.

To hell with the consequences.

I couldn't say I regretted my decision. In fact, I was starting to believe it was the best damn one I ever made.

A shiver ran through her body, and I held her close and whispered soothing words and phrases, sweet nothings, as she cried herself to sleep against my chest.

"It's okay if you change your mind, Marat. I'll understand," she whispered.

I knew exactly what she meant, and it stopped my heart in my chest. Did she think I wanted out because I knew she'd been married before? Did she think I regretted choosing her?

"I'm not changing my mind, Dumplin'," I murmured against her hair.

But her body was completely relaxed against me, and I knew she'd fallen asleep without hearing me. I sat there for over an hour before carrying her to bed.

Even then, I couldn't bring myself to let her go. I held her soft, warm body in my arms even as my own self-disgust reached immeasurable heights.

What kind of monster am I?

Maybe she was right. Maybe I was the Devil. I looked down at my sweet wife's face, so peaceful in sleep, and I kissed her temple. It didn't matter.

Angel or Devil, Destiny was mine. Again, that same thought that had been on replay since I first saw the sweet temptation that was my wife played inside my head.

I'm keeping her.

CHAPTER THIRTY
DESTINY

Lunch at the in-laws was not something I looked forward to. But Marat asked me to go with him, and he'd been so sweet the past week, I couldn't refuse.

He'd come home early from the office every day. Well, early for him, but what I imagined was a normal time for most people, six o'clock or around then. We ate dinner together every night. Watched TV. Listened to music. And we always made love.

Shit. I had to stop thinking about the sex we shared as making love. It confused things, and I was already too emotionally involved as it was.

Marat was an unexpected foodie, and he took me to the best hole in the wall eateries Manhattan offered. He loved it all. And so did I.

"I can't believe of all the places we've been so far hot dogs are your favorite," he said, tsking and grinning at me as we drove to his brother's house.

"I just love a good hot dog. There's nothing like New York onions and spicy brown mustard on a dirty water dog. Besides, I have wonderful memories of that place. Bear used to bring me hot dogs and a papaya drink from there whenever he went to the city," I replied with a shrug.

Marat made a humming sound deep in his throat, and I squeezed my thighs together. I loved the sounds he made. Loved that he was just as noisy as I was in bed, always growling and purring like a great, big beast.

Nerves assailed me and I took several deep, cleansing breaths before climbing into the car. We didn't often drive places, but when we did, it was usually in an SUV driven by someone from Marat's vast security team.

But not today.

Marat had insisted on driving the sleek, metallic blue convertible himself, warning me the top would be down when he saw my hair loose. I'd quickly braided it, donning a silk scarf around my head like some movie star from the fifties.

"Did I already tell you how gorgeous you look

today?" he asked while we were stopped at a traffic light.

"Maybe, but I could always hear it again."

"You look good enough to eat, Dumplin'," he growled, tipping his glasses down and giving me a once over.

I was wearing a sky blue dress with a low scoop neck and flutter sleeves. It was so damn soft and light, and it made me feel deliciously feminine.

The dress was cinched at the waist, not my usual preference with my body type, but the way the skirt flared out was flattering. It landed mid-calf, my favorite length for dresses.

I completed the outfit with a pair of ballet flats. I had to admit I loved that most of the shoes Marat bought me in Las Vegas were low-heeled.

He was tall, and I imagined women often wore stilettos to try to match his height. It would be pointless to try, though. I mean, I could stand on a stepladder, and I would still be shorter than him.

Heels would make no difference. But I would wear them if he wanted me to.

"What are you thinking over there so intently?"

Remember the ground rules, I reminded myself.

"I was thinking about shoes," I said, clearly shocking him.

"Shoes? What about them?"

"I was wondering if you don't like high heels."

"Well, the truth is, Dumplin', I don't think I could walk in them," he said, and I barked out a surprised laugh picturing my gorgeous husband in a pair of ice pick heels.

"No, you idiot. I meant because all the shoes you bought me are low or flat."

"Oh, well," he said, and I could see him collecting his thoughts. "The night we met at Lux, you mentioned not liking the heels that jerkoff made you wear. I just figured you preferred them low. But if you want something else—"

My heart pounded so hard at his words, I thought it might beat me to death.

"No! I mean, yes, I do prefer low heels or none at all. That was sweet of your to remember. Thank you."

He glanced at me and dipped his chin, acknowledging my thanks but not speaking further. That was alright. I appreciated the time to get my emotions back under control.

The rest of the drive passed in comfortable silence, and it was minutes later that we pulled into the driveway. I started to get unbuckled, removing the scarf and running my fingers through my hair.

"Wait for me," he said.

There were several cars there, and a uniformed guard came over to take his keys. I worried my lip. I'd dressed for a small lunch with his family. Not a large gathering. Before I could stress any further, Marat opened my door.

"Marat? Is this a party or something?"

"I don't know. Maybe. It was on my calendar as lunch," he replied with a careless shrug. "Why? What's the difference?"

"Marat," I scolded him gently, annoyed with his nonchalance. "If I knew there was a party, I would have dressed more carefully. I don't want to embarrass you."

"Embarrass me? Dumplin', I already told you how beautiful you look today. In fact, you look too good. Maybe you should wear my jacket," he growled, and started undoing his buttons.

"What? Oh my god, no. Keep your jacket on," I said, shaking my head.

It was one thing for him to show up as he was. My husband always looked incredible. Even amongst good looking, powerful men like his brother and Josef, Marat stood apart.

Like a noble white stag. Beautiful, yet masculine. So damn handsome, he was otherworldly.

"Is my tie crooked?" he asked, trying to look down.

"No. But you have something here," I said, stepping closer, and pretending to wipe a spot of lint from his linen jacket.

"Mmm. You know you're the only woman I know who's ever pointed out a flaw in my appearance," he said, and I could tell by the tilt of his lips he was amused.

"Is that so? Well, *honesty*, remember? It's our number one ground rule," I told him, allowing him to pull me close.

"Honesty, right? Well, then I should tell you, you look utterly fuckable, Mrs. Volkov."

"I like when you call me that," I admitted, and I sounded breathless.

"Good. When you introduce yourself, make sure you use it. I want everyone here to know who you belong to."

His words were completely overbearing and borderline psychotic. They shouldn't have turned me on. But I clenched my thighs together, hoping to keep my arousal from dripping down my legs.

"I never met anyone like you," I whispered.

"No? Good. You know, I think you have something here," he said, repeating what I'd said to him as he bent his head, kissing me on the lips.

Our eyes remained open, focused on one another for the duration. Even though our mouths were closed, it was the single most intimate kiss of my life. I felt it down to my toes.

"There, that's better," he murmured.

"Better? I must look a mess now that you smeared my lip gloss."

"Not a mess in sight, Dumplin'. You look perfect now. Claimed. You look like mine."

Holy. Fuck.

Did women still swoon? Because I was about to. If Marat wasn't still holding onto me, I might have melted into a puddle at his Italian loafer clad feet.

After another long moment, he stepped away from me. His expression was far too serious as he held out his arm. I swallowed my nervousness and placed my hand in the crook of his elbow.

I walked up the stairs to his brother's house on my husband's arm and tried for a calm I wasn't really sure I was capable of.

Music and the sounds of people chatting led us around the porch to the back of the house where at least thirty people were gathered for an outdoor luncheon. I didn't know anyone except Adrik and Sofia and a couple of the guards.

"Guess it is a party," Marat whispered, and I glared at him.

The fucker.

He just shrugged. Sure, it was no big deal for him. He was used to mingling with people like that. But I sure as fuck wasn't.

What insights could I offer people whose conversations revolved around their millions? Just a couple of weeks ago, I was living in a shitty apartment, working as a waitress, for fuck's sake.

"You okay?" Marat asked, frowning at me.

"No," I said, pasting a fake smile on my face as the first group of strangers approached.

"Marat, darling!"

I jumped at the shrill voice of the older woman as she came barreling towards us. She was dressed in neon pink and gold silk from head to toe, her scarves fluttering in the breeze as she grabbed Marat's right hand and tugged him down.

He indulged her with an air kiss, but kept his other arm entwined with mine. My nerves were going berserk, but I stood beside him and allowed him to make the introductions.

"Mrs. Dartmouth, allow me to introduce my wife, Destiny."

"Destiny, darling, how did you catch the heart of our dear Marat? You'll have to share your secrets, my dear. He's the catch of a lifetime. Everyone is so jealous of you."

"Oh, it was just dumb luck," I replied, grinning at the older woman.

I didn't like that she called him a catch, like he was some prize and not a flesh and blood man. But she was harmless, so I let it go. Feeling protective of Marat was a gateway to deeper feelings I didn't want to acknowledge just then.

"I see, well, treasure her, Marat. I think maybe she is the real catch. Yes, I am sure of it," she replied, eyes twinkling with mischief.

"You're right about that, Mrs. Dartmouth. My wife is one in a million. Excuse us, please. We must go say hello to Adrik. He's glaring at me."

"Oh my, yes, please go. No one wants to draw the wrath of the Dark Wolf," Mrs. Dartmouth whispered conspiratorially.

"Dark Wolf?" I asked Marat, but he just shook his head.

"Later," he whispered, as we wove our way through the crowd.

My head was spinning with names and faces by the time we reached Adrik and Sofia. My brother-in-law spared me a nod and turned his attention to Marat, speaking in what I thought was Russian.

"How many languages do the two of you speak?" I blurted.

Marat blinked at me slowly, like maybe he did not realize he was speaking another language. It was Sofia who finally answered me.

"Don't bother asking," she said.

"They'll say they only speak three or four languages, but it's more like a dozen. Adrik and Marat are both terrible snobs when it comes to that sort of thing. They don't consider it *speaking another language* unless they're able to read and write in it," Sofia explained, rolling her eyes at her husband before handing him their baby.

"Hello, Princess," I cooed to the baby, before Sofia grabbed my arm and pulled me away from the boys.

"Please, come sit and talk to me. I need some grown up time, and I promise to feed you wine!"

Sofia begged, bribing me with booze, and I snorted a laugh. It was the perfect enticement. I really needed a glass of wine right about then.

Now, I obviously did not have any children, but I had a couple of friends in Vegas who'd experienced the same *adult time withdrawal* after giving birth. I was sympathetic. Really, I was.

We didn't really know each other. But the prospect of making a friend was too tempting to resist. I glanced at Marat, but he was still chatting with Adrik, his attention on little Micheala.

Fuck. When a man who looked like that played with a baby, it was enough to make women around the world weak-kneed. But when that man was also your husband, *double fuck*.

My ovaries were in a state of permanent hyper drive.

Sofia handed me a glass of red wine, topping it off with a splash of lime soda, and my mouth dropped open.

"Once I heard Marat mention you preferred red wine and lime soda, I had to try it."

I turned my head to Marat. He was watching me intently, and I mouthed a thank you, my cheeks burning when he dipped his head in recognition.

"And?" I asked nervously.

"Oh my gah! Gurl, you know this is so good," she said, making herself the same thing.

"Awesome. So, I apologize for not knowing this was a party," I began, tripping over my words but not wanting her to think I'd purposely come empty-handed or anything.

"Say again."

Sofia tilted her head, staring at me like I was daft, and I felt ten times dumber than I already had.

"Marat said we were coming here for lunch. But when we got here, I saw all these people, and I just wanted you to know he didn't tell me. I mean, if you were giving a party, I could have helped or I mean, were we supposed to do something? What is this party for? Should we have brought a gift?" I asked, wincing at the thought.

"You are so sweet! But no, no, this isn't my party. Andres, you know, he works for Adrik and Marat," she said, and I nodded because I had heard Marat mention that name even though I never met the man.

"He put together this lunch as part of an effort to involve Volkov Industries in the New York elite charity scene. All these people are members of the board for one big charity organization or another. They want our money, but they never asked. See, they were nervous about rubbing elbows with a former mobster," she whispered.

"Former mobster?" I blurted, almost spitting my wine out on the table.

"Didn't Marat tell you?" she asked, eyes wide.

"Um, no," I replied, shaking my head.

My heart pounded. Were Marat and Adrik gangsters? I mean, she said former, but what the hell did that mean?

"Look, it's no big deal. I mean, the guys grew up basically on the streets back in Russia. Their parents died, and they had nothing. I mean that literally. No home, no money, no food. Adrik did what he needed to do to provide for himself and Marat. You know, he's ten years older than his brother."

"No, I didn't know any of this," I murmured, aghast at how little I knew about my husband.

"The boys were involved with a certain Russian criminal organization. Bratva," she said, though I had no idea what that was. "Adrik did most of the heavy stuff since he was older. Marat ran numbers, acted as a courier. Adrik gained a reputation for being a brutal hunter. The Dark Wolf was his moniker. He managed to get out, taking his brother, Josef, and some of the men you see on our security team with him."

"So the money, the business, it all started as, um," I dropped off, not knowing how to finish that statement.

"Criminal connections aren't that different from business ones," Sofia replied.

"You know, Volkov Industries made their billions through mining rare earth minerals. The kind used to make cell phones and such. Of course, I won't pretend that other avenues were employed to gain capital. I'm sure they were. But it's all legit now, and with Andres' help, they've been doing more on the charitable front."

Sofia paused, and I felt her eyes on me while I absorbed this newfound information. I wasn't completely naïve about the world. I mean, I knew the mafia existed. Every country had their version. Las Vegas was ripe with old mobsters, the city having been founded by them.

It didn't bother me that Volkov Industries' origins were dark. In fact, when I dove deeper into my feelings, I was more concerned with Marat. The things he'd suffered. The trials he'd been through.

My beautiful husband was more than the face of the company. He was the fucking heart. He was the first reason his brother had for fighting so hard.

Marat was so damn important to Adrik, to Josef, and I wondered if he knew. I wondered if he was aware of the way those two men watched out for him.

"You know, Marat's been involved with an entire campaign to make the mines greener," Sofia added, and pride surged inside of me for my husband.

"He was never just the face of Volkov Industries," I murmured, and my new sister-in-law nodded.

"Exactly. You know, I've never seen my handsome brother-in-law look quite so content, Des. You're good for him."

"Des?"

I scrunched my nose. The sun was warm, but the courtyard was set up with an overhead sail and large slow-moving fans, so there was a breeze and plenty of shade. A small quartet was playing music, and half a dozen servers were moving around with drinks and finger food.

"Oh, I was just trying it out. Like a bestie thing. I mean, I think we should be best friends," she said, and offered an awkward smile that made me like her even more.

"I'll call you Des and you can call me Sof."

I allowed the idea of having a best friend, one with her very own nickname for me, to wrap around my brain. Suddenly, I didn't feel so alone.

"It's a deal, Sof. To being besties," I said, and clinked glasses with her.

Our bestie-fest was short-lived, however, once

the guys joined us. Micheala had grown fussy and not even her debonair Uncle Marat could soothe her.

"I'm sorry, please excuse me. She's teething," Sofia explained.

"I should have told Andres no," Adrik murmured, but his wife patted his shoulder gently and kissed his cheek.

"It's fine, Darling. I'll feed her and have Rosa sing to her. You know she loves that. Don't worry so."

"I will always worry about you Zaika, and our precious daughter. It's my privilege to do so," he replied.

The way he gazed at her, his dark eyes glittering. So familiar and not. I gulped.

The love between them was tangible. A living, breathing, pulsating force that I could reach out and touch if I tried, I was sure of it.

I had to look away. Marat must have felt something similar, because he cleared his throat. A sign he was uncomfortable. The arm he had around my shoulders loosened, and I couldn't help despair from filling me.

Awareness was a cruel bitch sometimes. Crushing dreams and bulldozing hope. It slapped me in the face, hard, just then, and I felt the sting all the way to my marrow.

I will never have what they have.

"Excuse me," I said, standing up.

"Dumplin', are you okay?" Marat asked, sounding concerned.

"Yes. Sorry, I just need the restroom."

"It's on the way to the nursery. Come on."

Sofia offered to show me, and I waved away Marat's offer to accompany me. I didn't need a babysitter. I could pee and find my way back to the party just fine on my own.

Fuck.

I liked to pride myself on being secure in my own skin. But right then, nothing felt right. Not my clothes or my shoes or my hair. Not the heavy sapphire on my finger. Or the ornate house and grounds around me.

There was nothing wrong with any of that stuff. It was me. I was the common denominator in all of it. I was the square peg trying to fit in the round hole.

I don't belong.

The feeling was overwhelming, and I blinked back the tears welling in my eyes.

Why did we have to come here?

I was almost okay with the lie I was living with Marat. Every day I pretended not to fall for him a little more. I took his touches and kisses with glee. Like a greedy child gorging on sweets, uncaring about the repercussions.

But I wasn't a child. I knew the price I'd pay for ignoring my heart, I just didn't know I was going to have to pay it so soon.

Yeah, I'd been fooling myself, thinking I could be okay with a loveless marriage. But that was not me. I led with my heart. And it wasn't like Marat wooed me. Hell, he didn't even propose. He just tricked me into this whole thing.

Anger surged, and it was better than the feeling hopeless. Goddamn him.

I should have demanded an annulment the second he told me what he did. But I didn't. So, we were married.

Just like that.

I was so pathetic. Tears spilled over onto my cheeks, and I wiped them absently.

I was so fucked up and so lonely. So sad and desperate that I was willing to believe this man— *with his fallen angel looks and billions of dollars, with his effortless charm and seductive smile—* wanted me.

A thirty year old waitress with too many curves and not enough scruples.

I was delusional. Or just plain dumb. You name it. That was me.

I gladly took the crumbs Marat tossed me and clutched them to my chest like they were something dear. He didn't love me. He never made me any promises. He didn't have to.

Hell, he barely had to crook his finger in my direction. I was putty in his hands.

This was all me. The hope I refused to look at was mine. Not his. Not put there or encouraged by him in any way.

I was the one who secretly nurtured it inside my innermost heart. The desperate wish Marat would one day fall for me was my own.

And as I walked down the beautifully decorated hallway of his brother's house that same private plea seized inside my chest, dying an agonizing death as I finally forced myself to face it.

Stupid. Stupid. Stupid.

Staying with Marat after he'd tricked me into marrying him had seemed like a better idea than being alone at the time.

But after watching that moment of tenderness between Adrik and Sofia, I wasn't so sure.

In fact, I was downright certain I couldn't continue with our sham of a marriage. I just couldn't deal with the fact he would never look at me the way Adrik looked at Sofia.

He wouldn't ever love me. Facing that simple truth just broke my heart.

"I can't believe you have the nerve to show up here. You know, I wondered if you would still be around," a sharp voice interrupted my thoughts, and I looked up to see someone exiting the bathroom I'd been on my way to use.

Sofia had pointed it out before hurrying off to the nursery to calm a crying Micheala. I'd been so wrapped up in my head, I hadn't paid any attention to the passing of time since I wandered down the hall to the large, distressed door. It looked like one of those things they found in an abandoned barn on the home improvement network.

Some interior designer, who probably charged a bajillion dollars, must have dug it out of some condemned structure in West Virgina or some such place. They likely brought it back to New York City, had it repurposed, and slapped a five-digit price tag on it.

Beautiful.

When I lived in Vegas, one of my roommates was addicted to the DIY channel. She loved shit like that.

The memory was fleeting as I took in the elegantly dressed blonde standing in front of the beautifully restored door. She lifted her pointed chin, staring down her nose at me like I was beneath her.

Maybe she was right. I was beyond caring.

Still, she looked vaguely familiar. I just couldn't place her.

"Do I know you?" I asked, then I remembered.

Tessa McNeil. That was her name. She was beautiful and bitter, like so many women. Too many.

"Oh, we met at the awards dinner in Vegas," I said.

"That's right, *Destiny*," she said my name like it was a joke.

Maybe it was. Maybe the joke was on me.

"I have to admit, I didn't expect Marat would keep you around this long. He can't be serious about a little nobody like you," she said, stepping closer.

Malice oozed from her, and I was in no mood. I straightened my spine. I wasn't a waitress here. I was Mrs. Marat fucking Volkov. And whether or not I remained his wife, this bitch had nothing to do with it.

"You know he's too good for you, don't you? You're just some flavor of the week. A full fat macchiato with extra calories. You'll give him everything you've got, and it won't be enough. He'll tire of you soon. He'll move on to a new flavor. He always does," she hissed with venom.

My empathy went only so far, and this woman was being rude and hostile.

"Is that what happened to you?" I asked, seeing through her bravado to the hurt woman beneath. "Did you give him everything, Tessa? And did Marat move on too fast for your liking? I'm sorry he hurt you," I said and meant it.

"W-what? Sorry? How dare *you* feel sorry for *me*?" she scoffed, stepping back.

"You're just jealous. He is one of the most sought after bachelors in the world! He's been courted by royalty, movie stars, billionairesses. His star is so bright, he couldn't even see you if you were traveling in the same orbit," she hissed.

I frowned. She wasn't wrong. Marat was in a class all his own. But the picture she painted was so sad.

Maybe he felt alone, too. Maybe that was why he chose me.

"*You* feel sorry for *me*? I'm beautiful, thin, and

rich. *I* am everything he needs on his arm. You'll be sent back to the gutter he found you in, and *I'll* be right here. Right in his path. I'll have him. Yes, I will," she announced like it was some sort of victory.

"You're right about some of it, Tessa. You know, once upon a time, you would have been everything I wished I could be. Thin, beautiful, rich. But that was before I knew better," I added, keeping my voice even. "Beauty fades and money comes and goes. You should know that, Tessa."

"What the hell are you on about—"

"It's not your turn to talk yet," I said, cutting her off and gritting my teeth. "You know, I worked really hard to like myself, to be okay with who I am, outside and inside. And that was before I met Marat. So, I am sorry to disappoint you, but no I'm not jealous of you. I feel sorry for you."

"You bitch!"

"Don't do that. Don't go there. It's beneath us as women to turn on each other just because someone else got the man you wanted. There are other fish in the sea, Tessa."

"But none like him," she said, stomping her foot like a petulant child.

"You're right about that. But could you really be

happy with a man who didn't love you?" I asked and turned my back on her before I revealed too much.

No longer interested in the bathroom or the party, I walked farther into the house, hoping to find an empty room. Instead, I found my brother-in-law. He'd been leaning against the wall, listening to the uncomfortable discourse between Tessa and me.

"Oh! You scared me," I said, lifting my hand to my throat.

"Apologies," he grumbled. "Tell me how you did it."

"How I did what?" I asked, not understanding.

"How you tricked Marat into marrying you," he explained.

I squared my shoulders and inhaled a deep breath.

"You know, I would have thought someone with a nickname like the Dark Wolf would have better resources when sniffing around for information," I snapped, crossing my arms.

Adrik raised his eyebrows, but he didn't interrupt. And I was on a roll.

"Josef can tell you all about the wedding ceremony since I wasn't even awake for most of it. Yes, you're right. There was trickery involved, but it wasn't mine," I stated.

"I believe you," he said after a long, drawn out moment, and just like that, my anger dissolved.

"Are you okay, *Korotyshka*?" he asked, his familiar dark eyes searching mine.

"I-I don't know."

It was an honest answer, and the only one I could give. Adrik just nodded, gesturing with his hand for me to walk in front of him.

"What does *Korotyshka* mean?"

"Hmm? It's nothing. Closest Russian word to Dumplin'."

"Oh."

"I would not call you that because it is my brother's word for you and he would be offended," he explained.

I stepped slowly, uneasy with the Dark Wolf prowling behind. But it was only a short distance back to the party. Back to Marat.

"There you are. Everything alright?" he asked, his eyes searching mine.

"I'm not feeling great," I told him.

"Are you sick? Do you need a hospital?"

"What? No. It's just a stomachache. But I'd like to go. I can catch a ride share or a cab—"

"No. If you're sick, we will leave together. I'll get the car, you wait here."

He leaned down and kissed my temple before he walked towards the valet. I closed my eyes and willed myself not to cry.

It was time for me to face the facts. If I stayed with him, he was going to destroy me. Tessa was a bitch for saying what she did. But she wasn't entirely wrong.

I was an oddity. Something new. And he was entertained for now. But what would happen to me when he grew bored? No, I couldn't handle that.

I was already half in love with the man. Staying with him would be emotional suicide. There was no other recourse.

I have to leave.

Volkov Towers was located close enough to the penthouse that I sometimes walked to the office.

In fact, I did just that morning. Destiny had gone to sleep early last night, and in deference to her stomachache I'd stayed on my side of the bed, allowing her to rest and recover.

It sucked. Big time.

But concern for my wife's health outweighed my need to fuck her. Another first. I couldn't remember a time when I gave two shits about someone's well-being.

I kept waking up with my body pressed against her soft curves. My cock ready to blow from the barest of touches against her sublime ass. I'd force myself to move back, to give her space. But eventually I'd find myself pressed back against her.

She was sick, for fuck's sake. And I was a fucking pig, getting turned on while she was suffering. I kissed her head and told her to stay in bed, I had some correspondence to take care of at the office, anyway.

I dressed, hauled my ass to the office, placing a bottle of water next to Destiny before I left. The woman was killing me.

I felt like the fucking Grinch, the Jim Carrey version not the cartoon, in that scene at the end where his heart was growing too fast. It hurt so bad the infamous character screamed and clutched at it with his furry fucking fingers.

The Grinch? Really? What the fuck was wrong with me?

My phone buzzed and I read the message Josef sent to Adrik and me. His second, Darius, was filling in for him over the next few days. Apparently, he had some emergency he needed to oversee.

That was odd and unlike him. The only real emergency I'd known Josef to have over the past couple of years was a spur-of-the-moment trip to Switzerland when his chocolate supplies ran low. He was fucking addicted to the stuff.

Speaking of addictions.

I grabbed my cell phone and sent a text to Destiny.

Wife, How are you feeling? If your stomach still hurts, I can have my personal physician come to the penthouse to check on you. Call me when you wake up, so I know what you want me to do.

I held the phone for a few seconds, expecting her to reply right away. But she didn't, and I shook my head. Of course not. She was probably still asleep.

I busied myself answering emails and checking over reports. One of our mines had experienced a significant increase in work related accidents and I frowned as I read the latest communication from the onsite manager.

Problems in this business almost always cropped up. Some were simply unavoidable, but I was working to change that. I wanted to improve conditions for the workers, and for the towns bordering the mines themselves by bringing in better waste management and clean water sources.

Another email came in on the heels of the last one. This one was marked urgent. And it was from the managers of one of our mines in the Murmansk region of Russia. The same mine I was using to test my greener initiative.

Shit.

I read his missive twice, needing to ensure I was translating correctly. There'd been an explosion at that same mine, located in eastern Russia in the Murmansk region. I had Adrik on the phone in seconds, and we plotted out a plan of action. We added Josef to the call, he was part of the planning after all, but there was no need for him to return from his *emergency*. Darius knew what he was doing, and he would be a fine fill in.

But there was no way around the fact I was going to have to go there to investigate the matter personally. The government needed reassurance, palms had to be greased, and more importantly Volkov Industries had to let the world know we would always protect what was ours.

If this was an attack from one of our rivals, or sabotage, we would uncover it. Nothing stayed secret for long in this world, especially not when you had our money and power.

Volkov Industries was a force to be reckoned with. But every now and again, someone had to test our strength. I didn't mind. I was more than fucking ready for it.

We would account for all our employees, ensure

their health and safety. And we needed to guard the mine.

My thoughts went back to my wife, and I frowned. If she was sick, I didn't want to bother her with all this. But I had to leave, and I could not go without saying goodbye.

I could check on her, then head to the airport.

Mind made up, I stood to leave my cell phone still pressed to my ear.

"Are you sure you can handle this, brother?" Adrik asked.

"I'm positive. It's time the world knew there was more than one wolf in our family."

CHAPTER THIRTY-TWO

DESTINY

Rain poured from the skies. Fucking spring.

But the gray damp matched the way I felt inside. I watched the branches bend with the wind as wetness cloaked the city.

The floor to ceiling windows were phenomenal, and I was really going to miss the view. But it was never mine to keep.

Just like him.

Boxes had arrived from Vegas with the rest of my belongings, and I kept them stacked by the elevator. It would be easy to get them delivered once I had a permanent address.

I'd already packed the few articles of clothing I'd brought with me. But I noticed a smaller box on the floor next to the others and I picked it up, frowning at how light it was.

"What is this?" I murmured, using my hands to peel off the duct tape.

It was the regular silver kind and not the beige threaded packing tape on the other boxes. Frowning harder, I opened the box and winced when I saw the four-inch stilettos I'd thought I left back at Lux inside.

I dropped them right in the garbage. There was literally no way in hell I'd ever wear those again. Marat must have had the movers double check my old work locker. That was thorough of him.

Sadness squeezed my chest. Thinking about Marat made it hard to breathe. I didn't want to leave him, but I had to. I didn't belong here. I didn't belong anywhere.

I'd already called Bear to ask him if I could use his couch for a few days. He had two roommates sharing the place, so there were no spare beds. But that was fine. I'd lived in worse conditions.

What was more important was the fact my big brother said yes. No questions asked.

That was nice. I hadn't expected him to agree so quickly. But he had. After meeting Marat and Josef that day in the diner, my brother had been super busy. Finally, he'd sent some strangely worded texts. Basically, Bear wanted me to thank them, and I deduced they'd put some things in motion for my brother.

I was not sure what they did, but my mother had been moved to a private facility that was ten times better than what we could afford. I didn't know how we were going to pay for that after Marat discovered me gone and he started divorce proceedings.

But maybe we could work something out. I was heartsick and full of melancholy. I let it envelop me. I let it fill my senses until I had nothing left to hold on to but grief.

But I refused to cry anymore.

Marat had been texting me since he left five days ago. Nothing earth shattering. Just checking in.

Good Morning. How are you feeling?

Hello, Wife. Just checking in. Did you see a doctor?

Have you been eating? Can you see my texts?

I stopped replying after day one. He acknowledged that by texting that he wasn't sure about the connection. He just hoped I was able to read his messages.

Miss talking to you. I'll check our data plan when I get back.

Are you being good, Wife? I'll call you from the SAT phone tonight.

I didn't answer his call. I just couldn't do it. I knew I was weak. If I talked to him, I'd confess, and he'd convince me to stay. That's what Devil's did. They made you think you had a choice, but you didn't.

This was all a goddamn setup from day one. Marat set me up for the fall. He saw me and wanted me and plucked me out of my life, thrusting me into his. He made me fall in love with him.

But he didn't believe in love. He wasn't capable of it. And that was more than I could bear. His inability to love was the end of me.

I wiped my face, feeling the wetness on my hands with wonder. When had I started crying?

When did you ever stop? My inner voice asked.

There was one more thing. One more weight added to the pressure on my chest. Every time Marat ended a text, he did it with the same sentence. And it was breaking my heart.

Talk to you soon, sweet Dumplin'. I miss you.

I'd just rolled the small suitcase I'd found in the closet and packed with my things when I heard the telltale ring of the elevator.

My heart pounded as I let go of the handle,

leaving the evidence of my betrayal right there on the floor as I went to check to see if it was him.

Did he really come home to catch me when I'd just found the strength to leave?

For days, I'd wandered around like a ghost. A half-empty shell of a human being who'd only just realized I wasn't really there anymore. I wasn't myself without him.

I couldn't help it. I missed him. I loved him. So damn much.

I'm so stupid.

I'd fallen in love with my husband, and it was the dumbest thing I'd ever done. But if that was him. If he'd returned just as I was about to leave, I knew I would never get out the door.

The elevator opened and instead of my fallen angel husband, it was Sofia.

"Des? There you are," she said, exasperated. "I've been texting you and calling and you don't answer! Some best friend you turned out to be," she said, and I don't miss the accusation.

She wasn't wrong. I'd been avoiding her. The last thing I needed was to have the great love story of Adrik and Sofia tossed in my face.

Ugh. That sounded bitchy. And I hated I felt that way.

"Sorry, I haven't been feeling well," I began, wringing my hands.

It was the truth. That stomachache I'd feigned started to manifest itself, and I didn't know if that was karma or if the idea of living without Marat was just making me sick.

"Des, what's wrong? You look terrible," she said.

"Thanks. Nothing. Look, can you keep a secret?" I asked, needing to tell someone.

"I think so," she answered honestly.

"I'm leaving him."

"What?" she whispered, and her crestfallen expression was my undoing.

"I-I just can't stay," I began, barely finishing my sentence before the tears started falling.

"What happened? Did Marat do something? Did he hurt you?"

"What? No, I mean, he tricked me into marrying him, made me fall in love with him when he knows he can't ever love me back. So yeah, he hurt me, but not that way. I just feel so stupid. This is my fault. I have to go, please, I just have to," I explained in a jumble.

"I know Marat. He's been spoiled by his damn good looks, so maybe he doesn't know how to show he cares. But I swear, Des, I have never seen him treat anyone how he treats you," she told me, and her words were comforting.

"That might be true, but I don't want to stick around till he gets tired of me. I don't want to be here when he realizes he made a mistake. I just can't handle that."

"Oh no. Okay, we will figure this out. Don't cry, Des."

Two seconds later, Sofia had her arms around my shoulders, and she was squeezing me tightly, promising to help. Her own eyes were filled with tears, and it just felt so good to have someone understand where I was coming from.

"Do you love him?"

I could only nod. I did love him. But I didn't want to say it out loud.

"Alright, what is your plan?"

"I was going to stay with my brother—"

"Your brother who lives with two other men. Don't ask how I know. But are you crazy? Marat will lose his fucking mind," she said.

"How would he find out?"

"Don't be dense. Look, I came here to see if you wanted to do some bookish things with me today. I'm going to meet with a couple of Adrik's friends who own a recording studio. They have some narrators they want me to hear, I'm interviewing for my next audiobook," she explained.

"I know it's over the top, but when you're married to Adrik Volkov, everything is over the top. But I've got a car and a driver at our disposal, and because I needed to get out of the house, I thought this might be a good excuse, so I don't feel guilty about leaving Micheala for a few hours."

"You are such a good mother! A few hours away from Micheala is literally nothing," I told her, wanting to chase away the cloud of doubt I saw flash across her gaze.

"Thanks. I appreciate that. It is so hard. Sometimes I don't even want to go to the bathroom because I'm afraid I'll miss something, or she'll need me. Adrik is with her now, and it is the cutest damn thing. He needs to learn to trust himself with our daughter, so this outing is for his sake too," she said.

"You two are amazing together," I told her, not really wanting to explain how her epic romance was pretty much what prompted me to run.

That could get awkward.

"Okay, so we're settled. You come with, and I'll find you someplace better than your brother's couch to crash."

Of course, I wound up doing everything she said.

Sofia was relentless when she wanted something. Apparently, she wanted to keep me as her best friend.

The recording studio turned out to be this cool little setup in some high rise owned by Volkov Industries. The guys running it were actually gals, and that made sense, seeing as how Adrik was homicidally possessive over his wife.

"Destiny, you've got a really unique tonal quality," Marjorie, one of the owners of Big City Voices had said during our visit.

"Why don't you get in there and give this passage a try?"

I did.

And I loved it. And Sofia loved it.

So did Marjorie and her wife Ally.

They offered me a job as an audiobook narrator, and the pay was beyond my wildest dreams.

Sure, Marat had buckets of money. But I wouldn't be his wife much longer, and even as that thought had pain slicing through me like a knife, I had to focus on the positive.

I needed to make a living. I'd been standing on my own two feet since I was eighteen, it wasn't anything new. But damn, I missed him.

The letter I'd left addressed to him sat on the

kitchen counter in the penthouse next to the bowl full of lemon sour candies I'd bought one day when we went food shopping.

It was as clear a goodbye as I could manage. Next to it, I placed the sapphire ring he gave me in Vegas. I loved that thing, but I had no right to keep it. Not when I was leaving him.

Shit. If I didn't stop thinking about him, I was going to cry again. And that wouldn't do. I refocused on my new job.

Narrating books? That seemed like kismet. I'd always loved reading aloud, acting out parts. Ever since I was a kid.

Hell, I spent years studying drama and theater. Practicing on my own. It was going to take a few sessions to learn everything I needed to learn about the equipment and how to use it to my benefit.

But I was up for the challenge. Getting to narrate Sofia's spicy books was just icing. That beyotch could write steamy scenes like nobody's business.

Sizzle, baby.

"We're here," Sofia announced.

The drive to New Jersey was faster than I expected. I looked out the window of the car at the neat little apartment building where the driver had stopped.

"Where are we?"

"This is it. Where you'll be staying," Sofia clarified.

The two of us got out, and fifteen minutes later I was sitting at a table eating a bowl of the best tortellini soup I'd ever had.

"This is delicious." I moaned around a spoonful of the delicious cheese filled dumplings swimming in piping hot chicken broth.

"Of course it is. Homemade," Nonna, Sofia's grandmother, said.

Apparently, the little old lady owned this building. After Sofia met Adrik, he'd seen to some repairs, and the whole thing ran smoothly. My sneaky new bestie had already said her goodbyes, and she was visiting her Dad who lived in the upstairs apartment before she went back home.

Meanwhile, I was treated to a full dose of Nonna in mama bear mode. It was no wonder Sofia made such an awesome mother.

"You look tired, dear. Why don't you go to your room and have a nice nap?"

I smiled and nodded, cleaning my plate before heading to the bedroom Sofia had shown me earlier.

I wasn't hiding from Marat, so it did not bother me that he would know where I was. I mean, I couldn't sign divorce papers if he couldn't find me, right?

Just thinking about not being married to him hurt so badly, my stomach turned, and I almost lost the lunch I'd just eaten. I held onto the wall, swaying on my feet.

I was staying in Sofia's old room. It was furnished with a pretty dresser and a full sized bed. Everything was pink and white, with matching curtains, bedding, and pillows. It was pretty and neat. But I felt detached from it all.

I was exhausted and sick. Really sick. And once again, I had only myself to blame. I knew better than to put things out in the universe that I didn't really want to happen. Served me right pretending to have a stomachache.

Maybe if I put it out into the universe that Marat loved me, he would?

I rolled my eyes at my idiocy. Sitting on the bed, I kicked off my shoes and undid the button on my pants. My phone buzzed. And I grabbed it, hoping it was him. But it wasn't. And I felt foolish for wanting him so badly.

It was a text from Bear. Turned out my brother's place was close enough he'd promised to visit after work.

"What are you doing with your life, Destiny?" I whispered, and for the first time in twelve years I hated the name I picked for myself.

Once upon a time, I thought I was going to have a wonderful future. I thought I was destined for happiness. But those dreams were gone, and they left nothing but sadness in their wake.

All alone again. But I have only myself to blame.

CHAPTER THIRTY-THREE
MARAT

I stopped texting Destiny after day five with no replies from her. Something had to be wrong with her phone, but I wouldn't bother worrying about it until I saw her in person. I could figure it out and change the data plan or get her a better upgrade then.

Goddamn, I missed her so much.

The softness of her. The temptation of having her near. Her bright sunshine flavor. Her warm body and big heart. My sweet Dumplin' had burrowed in deep. She'd slipped past my defenses and made a permanent home inside my very bones.

Destiny was a piece of me and being separated like this was leaching the life from my veins.

It was fucking killing me. It took another week in that godforsaken place to put all the pieces together.

I'd tried calling her, but the SAT phone was fucked up. The few messages I got to Adrik, he hadn't been able to return either.

Fucking mining towns. I worked tirelessly to close this thing. Hunting down leads and tracking down the fucking people responsible for the so-called accident. To the rest of the world, that was what had happened. A tragedy.

But it was sabotage. A deliberate attack to try to rattle Volkov Industries. Only we didn't get rattled. We got revenge.

The thing about being the face of a company I never appreciated was that I was an unknown quantity. A wild card. Our enemies underestimated me, and that alone gave me an advantage.

Whispers of the Devil Wolf made their way around the mining camp, and further still into every hellhole town nearby. Blood, sweat, and tears, not mine, were spilled to find the right information.

So, when I tracked down the perpetrator to a goon who once worked for an old syndicate long since dismantled, I was shocked. I didn't think the greasy little fuck had it in him. But apparently favors only got you so far.

Ferragamo didn't like being booted out of Sin City, and to exact his revenge he'd called in every marker, every favor he was owed. But no one wanted to go against the Dark Wolf face to face, so this last part, the actual wrecking of one of our mines, the soon to be dead man had to oversee himself.

"You can't be the Devil Wolf?" he'd asked when I first stepped through the door.

"Can't I?"

"You think you're so fucking smart," he snarled, which was pretty impressive considering the broken jaw I gave him two seconds after I'd entered the filthy room he'd been hiding in.

"We found you pretty easily, Ferragamo. Your little accident did minimal damage, and my plans are moving forward as before. So yeah, I would say I am pretty fucking smart," I replied, rolling up my sleeves before I got to the fun stuff.

A dozen of my men surrounded us, and the four he'd had with him were bound and gagged, two already dead. No, I was not the Dark Wolf.

But I was still a Volkov. Rumors of my actions had flooded the streets of this shitty fucking place. They called me by a new name here.

They called me the Devil Wolf.

Like Lucifer himself, I rained destruction on any and all associated with the bombing. All roads had led to this man. He'd threatened *mine*. And I was going to show him why you didn't dance with the Devil.

He owed a debt. He owed Volkov Industries, and me personally. And he would pay. Right fucking now.

However slowly was entirely up to him.

"Tough guy, coming into *my* club. Taking one of *my* girls. Telling me how to run *my* place. Then you fucking took it from me. Lux was my life! I poured my blood in that place."

"It wasn't worth your life," I replied, shaking my head.

"You stupid fuck. You don't even know," he smirked, and my fist pummeled his jaw.

"Know what? I don't know what?" I demanded, wrapping my hand around his sweaty fucking throat and squeezing.

The Devil Wolf's rep revolved around the singular focus of my attacks. I wasn't uncouth in my violence. I was controlled. Deliberate. He would talk. I knew he would. I would make sure of it.

Ten minutes later, I was not disappointed. My

men surrounded us, ignoring the acrid stink of the filth in Ferragamo's pants. Fucker had actually pissed himself.

"Last chance. What don't I know?" I asked, tapping my fingers over the curved blade strapped to my thigh along with several others.

"This was j-just a distraction. Your whore wife is going to pay what you owe me."

The world went dark at his words. I canted my head. Not sure I heard right.

"What did you say?" I whispered.

"I sent Royce after her. He's been wanting her awhile now. And I just gave him the go ahead before you knocked down this door. It's my final fuck you to you, you fucking Volko—"

That was as far as he got before I shoved the nine-inch blade I'd been tapping with my fingertips right through the bastard's neck. I'd had every intention of dragging out his torture. But when the greasy fucker mentioned my wife, he'd signed his own death certificate.

"Call the airfield. I want the plane ready ten minutes ago!" I barked the order, grabbing the satellite phone from Darius to call Adrik.

It took three tries. But I got through.

"What is it?" my brother's voice sounded even rougher over the weak connection.

"I need you to send men to protect Destiny. Don't let her leave the penthouse—"

"She isn't there."

"What?" I froze, one foot caught in the air, hovering over the disgusting floor of the hovel I'd found Ferragamo in.

I fucking hated this place. Hated this part of what was really a beautiful country. Not that any of that mattered. I was still trying to process what Adrik had just told me.

"What do you mean she isn't there?" I asked.

"Marat, Destiny is gone. Now, tell me what's happening."

But I couldn't. I couldn't form a fucking word for all the thunder roaring in my ears.

She wasn't there?

I couldn't even understand what that meant. Of course she was there. I left her right there.

She was wearing a pair of cotton pajamas and was asleep, curled up on her side in our bed the last time I saw her.

My heart felt heavier than it had in, *well,* ever as I tried to make sense of Adrik's words.

"Why does she need protection, Marat? Explain," Adrik repeated, louder that time.

"She has to be there—"

"Marat! What the fuck is happening?!"

"Ferragamo was behind the mine attack. He knew this was the mine I'd been testing my greener plans on, and he wanted me to fail as revenge for taking Lux from him. My wife is part of his revenge plan. He sent a guy named Royce after her. Fuck. You need to find Destiny!"

"Who is Royce?"

"One dead motherfucker," I snapped.

"Understood. But who is he, Marat, so the men have someplace to look?"

"He was her old manager," I growled, black rage blurring the edge of my vision.

"Okay, I am on it. I will send our best men to her location, but there are already some stationed where she is. Do not worry, brother," Adrik said.

"Where is she?" I asked, seconds from falling apart.

"Safe. She is at Nonna's," he told me, and I exhaled.

Sofia's grandmother had basically adopted everyone associated with her granddaughter. She was Nonna to us all. She would take care of my Dumplin', I knew it. But I hated that she left me.

I felt betrayed. Lost. So fucking hurt.

"Did she say why she left?" I whispered, sounding so much like a little boy I wanted to puke.

Adrik let loose a stream of Russian, and because my mind was so fucked thinking about Dumplin' leaving me, I needed him to repeat it twice before I understood.

The whole flight back to New York I was caught between grief and rage. One second away from putting my head through the fucking wall just so I'd be out of my misery.

She couldn't leave me. I wouldn't let her. I was going to get her back.

Volkov meant wolf, and I finally understood what that meant. I'd accepted my fate. Learned who I really was. More than a face. More than a bored billionaire playboy.

I was Marat Volkov.

I was the Devil Wolf.

And I was never letting my wife go.

All facts. All immoveable truths.

My wife. My Destiny. My sweet Dumplin' was never going to be rid of me.

When I'd found her in that club, I had no idea

what a prize my sweet, welcoming, beautiful little wife would be.

Her soft body tempted me like no other. Her beguiling blue eyes had me mesmerized. And her big heart brought me to my fucking knees.

I was nothing without her.

She was the only woman who'd ever cracked through the shield I'd built around my heart. Like a goddamn cannonball, she busted through my barriers, leaving me no choice but to let her in.

My lips quirked, and I wondered what she'd say if I told her that. If I confessed my suspicions about my feelings for her.

Maybe that was the problem all along. I'd been fighting the truth. Keeping it from the both of us.

Fuck. I'm such a shithead.

I'd never said I love you to another human being. Not once in my whole life. It didn't look hard. I mean, I heard Sofia and Adrik say it all the time.

I should have told her. I should have let Destiny know what she meant to me. It was too fucking late now.

She'd left. She was gone. Destiny walked out on me, and I was all alone.

The realization hit me like a fucking hammer,

and I'd never been more fucking miserable in my life.

I'm gonna get her back.

It was a promise I made as I boarded the jet. I was going to get her back.

CHAPTER THIRTY-FOUR
DESTINY

The cool dirt felt good beneath my torn jeans as I dug holes for Nonna's basil plants. She was adding three more rows of herbs to the already impressive garden she'd planted in the back courtyard of the apartment complex she owned.

I'd finished recording for the day and had just come back from the city when I saw the old woman hauling bags of dirt outside. She had plenty of helpers, but Nonna wasn't one to sit back and watch. But I managed to distract her by telling her I was hungry.

The woman had some sort of inner sensor and letting her know if anyone within a twenty-foot radius of her was hungry. Once she'd established that, it was only a matter of time before she had something homemade and delicious sitting in front of you.

"I'm going to go grab some more fertilizer from the truck. I'll leave the side gate open," Vince, the building manager, told me,

He and his wife were an absolute godsend. Trudy was inside with Nonna, mixing a pitcher of her special lavender lemonade, which I was completely addicted to. I wiped my brow, wondering if my tummy would cooperate with me today.

I hadn't seen Marat in almost two weeks, and I wasn't stupid. We'd had unprotected sex several times during our time together, but my period wasn't regular.

The doctor diagnosed me with polycystic ovarian syndrome when I was in my twenties. The likelihood of me getting pregnant without the help of a fertility specialist was slim to none. But miracles did happen. I just wasn't ready to find out just yet.

It was difficult enough just learning to live without him. Sure, I had Nonna, Vince, Trudy, Matt, Sofia's father, and his sister, Linda. Everyone in the building was family by blood or marriage or choice.

It was a great mishmash of people, but it worked, and I was happy I was there. Even though it was only temporary. I mean, I couldn't just plant myself in Nonna's spare room and grow roots.

The sun was low in the sky, evening would settle soon, and I was not looking forward to another night alone. I missed Marat. I was so lonely even with all those people there.

I knew it was crazy, we'd only known each other for barely a couple of months, but goddamn, I missed him. Without his arms holding me at night, I slept fitfully. My dreams were horrible. More like nightmares.

My heart ached all the time. I felt so empty, I couldn't focus. It was like my soul was crying out for him. Like that piece of me that bonded to him was stretched across oceans, across continents.

I was still tied to him. Even a world away. I still felt it, and I wondered if he did too.

I glanced down at my bare finger and teared up. I should have kept the ring. At least until we had the chance to talk.

Honesty. That was our rule number one. And I'd broken it. I'd hidden my real feelings from him, and I ran away like a coward. Lost in my own tumultuous feelings, I didn't hear the gate open or notice the foul man creeping towards me until it was too late.

"Well, well, well. Look what we have here."

I froze as a big, grubby hand closed around the back of my neck.

"I gotta say, you look like shit, Dollface."

I turned my head, trying to shake off his hold, but he was strong. Immovable.

"Did you miss me?" he asked, his nasty mouth pressed against the side of my face.

Roger Royce's stale breath invaded my nostrils, and I wanted to gag.

"Easy," he grunted and tightened his hold when I tried to get away from him.

He pressed the barrel of his gun against my head. It was cold and hard, and it did nothing to instill a sense of calm in me.

Fear had me whimpering, and I hated the sound, hated Royce for causing it.

"I asked you a question, bitch."

"No! I haven't even thought about you since I left that job. Get the fuck off me," I said, elbowing him in the side.

Royce grunted and pitched forward, but he recovered quickly, pulling my hair hard. I yelped at the pain as he dragged me towards the gate to where he likely had some vehicle to kidnap me.

To take me away from here. From Marat. Forever.

I struggled, but he pulled harder on my hair. I tried to lean into his hold to stop it from hurting. But I dragged my feet, using my weight to try to slow him down.

"What do you want with me?" I asked, gasping at the pain radiating through my head.

"What do I want? You stupid fucking bitch! You wanna know what I want? I want my life back," he shouted in my ear, making my head hurt even more.

"I was somebody. I had money, power, girls, all at my disposal. Then your pretty boy had to go buy the club out from under Ferragamo. He fired all the managers, all the old bosses," Royce said, and I was stunned.

"But don't worry, Mr. Ferragamo has a special treat for him overseas," Royce said, breathing in my ear as maniacal laughter sputtered from his chest.

Worry sliced into me. Real fear, the likes of which I'd never known filled me, but not for my situation.

I was scared for my husband. For Marat.

If Ferragamo was behind whatever emergency that sent Marat to Russia, it couldn't be good.

God, no. Please no.

I knew the club owner was a former gangster. He likely still had connections.

Oh my fucking god.

This was all my fault.

Marat bought the club *because of me.*

He was in danger. He could be hurt *all because of me.*

"No! Please, Royce, you have to stop him. Call Ferragamo. I'll do anything you say," I begged and fell to my knees, forcing Royce to bend with his fist still wrapped around my hair.

"What are you doing? Get up," he demanded, pointing his gun at me.

"Take your fucking hands off her!" a roar sounded from the gate.

I turned my head towards the familiar voice, no longer caring about Royce's tight hold on my hair.

It was him. My very own fallen angel. My husband whose menacing beauty rivaled that of the Devil himself.

"Marat!"

I called out his name, so damn grateful he was whole, and he was here.

Marat was okay. And he was right here. But he was running straight into danger. I shouted a warning, and Royce fumbled with the gun.

But the bastard still managed to aim and squeeze the trigger. I screamed and slammed my fist into the side of his knee, causing him to buckle at the same time he fired the weapon.

The shot went wide, hitting one of the gnome statues Nonna had surrounding the garden like miniature sentinels. Shattered bits of concrete flew in every direction, but the broken gnome was still standing.

And so are we.

"Sonovabitch," Marat snarled.

He slammed into Royce, knocking the squat man to the ground. Ironclad fury, brute dominance, and raw masculine energy vibrated from Marat.

Eyes wide as I couldn't look away as my normally cool, calm, sophisticated husband beat the living shit out of my former manager.

Too close for my liking, I rolled away from the brawling men. Marat's dark eyes were wild as he straddled Royce's chest, raining his pain down on the man's face and body.

Royce stopped struggling a while ago, but Marat's anger was still going strong. A group of men in tactical gear came running into the courtyard, but he didn't even flinch.

"Boss! We got him, boss!"

I exhaled, relieved they were on our side. Marat

hit Royce one more time, and the crunch of bones breaking echoed in the courtyard.

My fallen angel stood up, his dangerous beauty a stark contrast to Royce's destroyed face. He spared the man one last glance before his guards hauled him out of there.

I didn't know where all the men had come from, but I was glad they were there to take over. My entire body hurt, and I realized tears were rolling down my cheeks.

I needed my husband. I needed Marat.

Adrenaline and fear, or maybe relief, had my body shaking like a leaf caught in a windstorm. Marat's gaze found me with unerring accuracy, and he approached slowly, his chest still heaving.

His knuckles were cracked and bleeding, and there was splatter on his shirt and suit jacket. It was the first time I'd ever seen him looking anything but perfectly put together.

And he'd never look so good.

My heart squeezed with emotion, and it was all I could do not to throw myself at him.

"Destiny, Destiny," he whispered, repeating my name like a prayer spilling from his beautiful lips.

"Are you good? Baby, talk to me. Are you hurt?" he asked, crouching down.

He raised his hands, arms wide, palms up, like I was a frightened animal he was trying to keep from bolting. But I wasn't scared of him, and I wasn't running.

Not anymore. Not after that.

CHAPTER THIRTY-FIVE
MARAT

*G*oddamn prick. *That fucking motherfucker.*

I'd just killed the man in front of my wife. And I wanted to do it again.

I should have been fucking terrified of her reaction to the unmitigated violence pumping through my veins. I didn't know how she was going to handle it, or if I even had the right to ask her to.

But I was too amped to think about it. And if I had to do it all over again. I would.

With no hesitation.

I would kill Ferragamo, Royce, and anyone else who threatened her a hundred times over.

I would burn the whole fucking world to keep her safe.

Hell, I'd already put plans into motion to bury

every one of Ferragamo's contacts. Anybody who had a hand in hunting my wife and targeting her would be dust by the end of the week.

The entire world needed to know Destiny was *mine*. No one fucked with *mine* and lived. I was the Devil Wolf now. I wasn't one to be trifled with.

It was time my wife learned who I was. And it was past fucking time I reminded her who she belonged to.

Me. Mine.

Trying to disguise my fury, I approached slowly, carefully, giving her time to get used to the fact I was going to invade her space. She was shaking, and her face was soaked with tears.

But nothing could detract from her innate beauty. She was stunning. Wearing ripped jeans and a baggy t-shirt, her hair in a ponytail, and dirt beneath her nails from gardening. She looked perfect.

Goddamn. So beautiful. Sweet. Mine.

I wanted her so fucking much.

"Are you good? Baby, talk to me. Are you hurt?" I asked, keeping my hands where she could see them.

I watched her face for any hint of feeling. Not wanting her to run, I crouched in front of her. I had one split second before I read her intentions. One moment to brace myself before she threw her arms around my neck and knocked me on my ass.

"You came," she said, crying harder as I wrapped her up in my arms.

"Of course I did. You're mine," I told her, kissing her tears away.

"You left me, Dumplin'. Fuck. How could you leave me?" I snarled the question.

"I'm sorry."

Destiny sniffed, tears clung to her long eyelashes, making her blue irises match the sapphire she left on our kitchen counter. I was going to fucking tattoo a ring on her before I was through.

I missed her so fucking much. She was coming home with me. And I was going to make her stay.

Somehow. I just had to.

"Marat, I'm sorry," she repeated.

"Not yet, you're not. But you're going to be," I growled, letting anger take over.

I stood up and bent down, lifting her in my arms. She was coming home. With me. I wasn't going to give her a choice.

And if she fought me, that was fine. I could wrestle her into submission.

In fact, I might enjoy that.

"Hold on," I grunted, lifting her into my arms.

Her legs wrapped around my waist as she held on to me, and I squeezed her tighter. The ride to the city was going to be fucking torture. But I needed her home, and I needed her naked.

"Darius. Take us home," I told my man, and he nodded, getting in the front seat while I slid Destiny into the back, buckling her in before joining her on the other side.

"Marat—"

"No. Not one word. Not till I get you alone," I said, my anger palpable.

My cell phone vibrated, and I picked it up, speaking in Russian I informed my brother of what had happened, explaining the emergency cleanup crew needed to rid the area behind Nonna's building of any crime.

Lucky for me, we owned that building and the neighboring two. The only people who could see into the yard from their apartments were Nonna and Sofia's father, neither of whom were looking at the time.

All surveillance was ours. It could and would be wiped.

I told Adrik everything, ignoring my wife who was staring up at me with glassy blue eyes. I loved the color of her eyes, so bright and startling.

She was so damn pretty.

And I was so damn angry.

Angry. Scared. Terrified of losing her. Did she know how close she came to being hurt? To leaving me for good? What if I'd arrived a minute later?

Fuck. Fuck. FUCK.

Darius pulled in front of the building half an hour later. I was seething inside, but I refused to speak. I couldn't. Not yet.

"Wait," I gritted the word, walking to her side of the car.

I opened the door, pulling her out with one hand on her arm, the other on her neck. I walked with her like that, as close to my side as I could get her until we were inside our private elevator.

"Marat—" she tried to speak again.

"No. You don't get to talk. You don't get to speak one fucking word, Destiny. Not one! Not until you listen," I growled.

"But I—"

"That's it," I growled, and leaned down, grabbing her around the waist and lifting her off the floor as the doors opened.

She squeaked, holding on to my shoulders as I frog marched her to the sofa.

"Sit there and close your mouth," I growled, plopping her down with zero delicacy.

I stood to my full height, arms crossed, and stared at her. At Destiny. My wife, who'd come into my world, tearing down walls, making changes.

My sweet temptation who'd had the gumption to walk out on me when I was halfway around the world.

Fuck that. No way.

She wasn't going to get away with this. I wouldn't let her. I'd tie her to the fucking bed if I had to. Remind her who she belonged to. That she was my wife.

Mine.

I was unhinged, and I knew it. But I was also beyond caring. She could have been hurt tonight, and it was more than I could stand.

Destiny had some serious fucking explaining to do.

But first, it was my turn.

CHAPTER THIRTY-SIX
DESTINY

Goddamn. Holy. Fuck.

I was married to one beautifully dangerous man.

Jesus. Fuck. He looked like he'd just stepped through the gates of Hell. An avenging angel. A conqueror with domination on his mind.

Looking at him was difficult. He was just that beautiful, but I'd suffer gladly for the privilege of doing it.

I missed him so much.

I knew I should feel something about the fact Marat had just beaten a man, *probably to death*, right in front of my eyes. Something other than lust.

But I didn't. I couldn't.

Who knew I was such a bloodthirsty little thing?

And really, what about what he did was shocking compared to the rest?

The logical part of my brain knew Marat's behavior since day one was one huge red flag. But watching him rush into the courtyard, teeth bared, fists raised, saving my fluffy ass from that prick Royce—well, that was just all kinds of hot.

And he did it all for me.

I knew his ego didn't need more fuel, so I kept all that to myself. But I thought maybe his soul needed something. And I wanted to be the one to provide it.

I wanted to throw myself upon his mercy. To hug him to my breast and offer him everything I had. To beg him for forgiveness.

"Marat, I know you're mad—"

"Mad? You think this is mad? I'm so fucking furious, I don't know where to begin," he growled, and my heart squeezed.

He looked every bit like the Devil he was as he glared down at me. I saw the pain reflected in his obsidian gaze, and it gutted me. I put that look there.

Too often I thought I saw shadows in his eyes, emptiness and despair. But right then, he looked furious and so fucking hurt, and I hated it. I hated that I did that to him.

"I named you Dumplin' cause you were so

fucking tempting, but I should have called you Monster. I should have called you Siren. My walking temptation trying to lead me to ruin!" Marat shouted, making me jump.

"I didn't mean to—"

"You damn well did! You bewitched me with your perfect, soft body, and your big eyes, and your easy smiles. You made me wild for you," he accused.

"Marat, just listen—"

"No, it's time for you to listen," he said, leaning forward and grabbing my ring finger.

I gasped, looking down as he pushed the ring, the same cornflower sapphire ring I'd taken off and left on the counter, back on my hand roughly.

"Now we match, Baby," he grunted, and I looked at his ring finger, gasping when I saw a platinum band that matched mine.

He dropped a hand on either side of my head on the back of the couch, forcing me to lean back.

Baby? He has to still care. Please, please, say you care.

"You let me have you. You let me hold you. I might have tricked you into marrying me, but you never objected. Not once. You gave me ground rules. You said you'd tell me when something was wrong. You said you would be honest, Destiny, and you said you would let me know when I fucked up. But you waited for me to leave the country, then you just fucking left."

"I'm sorry," I cried softly.

"You. Left."

He tossed the accusation out again, and I sobbed. I nodded. He was right. I did all those things.

"You half-assed this, Destiny. You tried to cheat us, and I am so damn mad at you. But I did fuckup. And you didn't reach that decision alone, did you Baby?"

"Marat," I whimpered.

"No, no more, crying. No more leaving, you hear me?" he said, his hands moving from the couch to cup my face.

"You're home now. Where you belong. And you are staying right here. With me. Like you said you would. Understand," he growled.

"I don't," I started, but he misunderstood.

He pushed himself between my legs, kneeling on the floor, and pulled me against him. I felt his chest rising with each breath, and I swallowed.

His spicy scent filtered through the haze fogging my brain, that sensual fuzziness that always happened when he touched me.

I was going to say *I don't want to be anywhere else,* but Marat's rock hard length was pressed against my core, and too many nights had passed since I'd had sex with my husband.

His lips were moving though, so I forced myself to listen. Leaning into his touch as he held me tight to him.

"Yes, you fucking do. You belong here. With me. You're my wife. And I'm not letting you go. I don't care what I have to do, you're staying," he said, shaking his head.

His dark eyes shone like glass, and I gasped when I saw his emotions overflow. His hurt washed over me, drowning me, and I cupped his face. I couldn't handle seeing tears on my fallen angel's face.

"I'm begging you for mercy, Destiny. You're the only woman I want. I know I ruined things. I was guarded and fucking stupid. I just didn't expect you," he confessed.

"You snuck past my defenses, found all the cracks and breaks inside of me, and you filled them with your light, with your beautiful fucking warmth."

This man. He was wrecking me. But in a good way.

I was more than ready to tell him the truth. To tell him I loved him. Explain I had no plans to leave him again.

Also, I probably needed to tell him there was a

slight possibility I was pregnant. But that all had to wait because my Devil was not finished pouring his beautiful black heart out to me yet.

I waited with bated breath, hanging on his every word.

"I can't live without you. Please, don't make me try," he said, pressing his forehead to mine.

"I'm sorry I left," I whispered. "I just, it hurt, seeing how different our lives really are, and knowing you could do so much better than me."

"There is no one better than you. Don't ever talk like that again," he said, his black irises growing even darker with anger.

"I still don't know why you married me," I said.

"Haven't you figured it out yet, Dumplin'?" he asked, and I shook my head.

"I love you. Since the first time I saw you. I just didn't know what it was," he said, and my soul soared.

He was so close. And it had been so long. I pressed my lips to his, needing that connection.

"Are you sure you want this? You want me?" I asked, needing to know.

"What do I have to do to prove it to you?"

"Just keep loving me," I told him, pressing him down onto the floor.

dmitting I was in love with my wife was the single most liberating act I'd ever committed.

Easily.

Having her push me down onto the floor, crushing her lips to mine, admitting without words how she felt about me was the second.

Goddamn. Fuck. Yes.

She wanted me. My gorgeous wife wanted me. It wasn't a declaration of love, but it would be enough for now.

I'd never tried to make someone fall in love with me. Sure, women had claimed to have intense feelings for me over the years, and who knew, maybe they did. But none of them were her.

She was the only woman whose feelings I cared about. I wanted them. I craved them. I'd fucking have them. No matter what I had to do to earn her heart.

Destiny moaned, rocking her hips against mine, and it was all I could take. I reversed our positions, straddling her thighs as I pulled off her shirt and unclasped her bra.

"You've got the most beautiful fucking tits," I moaned, cupping them in both hands and kneading her soft flesh.

Goddamn. She was killing me.

I moved down her body, kissing her mouth, tasting her, as I undid the button of her jeans. She was so soft. So perfect.

"You taste so fucking good, Dumplin'," I growled, ravenous for her.

Licking a trail between her tits, I kissed and nibbled my way down her belly to her navel. I tugged the tight denim down her hips and thighs, groaning when I saw her cute as fuck panties. The pink heart pattern shouldn't have been sexy, but it was.

Cute, sexy, perfect. And just so *her*.

I glanced up to catch Destiny's crystalline gaze as she watched me, her lower lip caught between her teeth. Her chest was heaving, and my heart damn near stopped.

I was so fucking in love with this woman.

"You're so fucking perfect, Baby. So mine."

And because I was salivating, I pressed her thighs wide, and closed my mouth over her cotton covered cunt. My chest rumbled with how hard I groaned. Even through the fabric, the taste of her sweet essence rocked me to my core.

"Marat, please," she said, rocking her hips against my mouth.

"What do you need, Dumplin'? Tell me. I'll give you anything you want."

"I want your tongue. I want your mouth, please," she begged, and who was I to refuse her?

I wouldn't even try. Gripping the cotton, I pulled it to the side and dove right in, licking her slit and closing my mouth over her tiny bundle of nerves.

Fuck. She was so hot. So good.

I never wanted anything like I wanted her. She was mine. My sweet temptation. My Dumplin'. My whole fucking heart.

She was so damn sexy, writhing beneath my mouth. I couldn't help myself, I unzipped my pants, freeing my cock, and gave myself a good, hard squeeze.

Fuck, it felt so good, I did it again. Stroking my dick as I lapped at her core, my wife was so fucking good, eating her out was going to make me come.

She tasted like heaven. She tasted like pure sin. She tasted like home.

And for the first time in my fucked up life, I knew what it was to truly be in love. To be vulnerable. To be open to hurt. To care about the needs of someone else. To be willing to do anything to protect that person. To give them what they needed.

I was head over heels, insanely in love with my wife. Destiny was everything to me.

"I love you, too, Marat," she said, whimpering with need, and I froze.

I must have said it out loud. And that was fine. I'd already told her. But this was the first time she told me she loved me, and I couldn't believe my ears.

"You do? Since when?"

I had to know.

"Since day one, I think. I love you," she repeated, and I saw it shining there in her blue eyes.

She loved me. Really loved me. Not just my face. Not my money. She loved me. The real me. Her Devil Wolf. And my heart felt so fucking full.

"I'll love you forever," I vowed.

This woman had changed everything for me. She

brought color and beauty to my world when I didn't think it was possible. She'd been through so much, but she still had a heart so goddamn big.

She was a walking miracle. My miracle. And I was so lucky I found her. My sweet Dumplin'.

My wild temptation.

Destiny was my light. My dark. My angel. My devil. My breath. My body. My purpose.

Mine.

She was mine.

I groaned as her pussy began to flutter, swallowing her orgasm. Needing to feel it on my cock, I slid up her body, spreading her wide and filling her in one hard thrust.

Fuck, she was still coming, and it felt so damn good. Untold pleasure filled every fiber of my being as I pumped my hips, joining her in sweet oblivion.

"You're mine, Wife. Fuck, I fucking love you," I roared as her sweet cunt pulled the cum from my body.

Yeah, I fucking loved her. She was my sweet Dumplin'. She was my home.

And I was hers.

EPILOGUE ONE
DESTINY

One *month later...*

Sun filtered in through the windows and I realized I must not have adjusted the setting to keep all light out. That was okay. I liked the way the rays of light bounced around the room, casting shadows on my handsome devil of a husband's face.

He was even more beautiful in sleep, if that was possible. If I'd been more conceited, or less sure of how much he loved me, I'd probably be annoyed that he was prettier than me.

I loved him so much, though. How could I feel anything but pleasure when I looked at his face?

"What are you looking at, Baby?" he asked, his

lips quirking up in a way that told me he was amused.

"Just admiring my husband," I said, biting my lip. "And wondering if our son or daughter will have your eyes or mine?"

"What?" he asked, sitting up abruptly and almost sending me flying off the bed.

Good thing he was fast. Marat caught me before I could tumble to the floor, and I was as grateful for that as I was for the fact he'd pulled me onto his long, hard body. He flipped us over, hovering over me, disbelief on his features.

"Say that again," he whispered.

I lifted my hands, tracing lines from his eyebrows to his cheekbones, down to his beautiful lips. He kissed my fingertips one at a time.

The night he came back from overseas, after the rescuing, the crying, and confessions of love, I'd told him about the possibility. He'd been stunned, of course. And he cried like a baby in my arms.

I got my period two days later, and I cried about it. But after we talked, we agreed our baby would not be made by accident. We both wanted a family. Marat had only ever had Adrik and Josef, but he loved Sofia like a sister. And he adored Micheala, our niece, to death.

As for my family, well, my relationship with my brother was getting better by the day. And although my mother did not recognize me on most visits, sometimes she did. Those were good days.

The care she received at the facility Marat had her moved to was phenomenal. It made me sad that kind of treatment was not readily available for everyone. Older people were so often overlooked and dismissed, but without them, where would any of us be? It hurt my heart when I thought about it. But maybe someday it would get better. It had to, right?

The past was in the past, and I could not change that. I did not regret running away with Timmy or the life I'd led after my parents cut me off. But I felt much better now that I had them back in my life.

But Marat was the family I chose. He was my husband and together we made the decision to try for a baby.

Of course, practice made perfect, and I sure loved practicing baby-making with my husband. He was super good at practicing.

With my PCOS, getting pregnant was always a long shot. But ever since Marat walked into my life, my very own Devil in disguise, I'd started to believe in miracles.

A few days ago, I noticed my stomach was queasy and my slacks were a little tight. Science being what it was these days, they were able to tell me fairly early that I was expecting our very own little miracle.

"We're pregnant," I told him.

The look on his face. The way his dark eyes teared up, and his features tensed. God, I wish I had a picture. He was so beautiful.

Marat beamed at me before he crushed his lips to mine, careful to keep his weight off me. I didn't like that, so I pinched him, and pulled to get him to hug me good and proper.

"Ow! Dumplin', I don't want to hurt you," he muttered against my mouth.

"You won't. I'm completely healthy," I said, swiping my tongue inside his mouth.

"Mmm. Are you happy?" I asked.

He looked at me affectionately then, his obsidian gaze tender and warm. He nuzzled my face and kissed me again, slower this time.

"Happy isn't enough to describe how you make me feel. You really going to have my baby?" Marat whispered the question, and the feel of his warm breath on my skin made me shiver inside.

"I am," I said, smiling through tears.

His entire body trembled against mine, and I tightened my hold on him.

"You've given me everything. I love you so fucking much," he said, his breath catching.

Before I knew it, I was on my back and my big, sexy husband had his cock lined up with my aching pussy. I was always so wet for this man. So ready for him.

"You're so perfect, Dumplin'. Ever since I met you, I can't think without you filling my head. I can't breathe without smelling your citrusy fragrance. I can't see anything but you. I'm consumed by you. Possessed with the need to have you. You're my everything, Wife."

Goddamn.

His words were an aphrodisiac on their own. He pushed his hips, joining them to mine, making me so full all I could do was feel.

"Fuck, Wife, you're soaked for me."

He was right. I was dripping. Clutching his bulking shoulders, I held on while Marat moved his lips, pressing them over mine, stroking his tongue inside my mouth in perfect time with his pistoning hips.

I scratched at him with my nails, careful of the new tattoo he'd gotten in my honor. A pair of black wings that covered his entire back with Destiny written in scrawling ink.

It was beautiful. Like him. And I loved it.

"I love you so much," I moaned.

"I love you too. I know I fucked things up before, but I'll fix it. I swear I'll fix it."

He was making promises. Telling me with words the way he's been making me feel for weeks now.

Christ, I loved him.

I pressed my hands over his mouth, silencing his tirade as he pushed us up the bed, his strokes getting deeper, longer. He moved to his knees, hooking my legs over his arms, and spreading me wide.

"You don't have to fix it, Marat. You just have to love me, *us*," I corrected myself. "You just have to love us."

"I can do that in my sleep," he growled, his eyes flashing with his promise.

"Show me," I demanded, keening as he started to rut into me in earnest.

And he did. He put all his love, all his energy into melting our bodies together. I saw stars by the time he finished.

Yes, my husband showed me just how much he loved me without words. All night long.

He showed me with his kisses. His touches. With his laughter. And his tears.

Marat showed me by making me part of everything he did. By gifting me his confidences and listening to mine.

He showed me by being there for me when my mother finally succumbed to her illness. By holding me through my tears and lifting me up when I needed him to.

He showed me by sharing his successes and failures in the fresh changes he was making to Volkov Industries. And by supporting my new career as an audiobook narrator. Something I could do from home now that he set me up with my own studio.

He showed me he loved me by wanting our family with just as much fervor as I did.

And he kept on showing me. Every day since.

For the rest of our lives.

Eight months later...

"It's too early," I said, worry making me impatient and agitated.

"It just happens like that sometimes," my beautiful wife said, comforting me as I held her hand inside the ambulance.

The vehicle slowed, and I barked at the EMT.

"What the fuck is going on? My wife needs to get to the hospital!"

"It's traffic, sir. But no worries. We handle deliveries all the time if it gets too close."

"Deliveries? That's my baby, not a fucking pizza!" I snapped.

The young man paled, but I didn't spare him

another glance as my wife squeezed my hand and yelled for all she was worth.

"Oooooh god! Marat!"

"Her contractions are coming faster. Um, sir, I have to check to see how dilated she is," the EMT said, and he had every reason to look afraid.

Even after almost a year of marriage, I was still a jealous fuck when it came to my wife. The second Destiny started to complain of backache I made a call to her OBGYN—*who was a woman.*

But when she keeled over in pain at the dinner party we'd been attending, I called an ambulance. She'd calmed down a little while she was being strapped in, but her water broke, and her contractions were increasing in frequency.

The thing they don't tell you about labor was the fact everyone and their goddamn uncle had to look at your wife's sex in order to check the progress. The second I saw this motherfucker put his hands between her legs, I lost my shit.

"It's okay, Marat. It's his job," Destiny tried to explain, but I wasn't having it.

I'd check her fucking cervix myself. So, I did. Yes, I was an overbearing lunatic. Destiny looked at me like I was crazy, but I just shrugged.

Deal with it.

"Okay, she's fully dilated," the EMT said, eyes wide when I showed him what I'd felt.

"Sir, I need to see if the baby is crowning."

Destiny's wail wrenched my heart, and I relented then, allowing the pissant to do his job. I warned him about touching though, and he nodded.

The ambulance was fucking stopped, and my phone was ringing. Adrik and Sofia were stuck somewhere in the traffic behind us. I put the call on speaker.

"Des, are you okay, honey?"

It was Sofia. I smiled, knowing she'd wanted to be in the room when Destiny delivered.

"Y-yeah—ohmyfuckinggod, no! I am not okay, Sof. Marat!" she cried aloud.

"It's okay, Dumplin'. You can do this," I told my wife, glaring at the EMT who was checking the baby's progress.

"Okay, Mrs. Volkov, we aren't going to make it to the hospital."

"What the fuck does that mean?" I shouted.

Sofia was busy offering support and encouraging Destiny. Thank god, because I was frozen somewhere between angst and pure fear.

I met my wife's frightened gaze and pushed my

own fear and shock down. She needed me to be strong. And I wasn't going to fucking let her down.

"I'm going to need you to push with your next contraction," the EMT confirmed.

Fuck. I wasn't ready for this. I couldn't be a father. I never had one. How the fuck—then I saw the worry and fear in my wife's eyes, and everything changed.

I could do this. I had to. I wouldn't let her down.

"Listen to me, Dumplin', you are going to deliver this baby right here, right now, with me. You can do this. You are the strongest woman I know," I told her, watching her nod. "You ready?"

"Yeah. Okay. I can do this," she repeated, her blue eyes shining with pain, emotion, and adrenaline.

"Okay, push!" the EMT yelled.

"That's it, Baby. Push. Come on. Good Girl. You're doing so good, Dumplin'," I praised her.

She was marvelous, my wife. Fantastic. Amazing. Better than I deserved.

It took twenty-seven minutes and countless pushes and deep breaths for my daughter to arrive. And when she did, it was nothing short of miraculous.

"Is she okay?"

"She's perfect! Look, look what we made," I said, awestruck by the tiny, squalling infant in my arms.

"I want to name her Lucy," Destiny said softly, exhaustion creeping over her face.

She never looked more beautiful.

"Lucy it is," I replied, grinning.

We'd had this talk countless times. Baby names and why we wanted them. It wouldn't have mattered to me what name Destiny wanted, I'd always let her have her way. But she wanted to call our daughter Lucy because she said the first time she saw me, my sweet wife thought I was more beautiful than the Devil himself.

I'd laughed my ass off at that description, flattered and amused. But Lucy was a good name. I liked it. And if it was what my wife wanted, then that's what we were going to call our little one.

The ambulance had pulled over onto the shoulder, Adrik and Sofia had arrived at some point and were waiting behind us. Once Lucy was born, they followed us to the hospital where mother and baby were being looked at by the best doctors.

I stepped into the hall after being ordered out of the room by my wife who was likely exhausted and tired of me wanting to kill every single member of the staff who had to see her naked to check her out.

"Congratulations, brother!" Adrik greeted me with a hard, back slapping hug.

"Thank you."

"Are they okay?" Sofia asked, and my sister-in-law's face looked flushed, and I knew she'd been crying.

"They are perfect. Just perfect," I said, my voice cracking.

"Adrik, I, uh, I never thanked you for everything you did for me, for us," I started.

"You are my brother, Marat. No thanks necessary. However, I would like to know the story of the Devil Wolf," he said, eyebrows raised.

I guessed the rumors had finally made it back to the states. I nodded, promising to tell him the tale later. I did not want to spoil my daughter's birthday with the details of how I hunted and slaughtered the men responsible for attacking the mine in Murmansk.

That prick Ferragamo and the old holdouts from that outdated mafioso family had worn out their welcome. This was the 21st Century. The world didn't need criminals and gangsters to run things anymore.

Corporations and conglomerates had taken over their positions and were every bit as ruthless as the old mobsters were. Volkov Industries was one such enterprise.

I was almost positive the little attack on the Murmansk mine would not be an isolated incident. There would always be those who'd want to test us for weakness.

But the things I did there were making the rounds with the right people. The rumor of another Volkov Wolf would hopefully be enough to keep those pricks at bay for a little while.

At least, until Lucy started college.

"Congratulations, brother," Adrik repeated, and I saw raw emotion in his gaze.

I nodded at him, too worked up to speak. Adrik clapped a hand on my back, and I bent my head and kissed my sister-in-law's cheek. I needed to get back to my wife and daughter. To my family.

I rushed through the hall back to the private room where they waited for me. The need to be at my Dumplin's side stronger than ever.

That was where I belonged. Where I felt the most grounded.

"Dumplin', how do you feel?"

"Good. So good, Marat," she said, sighing my name.

I swallowed and watched as she nursed our child

at her breast. Pride surged in my veins and a love so strong, I thought my heart might beat right outside my chest.

I'd never known true joy until I'd met this woman. She was my heart. She was my life. My wife was truly my destiny in every sense of the word. She'd given me everything.

Her body. Her heart. Our daughter. And I gave her all of me in return. All I had to offer. My body, my soul, my heart, my life.

I was her Devil Wolf, and she was my wild temptation. She was my everything. I'd never loved anyone before. Never knew I could. But I loved her.

And I would spend the rest of my life proving how much.

EPILOGUE THREE
JOSEF

When Meredith reached out to Volkov Industries with a request to meet to discuss terms regarding the default on the loan her father had taken out with his business as collateral, I was the one who received the message.

She was the only woman who'd ever brought me to my knees, and it wasn't a past I liked to remember. But our positions were reversed this time, and I knew the second I walked into the boardroom I'd do anything to keep my Little Red from getting the upper hand again.

Her gorgeous mane of bright red waves was fastened at her nape. The style should have looked severe, but her hair was never one to be tamed.

Her emerald eyes sparked surprise, then anger, as I took my seat across from her.

"Josef," she said my name and I had to close my eyes at the emotions roiling through me.

"What are you doing here?" she asked.

"I represent Volkov Industries and I am calling in your loan in full, Miss Gray."

"What? You can't!"

"I can. And I am," I replied, fury feeding my desire to see her squirm.

My gaze roamed her face, absorbing the shock, taking in the changes time had made. It had been fifteen years since I'd seen her. She was little more than a child then. But goddamn it, how I'd loved her.

The curve of her lips was the same. But there were fine lines around her mouth.

Not smile lines. These were different. Sadder.

The dead organ inside my chest squeezed, and I nearly grunted at the pain of it.

"Where is your father? I should be discussing this with him."

"He's in the hospital. Heart attack."

"What? I hadn't heard."

"Why would you?"

My phone beeped, and I looked down to see a

message from Adrik. Oh shit. Marat's daughter was just born.

A mixture of disbelief, happiness and envy filled me, but happiness won out, outweighing the others. I had no family of my own, and the Volkov brothers were the closest thing to it.

Adrik and Marat were the family I chose, who chose me. I was sorry I'd missed the part where Marat had gone rogue wolf and hunted the mother-fuckers who'd sabotaged one of the Volkov mines.

But since I'd trained the man myself, I believed every single rumor of the Devil Wolf I'd heard since then.

Well done, brother.

It was a good thing Marat was younger than Adrik, or he'd have given his brother's rep a run for his money. I smirked. It was about fucking time he realized what he was capable of. And how very interesting that a woman had shown him the way.

"Is that a smile for another life you ruined?" Meredith spat.

I looked up, schooling my face to show no emotions. She looked hostile, angry. And I was confused.

"You can't mean you think *I* ruined *your* life, Little Red."

What the fuck was she talking about? I was there all those years ago, rooted to the spot we'd promised to meet. I'd waited hours only to have her father come with some shitty little note from her saying she didn't mean any of it.

Not the declarations of love. Not the giving of herself to me in the moonlit garden behind her bedroom. Not the promise to leave with me.

Franklin Gray promised not to press charges against me if I left that night, so I did. I was young. Stupid. Not the powerful man I was today.

But none of that explained why she was staring daggers at me, pissed as all hell.

Fuck. She was still so damn pretty when she was angry. Her emerald eyes spat green fire at me, and that red hair seemed to glow like flames.

My cock stirred and only through the extraordinary self-control did I manage to sit there seemingly unaffected.

"Ha! You're the one who walked out, and I was left to pick up the pieces," she said, stunning the fucking shit out of me.

I frowned. I had a feeling maybe neither of us had the full story. Something was not right in the way things had gone down all those years ago.

True, it had taken me some time to find a weakness in Gray Corp. Years, actually. But once I'd fooled her father into taking out a loan at a bank I happened to have a controlling interest in, the rest was easy.

It just took patience. Eight months was nothing after I'd spent the past fifteen years in torment, waiting for the chance to pay back the woman who almost broke me.

Goddamn her for still looking so beautiful.

Once upon a time, I was mad for her. But she threw me away.

I'd been a *fun distraction*. Just something she'd used to scratch an itch. She'd wanted a bad boy between her legs to piss Daddy off, and I stupidly ran to fill the position.

Once upon a time, Meredith Gray used me.

Now it was my turn.

EPILOGUE FOUR
DESTINY

The bed was warm and I sighed, opening my eyes slowly as I floated in that place between wake and sleep.

The sound of humming was soothing and I turned my head, focusing in the darkness on the familiar figure of my handsome husband, his tattooed back towards me as he rocked our baby girl in his capable arms.

I didn't know what I love more. That the billionaire playboy who looked like a fallen angel had turned into such an incredibly possessive, loyal, and faithful husband or that he was so completely devoted to me and our Little Lucy.

Maybe I just loved how good he was at loving us.

"I tried not to wake you," his soft voice reached

my ears and I smiled as he placed the now sleeping baby back in her bassinet.

"You didn't," I assured him, scooting back so he could crawl in beside me.

"Did I ever thank you?" He asked suddenly and I frowned as I snuggled into his side.

"Thank me? For what?"

"Just for being you," he said, kissing me so sweetly if I didn't already love him like crazy I would have fallen right then.

"I love you," I said, and smiled at the appreciative rumble that reverberated through my husband's sexy as sin body.

"I love you too, my sweet Dumplin'. Always."

I fell asleep just like that. With Marat's strong arms wrapped around me, safe and secure in the knowledge that our love was real and true. I'd never known happiness the way I knew it now. And I never regretted a single thing about the way we came together.

How could I when he was everything I'd ever wanted? Marat was my home. My heart. My very soul.

He called me his wild temptation, but the truth was, he was mine. I'd never stop wanting him. Not as long as there was breath in my body.

The end.

Did you enjoy this contemporary romance book?
Please consider dropping a line or two in a review so other
readers can enjoy it, too.

Look for the next book in the series, His Wild Seduction,
featuring the sexy and intimidating head of security for
Volkov Industries, Josef Aziz.

Want more Wild Billionaire Books? Visit my website for
more: https://www.cdgorri.com/series/wild-billionaire-
romance
Thank you and happy reading!

del mare alla stella,
C.D. Gorri

P.S. Indie authors like me count on word of mouth to get
my books seen, so if you have a blog or a social media
account and you want to post about my books, be sure to
include #cdgorribooks so I can see it and I will share to
too. THANK YOU.

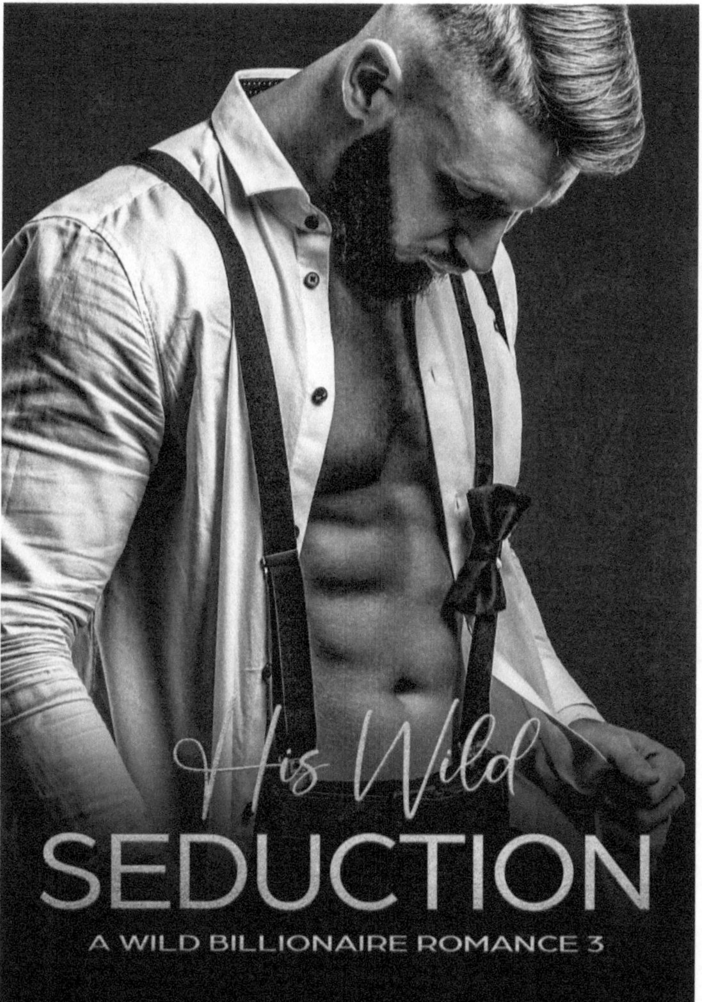

His Wild
SEDUCTION
A WILD BILLIONAIRE ROMANCE 3
USA TODAY BESTSELLING AUTHOR
C.D. GORRI

Merciful Lies by C.D. Gorri

Lies can be merciful. It just depends on the why.

Meredith

I knew the second I saw him, my life would change forever. When my brother offers me as payment to Nico Fury, the king of the Vipers, how can I refuse? Tattooed, built, and tall, he was the only man I saw when I walked into the room. It was like he occupied all the available space, sitting on his throne of blood, sweat, and lies.

Nerves assailed me, but I owed my brother too much to let anything happen to him. One night. That was all. But it would leave me wrecked. Actions always had consequences. Six months later, my brother was killed by a rival organization, and now they were after me.

There was only one place I could go to keep my unborn baby safe. I just hoped the king would be merciful.

***

Nico

Perfect things didn't exist, at least not in my experience. But she was pretty close. I had her in my bed for one night, and I couldn't shake the memory. No, I wasn't meant to keep soft things like Meredith Keller. My life belonged to my crew, and we were a vicious group. Hell, we weren't called Vipers for nothing.

But she was different. She made me want, and I loved and hated her for it. Meredith was light in a world of constant darkness. She was all warmth and beauty like no other. And I craved her like a drug. Six months had passed since I took her in return for clearing her brother's debt to me, but that man attracted trouble like honey did flies. It wasn't long before I learned Sam Keller had gotten himself killed. Less than an hour later, Meredith came back to me, on her knees, asking for sanctuary.

I knew the moment I saw the swell of her stomach she was carrying my baby. Meredith thought coming here would protect her, but she was walking right into the Viper's nest. Before I was finished, my little runaway would be begging me for mercy.

Merciful Lies is the first in the contemporary

romance series of connected standalones, Jersey Bad Boys. This series features familiar tropes such as enemies to lovers, forced proximity, arranged marriages, secret babies, and contains some violence and explicit scenes.

I looked around at the highly polished mahogany bar top, satisfied with the pristine sophistication of my establishment. It took me years to find just the right location, and Montclair, New Jersey, was simply ripe for this kind of place.

No, it wasn't my first rodeo. I'd spent years helping entrepreneurs open bars up and down the east coast. Was pretty damn good at it, too. Especially when it came to marketing. But this place was special. This one was *mine*.

The Whiskey Bar had its first soft opening a few months ago, and so far, so good. The reviews were amazing, and we were bringing in crowds all the way from New York City to our little Jersey town.

We featured premier whiskey, bourbon, scotch, with a special section for local artisan liquors.

Oh sure, we serve other stuff, beer, and spirits, but whiskey, that was the star. There was just something about it that spoke to a clientele with a refined palate. I wanted to reach that customer base. Men and women with good taste and money to spend, who wouldn't scoff at a $35 glass of the good stuff.

Something was missing, though. I knew it and my staff knew it. But fuck me if I could figure out what.

"Yo, Sonny, the guy's here to fix the ice machine," Eddie, one of his bartenders, said from the doorway to his office.

"Great. You got this or you need me?"

"Nah, I'm good."

I nodded and watched him go, steepling my fingers as I thought more about the issue. I'd just signed a contract with a very popular New Jersey whiskey distillery and was planning an entire marketing campaign around them. Bite was a damn good whiskey. Older, established, it was the perfect foil for my own upcoming label.

But none of that mattered if I couldn't get the right crowds in. I closed my eyes, shaking my head when a now familiar scent reached my nostrils.

Fuck. It must be late afternoon already. That was usually when *she* started mixing her sinfully sweet confections. I growled and rubbed my hand over my face.

Ever since she moved in, I was having the hardest fucking time concentrating on work—and I meant that literally. My dick twitched behind my pants, and I flicked the thing to get it to behave.

Last thing I wanted was for one of my staff to accuse me of something untoward because I couldn't control my boner every freaking time I got a tantalizing whiff of what my new neighbor was whipping up next door.

Fuck me.

No, really. Would she? It's been the only thing on my mind ever since I first saw that delectable ass hauling a fifty-pound sack of sugar inside her small confectionary shop. Of course, I helped her. Flashed her my best smile, too.

You know the one. Guaranteed to melt a pair of panties at 100 yards or more. But Delani wasn't like other women. She smiled sweetly, said thanks, then turned around to introduce me to her boyfriend. The asshat was on the phone, sitting in the corner while she did all the work.

Apparently, the woman was taken by some loser

who didn't deserve her. But that wasn't my business. No. My business was getting The Whiskey Bar off the ground. As it was, I was bleeding money into advertising that simply wasn't working.

What was I doing wrong? Why was this so easy for me when it was someone else's bar on the line? And what the fuck was she making today?

Holy hell. My eyes crossed as the tempting fragrance of fine dark chocolate, sweet sugar cane, Tahitian vanilla, and something dark and subtle filled my office. I closed my eyes and let it sink in, grimacing when I started to imagine Delani Whitman wearing that cute little red apron of hers—*and nothing else*—while she fed me one of her tasty little morsels.

Fuck. I was sick. Delani was not for me. She had a man, and I had a bar.

Best remember that.

The phone rang, and I answered it on autopilot. Straightening in my very comfortable leather office chair when the caller provided her name.

"Hello, Mr. Delgado, this is Cynthia Blair of Blair Investment Group," she said.

"Yes, Ms. Blair. How are you?"

"Very good, Sonny. Can I call you Sonny?"

"Sure. Of course."

"And it's Miss Blair, I am single," she said, and her voice held that familiar note of invitation I'd received with increasing regularity ever since my balls had dropped.

But this was not a pleasure call. I had been waiting for Blair Investment Group to get back to me with their answer to my proposal. You see, I didn't just serve whiskey. I made it. I just needed the right backers to support my brand.

"Okay, Miss Blair. What is your news?"

"It's good, Sonny. Blair Group would like to come to a tasting at your bar on Valentine's Day," she said, and my heart stopped.

"A tasting?"

"Yes, all the brands do it these days. Expect us at around seven, and I can't wait to see what pairings you offer, Sonny. Until then."

"Yes. See you."

Fuck.

I had no idea what she meant, but I knew the names of some talented chefs in the area. Blair Group wanted a tasting party, so I guess had to give one. *The Whiskey Bar,* and more importantly, *Whiskey Neat,* my label, needed their support and if that meant some wining and dining, I could sure as shit provide that.

Afterward, everything would be gold. The scent of chocolate got stronger, and I frowned. I just had one annoyingly sweet problem. It seemed avoiding my neighbor would not work anymore. I readjusted my dick and gave my balls a pinch to keep the damn thing under control.

When I walked into the tight alley that connected our properties. I overheard a telephone conversation she was having with someone, a woman, I quickly discerned. Shamelessly eavesdropping, I leaned closer to the door. Once I heard what was being said, I couldn't have walked away if I tried.

Holy. Fuck.

She'd broken up with that asshat. Finally, I had an opening. But what was she going to say when I asked her to close for a few days? I pursed my lips and cleared my throat. There was nothing else to do, so I raised my hand and knocked.

Time to confront the buxom beauty to find out.

Read more www.cdgorri.com/books/her-chocolate-his-bar

ALSO BY C.D. GORRI

<u>Contemporary Romance Books:</u>

<u>Cherry On Top Tales</u>

Her Yule His Log

His Carrot Her Muffin

Her Chocolate His Bar

<u>Wild Billionaire Romance</u>

His Wild Obsession

His Wild Temptation

<u>Jersey Bad Boys</u>

Merciful Lies

***

<u>Paranormal Romance Books:</u>

<u>Macconwood Pack Novel Series:</u>

<u>Macconwood Pack Tales Series:</u>

<u>The Falk Clan Tales:</u>

<u>The Bear Claw Tales:</u>

<u>The Barvale Clan Tales:</u>

<u>Barvale Holiday Tales:</u>

<u>Purely Paranormal Romance Books:</u>

The Wardens of Terra:

The Maverick Pride Tales:

Dire Wolf Mates:

Wyvern Protection Unit:

Jersey Sure Shifters/EveL Worlds:

The Guardians of Chaos:

Twice Mated Tales

Hearts of Stone Series

Moongate Island Tales

Mated in Hope Falls

Speed Dating with the Denizens of the Underworld

Hungry Fur Love

Island Stripe Pride

NYC Shifter Tales

A Howlin' Good Fairytale Retelling

Witch Shifter Clan

Young Adult/Urban Fantasy Books

The Grazi Kelly Novel Series

The Angela Tanner Files

G'Witches Magical Mysteries Series

Co-written with P. Mattern

Witches of Westwood Academy

with Gina Kincade

ABOUT THE AUTHOR

USA Today Bestselling author C.D. Gorri writes paranormal and contemporary romance and urban fantasy books with plenty of steam and humor.

Join her mailing list here: https://www.cdgorri.com/newsletter

An avid reader with a profound love for books and literature, she is usually found with a book in hand. C.D. lives in her home state, New Jersey, where many of her characters and stories are based. Her tales are fast-paced yet detailed with satisfying conclusions. If you enjoy powerful heroines and loyal heroes who face relatable problems in supernatural settings, journey into the Grazi Kelly Universe today.

You will find sassy, curvy heroines and sexy, love-driven heroes who find their HEAs between the pages.

Wolves, Bears, Dragons, Tigers, Witches, Vampires, and tons more Shifters and supernatural creatures dwell within her paranormal works. The most important thing is every mate in this universe is fated, loyal, and true lovers always get their happily-ever-afters.

In her contemporary works, you will find fiercely possessive men and the smart, confident, curvy women they are crazy about. As always, the HEA is between the pages.

Thank you and happy reading!
del mare alla stella,
C.D. Gorri

http://www.cdgorri.com
https://www.facebook.com/Cdgorribooks
https://www.bookbub.com/authors/c-d-gorri
https://twitter.com/cgor22
https://instagram.com/cdgorri/

https://www.goodreads.com/cdgorri
https://www.tiktok.com/@cdgorriauthor